PRAISE FOR **DANIEL KALLA**

WE ALL FALL DOWN

"A fast-paced thriller with an historical overlay and a dash of romantic tension."
Vancouver Sun

"A tightly plotted thriller, energetic and completely believable."
Booklist

OF FLESH AND BLOOD

"[Kalla] plunges us straight into the frenzied pace of the OR and [into] a medical drama that spans a hundred years. He's a strong storyteller who keeps his characters moving and struggling, and we're right there, struggling with them, rooting for them."
Vancouver Sun

COLD PLAGUE

"Similar in many ways to Michael Crichton and even Dan Brown's bestsellers, *Cold Plague* is testament to just how good commercial fiction can be: entertaining, informative, and downright fun."
Winnipeg Free Press

"Plenty of suspense and layering on the kind of scientific detail that fans of medical thrillers crave. Recommend this one to fans of Robin Cook and other such A-listers."
Booklist

BLOOD LIES

"Kalla strikes again with another perfect page turner."
LEE CHILD, *New York Times* bestselling author

"Fans of *Presumed Innocent* will find welcome echoes of that modern classic in *Blood Lies*." *Publishers Weekly* (Starred Review)

RAGE THERAPY

"[Kalla's] first novel, *Pandemic*, was as fine a medical thriller as I've ever read; his newest, *Rage Therapy*, is a taut psychological thriller that will pull you into a world of sexual deviancy, murder, and mind games. A very good read."
NELSON DeMILLE, #1 *New York Times* bestselling author

RESISTANCE

"Daniel Kalla's prescription for a perfect thriller includes snappy characters, a pace that sweeps up a reader, and not too much technical jargon. . . . The kind of magnetic story you can't put down."
Vancouver Province

PANDEMIC

"Michael Crichton ought to be looking over his shoulder. He has some serious competition in Kalla." *The Chronicle Herald*

"Kalla expertly weaves real science and medicine into a fast-paced, nightmarish thriller—a thriller all the more frightening because it could really happen."
TESS GERRITSEN, internationally bestselling author
of the Rizzoli & Isles books

"Very much in the Michael Crichton school of cutting-edge scientifically rooted thrillers. *Pandemic* is an absorbing, compulsive thriller, the sort of book you could stay up too late reading."
Vancouver Sun

THE LAST
HIGH

A THRILLER

DANIEL KALLA

PUBLISHED BY SIMON & SCHUSTER
New York   London   Toronto   Sydney   New Delhi

SIMON &
SCHUSTER
CANADA

Simon & Schuster Canada
A Division of Simon & Schuster, Inc.
166 King Street East, Suite 300
Toronto, Ontario M5A 1J3

This Simon & Schuster Canada edition May 2020

SIMON & SCHUSTER CANADA and colophon are trademarks of Simon & Schuster, Inc.

For information about special discounts for bulk purchases, please contact Simon & Schuster Special Sales at 1-800-268-3216 or CustomerService@simonandschuster.ca.

Manufactured in the United States of America

10 9 8 7 6 5 4 3 2 1

Library and Archives Canada Cataloguing in Publication

Title: The last high / by Daniel Kalla.
Names: Kalla, Daniel, author.
Identifiers: Canadiana (print) 20190101067 | Canadiana (ebook) 20190101075 | ISBN 9781501196980 (softcover) | ISBN 9781501197000 (ebook)
Classification: LCC PS8621.A47 L38 2020 | DDC C813/.6—dc23

ISBN 978-1-5011-9698-0
ISBN 978-1-5011-9700-0 (ebook)

For my aunt Alisa, who's as kind and selfless as she is stoic

PROLOGUE

The house music courses through Alexa. The hypnotic beat and melting layers of sound feel as if they come from within, as if her heart is the amplifier. And the warmth is so enveloping. Like being lowered into the most perfect bubble bath. The bliss is almost unbearable.

Alexa can't lift her head off her chest, but she can move her eyes. With a quick sweep of the room, she sees all the friends who matter most to her—Rachel, Nick, Joshua, Grayson, and Taylor. *The only ones who matter at all, really.*

Taylor, her very best friend, is slouched at a weird angle on the couch beside her. Taylor had promised to ensure Alexa got some alone time with Josh at the party, even though she has a crush on him, too. Typical Taylor, always putting friends first. Her eyes are still open, but the pupils are tiny as pinholes. And her complexion! It's grayish blue, while her lips have turned almost purple. *So strange, but so beautiful.*

Alexa shifts her gaze to the left and sees Josh and Gray sprawled out on the other couch, propped up only by their abutting shoulders. Josh's eyes are as glassy as Taylor's, while Gray's are shut altogether.

They're both so still. And Josh's exposed arms are mottled deep dark blue. Alexa wishes she could tell him just how much she loves him. Tonight was supposed to be the night.

Alexa looks down at her own hands. Her fingers feel foreign to her, and the color of her nails matches that of Taylor's lips. She knows it's not right, but it's still so wild.

The floating warmth intensifies. Alexa feels as though she's falling off the couch, even though she's not moving. She's never drunk anything more than a beer or two in her sixteen years. How could one cup of Nick's punch make her so woozy?

Somewhere in the back of her brain she can hear her mother's panicked voice—a distant scream—telling her to breathe. But her mom's nowhere near the party.

Alexa finds it all kind of funny. She wants to laugh. She wants to tell Taylor how exquisitely wrong it all is. But she can't even move her lips. Besides, dreams are stealing over her now. And she can't hold on any longer.

CHAPTER 1

"This one, Julija, you never will believe."

The refrain is familiar. Goran Veljkovic loves to weave yarns, few of them short. But Julie Rees has a soft spot for the sixty-year-old bear of a man, from his hulking six-foot-five frame to the hair matting his exposed arms and spilling over the neck of his scrubs. After all, he helped see her through her darkest time without making her feel judged.

Handover rounds rarely last more than ten minutes with other colleagues, but Goran's chattiness will often set Julie behind twice as long at the beginning of a busy shift. This Friday night, though, is oddly quiet in downtown Vancouver—at least based on the relative emptiness of the usually crammed waiting room in St. Michael's ER—so she is happy to indulge him. "At this point, Gor, there's not much I wouldn't believe," she says.

"So the presenting complaint on this patient's chart reads 'rectal foreign body.'" Goran rolls his massive shoulders. "No biggie, right? I could fill a sizable trophy case with all the misadventures I've had to pull out of people's bottoms."

Though Goran's Croatian accent isn't strong, Julie still gets a kick out of his idioms—a unique cross between hip and archaic. "But . . ." she prompts.

"I ask him how this particular gem ended up where it did. He says he doesn't remember. He had been drinking. You know how it is . . . you get drunk and next thing you know you've wedged a garden gnome up your backside."

"Gor . . ."

"I look at the X-ray. There's nothing there, Julija. Zip. His rectum is as empty as my bank account. So I go ask him. 'What convinced you something might be up there?' He says, 'When I woke up this morning my toy wasn't in the bedside drawer where I always keep it.' I say, 'And you just assumed it must be inside your rectum?' He looks at me, mouth open, as if staring at the biggest moron he's ever run across. 'Where else would it be?'"

Goran howls so hard that Julie could swear she feels the floor shake, and she can't help but join in the laughter.

"'Where else would it be'!" Goran repeats, still laughing. "Stretcher Twelve is an inferior wall non-STEMI," he says, turning abruptly back to business as he describes the insidious form of heart attack suffered by the wide-eyed, gray-haired woman he's gesturing to. "Cardiology will admit her. To the ward only. They're in no hurry to take her to the cath lab." He glances skyward, showing his disdain for their conservative approach. He then motions toward the man writhing on the next stretcher. "Stretcher Thirteen is a renal colic. Huge kidney stone. If he was in North Dakota, they might carve a president's face onto it."

"South."

"Huh?"

"Mount Rushmore's in South Dakota."

"North, South . . . either way, Urology will admit." He looks over his shoulder to the middle-aged nurse charting at the desk. "Doreen, a smidge more hydromorphone over here."

Doreen rises from her desk with a syringe already in hand. "And how much exactly is a smidge, Dr. Veljkovic?"

"Halfway between a drop and a pinch. One cc. Don't you speak metric?" he teases.

They move from one stretcher to the next, stopping long enough for Goran to describe each patient's condition in more detail than necessary. The younger ER docs prefer to do rounds at the computer, reviewing patients on the electronic bed board, but Goran is old school—he insists on laying eyes and sometimes hands and even a stethoscope on each person he hands over.

Julie can hardly remember how much Goran once intimidated her. When she first started at St. Mike's, the larger-than-life Croat terrified her. She mistook his sarcastic wit and excitable boisterousness for judgment and disappointment. She dreaded working under him. Little did she expect that, within a few years, he would become her mentor and, soon after, one of her best friends.

Julie and Goran leave the last stretcher and return to the central nursing station. "Dinner Tuesday, right?" Goran asks. "I promised the missus I would double-check."

"I wouldn't miss Maria's cooking for the world."

"Julija," he tsks. "There's no call for lying."

"I love her food," Julie says with a roll of her eyes. "Her company, too. More than yours, for sure."

"Join the club." Goran pats his thick chest. "Took one heck of a con job to have sold her on this."

Julie understands that as much as Goran loves Maria, his first wife, Lada, was his soul mate. When she died of breast cancer five years earlier, Julie was convinced he might soon follow. Then Goran met Maria, one of the hospital pharmacists. The much younger Filipino woman has proven to be his redemption. But she hasn't replaced Lada. No one could.

"Are we setting the table for three or for four?" he asks with an arched eyebrow.

"Three."

"Pity. Such a waste of this flawless youth. Well, perhaps a little too skinny. Still, it's a crime how rarely you date."

"Enough." Julie wraps her arms around him and pecks him on the cheek. "You've put me far enough behind already. Go home."

As soon as Goran leaves, Julie heads over to the nearest computer screen and eyeballs the list of presenting complaints of the patients waiting to be seen: "flank pain," "difficulty swallowing," "numbness in limbs," "nausea and vomiting," "shortness of breath," "chest pain," "headache," and two others with "abdominal pain." There are only nine in total. None have waited more than two hours. A slow night, indeed. She clicks open the electronic chart of the patient with numbness in her limbs and reads the triage note. The symptom could portend a true emergency—a stroke, rupturing aneurysm, multiple sclerosis, or even a tumor—but based on the healthy vital signs and the additional complaint of being "unable to breathe," Julie suspects that a panic attack is the most likely cause.

She's taken one step toward the patient's stretcher when the speaker booms overhead. "Resuscitation! Five minutes. Multiple."

She swivels and darts for the three-bed resuscitation room down the hallway. "Multiple" almost invariably means traumas, usually of the motor vehicle variety.

Sandy May, the wafer-thin charge nurse, waits inside the brightly lit room along with four other nurses, a respiratory therapist, and a radiology technician. No one speaks, but all are in motion, swirling around the three empty resuscitation bays—slots with the same high-tech monitor mounted above each stretcher and surrounded by matching gadgetry—in a silent dance of preparation.

Julie picks up on the unusual collective grimness. Resuscitating is as fundamental and, often, routine to ER staff as casting or stitching. But she senses something ominous about this particular call. "What are we getting, Sandy?"

"Overdoses." Sandy nods without looking away from the pre-loaded IV bags on poles that she's inspecting. "Lucky we have someone so good with poisons on."

"You make me sound more like a poisoner than a toxicologist." Julie laughs nervously. "How many?"

"Five or six. At least."

"Five or six? Was it an industrial spill or leak or something?"

"Teenagers at a party. Two pronounced dead at the scene. At least three others are in cardiac arrest with CPR ongoing. Likely others."

"What the fuck, Sandy?" In her experience as a clinical toxicologist and an ER physician—and as a user before that—Julie cannot recall a single recreational drug overdose of this magnitude.

Sandy only shrugs.

Julie hears the distant wail of the first siren. "Have we called for backup?"

"I told Goran to hang around. ICU is aware. They're sending two fellows down," Sandy says of the senior medical trainees who have completed their residencies and are now subspecializing in critical care.

"Everyone wears protection," Julie calls out as she reaches for a waterproof gown herself. "Some of those ultrapotent opioids can penetrate skin. We also need massive doses of naloxone ready," she says of the opioid antidote.

Sandy motions her pen to the IV poles above her. "Check."

"We'll need tons of epinephrine, insulin drips, bicarb, magnesium, IV fat emulsions, diazepam, and charcoal at the ready, too."

"Not my first rodeo, Julie," Sandy says, but there's something forced in her cynicism. Julie can tell that she's scared, too.

The sirens are screaming now. Julie bolts out to the entrance to meet them, arriving just as the first paramedic crew flies through the open doorway with the first stretcher.

A gangly teenager lies on it with a mechanical CPR device the size of a toaster oven strapped to his chest. Its noisy arm thumps up and down like a piston, compressing the boy's chest deep enough to rattle the stretcher with each thrust. A barrel-chested paramedic steadily squeezes a bag in both of his long hands, pumping oxygen down the endotracheal tube and into the boy's airway. It's clear that his heart is not beating on its own.

The other paramedic speaks as she hurls the stretcher toward the resuscitation bays. "Patient's name is Grayson Driscoll. Unwitnessed cardiac arrest. Unknown substance. Likely opioids. Found at eleven twenty-two with six other ODs on scene. Intubated. Naloxone four milligrams given. Multiple doses of epinephrine. No response."

Julie jogs beside the stretcher, noting the boy's bluish complexion and dilated pupils. With long curly hair and cyanotic coloring, he resembles Michael on the morning that she woke up to find him beside her, also in cardiac arrest. "What's the underlying cardiac rhythm?" she asks, shaking off the crushing memory.

"He was in v. fib," the paramedic says, describing ventricular fibrillation—the state when the heart's wiring is overcome with a chaotic electrical storm that renders the powerful pump into a useless bag of writhing worms. "Now his heart's in complete standstill. Asystole."

Goran is already in the resuscitation room, gowned and masked like the other staff. "Fentanyl, no?"

"Or an even stronger derivative," Julie says, as the paramedics seamlessly swing the patient from their gurney to the hospital stretcher.

Julie motions to the mechanical CPR device still pumping away on his chest. "Pause it for a rhythm check."

The paramedic hits a button and the machine stills. There's a moment of dense silence. Julie's eyes dart to the overhead monitor, which reveals the nearly flat line—"imagine a drunk trying to draw a straight line," as one of her favorite profs used to describe it—of asystole.

"Resume CPR!" Julie commands, and the paramedic flicks the device back into noisy motion. "I want epinephrine every three minutes. Two amps of bicarb. Magnesium two grams."

"I will insert an intraosseous line." Goran reaches for the bone drill. He wipes the patient's exposed upper shin with an alcohol swab and then presses the drill straight down on the same spot. It whirs to life and, with a slight crunch, the catheter screws into his bone.

Something slams against the doorframe. Julie glances over to see another paramedic duo jostling another stretcher through the doorway. A pale girl with flaming red hair lies on the stretcher, but instead of a machine, Wes—the bearded paramedic who's notorious for smoking beside his rig out front of the ER—leans over her and uses his interlocked palms to rapidly compress and decompress her narrow chest. "We shocked her back to life at the scene," Wes's partner, Nadia, says in a loud but calm voice. "We lost her pulse again just as we were pulling up."

Julie glances over to Goran. "Can you manage the first case?"

"Yes, I'll deal with the boy," he says. "You take care of her!"

Julie darts over to the second resuscitation bay and helps swing the patient's legs over to the hospital stretcher. The girl weighs practically nothing in her hands. With elfin features and smooth freckled skin, she looks to be prepubescent. "Pulse check!" Julie calls as soon as the girl hits the stretcher.

"Nothing," Sandy says, pressing her fingers to the girl's neck.

Julie glimpses the overhead monitor, which shows a frenetic squiggly line. "V. fib! Let's shock her with two hundred joules!"

A nurse reaches for the green charge button on the bedside defibrillator. It emits a rising whine as it charges, and then loudly beeps its readiness. "All clear!" she cries as she presses the red shock button.

The current jolts the girl enough to arch her back off the stretcher momentarily before her body slams back down. Julie checks the monitor again, but the line remains as chaotic as ever. She doesn't need to say a word before Wes restarts chest compressions.

"Epinephrine now!" Julie commands. "Amiodarone three hundred milligrams. Vasopressin forty units. Two more milligrams of nalox-one. Shocks every two minutes while we have v. fib."

A third set of paramedics bursts through the room's doorway with another gurney. This one holds a plump Asian girl, whose short hair is streaked blue. A mechanical CPR device thumps away on her chest, too, as the paramedics urgently wheel her over to the final resuscitation slot.

Goddamn it! "Where are the ICU fellows?" Julie yells.

"Over here," a shorter woman in scrubs says as she steps out from behind the two husky paramedics. "I'll take this one."

"Thanks." Julie nods, satisfied that the patients on either side of her have qualified physicians running their resuscitations. She turns back to the redheaded girl. "Know anything else about her?" Julie asks of Nadia and Wes.

"Name's Alexa O'Neill. Sixteen years old. That's about it," Wes replies.

Sixteen? She looks more like twelve. But Julie keeps that thought to herself as she continues her silent whole-body survey, noting the lividity in Alexa's upper arms.

"There were seven of them in that basement den. She was one of the two kids still with a pulse when we reached them." Nadia shakes her head grimly. "But she wasn't breathing. Dark blue as the others. Went into v. fib as soon as we got her on the stretcher. Came around with four shocks with a decent blood pressure. And then she arrested again in your parking lot."

"Two minutes, Dr. Rees," the bedside nurse, Leandra, an-nounces. "Another shock?"

"Yes."

The beep sounds again, and after a quick "All clear!" Alexa arches on the stretcher again. But the screen shows the same erratic tracing of ventricular fibrillations, and Wes resumes CPR.

Four more defibrillator cycles pass without effect. Julie tries "stacking shocks"—using handheld paddles to double the electricity coming from the pads already wired to Alexa's chest—but Alexa's heart resists all electrical intervention.

Julie can feel her patient slipping away. She can't help but think of Michael again, and how she continued to crunch his chest in CPR long after it was too late. But there's still one option left for Alexa. "Call for the perfusionist and the cardiac surgeon! We're putting her on ECMO," Julie says, using the acronym for extracorporeal membranous oxygenation, also known as heart-lung bypass, which is usually reserved for patients undergoing heart surgery.

Goran steps over from the bay beside her, where the nurse has just switched off the monitor and the mechanical CPR device, meaning his patient has already been pronounced dead.

Julie can tell in one glance what Goran is thinking, but there's no way she is going to give up on Alexa yet. "They got to her sooner than yours, Gor," she says. "This one still has a chance."

He nods, but his sad eyes brim with skepticism.

A woman in blue scrubs runs into the room, her ID tags flying, and introduces herself as only "the perfusionist," which means she's the expert at running the heart-lung bypass machine.

Moments later, an older bearded man in green scrubs hobbles through the doorway. Julie's heart sinks as she recognizes the chief of cardiac surgery. "What've we got?" Dr. Harold Mott demands of no one in particular.

"Opioid overdose," Julie says, leaning over Alexa. "She arrested with paramedics. Persistent v. fib. She should—"

Harold is vehemently shaking his head as he cuts her off. "You know the drill, Dr. Rees! Drug overdoses are not candidates for ECMO. Period."

"She's still in v. fib. Means the arrest is more recent. Her heart still has a chance!"

"Her heart might. But her brain doesn't. The protocol is clear. No drug overdoses."

"She's only sixteen."

"Age has nothing to do with it. She's excluded."

Julie whirls to face him. "I'll put the lines in myself, Dr. Mott. One way or the other, she's ending up on that bypass machine."

"In violation of protocol?"

"If it saves her life."

"Which it won't," Harold says, as he pivots and walks out of the room.

Julie turns to Leandra. "Get me a cannulation kit. And let's prep the groin."

"Julija . . ." Goran says. "Harold—asshole that he can be—is correct."

"Don't need him," she says as she reaches for the large syringe and connected needle inside the sterile kit Leandra has just opened in front of her.

"This isn't about the past," Goran says quietly.

"I know that!" she snaps, and then forces the defensiveness from her tone. "If it was your kid, would you want me to stop now?"

He wavers a moment. "How can I help?"

"Find me the vein and artery with the ultrasound."

Leandra pushes a stool beside the patient's right hip, and Julie sits down on it. As she wipes down the exposed groin with an iodine cleanser, Julie hears Goran wheeling the portable ultrasound closer. He positions the machine above her so that she can easily view the screen. He applies the lubricated probe to the skin, until two black tubes—the femoral artery and vein—appear in the center of the gray haze that otherwise fills the screen.

Julie wills away the butterflies in her stomach as she pokes the large needle through the skin overlying the groin and pushes it forward until she sees the bright flash on the screen, indicating the metallic tip has entered the major artery. The syringe fills with bright red blood, and she uncouples it from the needle. Blood pumps from the needle's hub with each chest compression, until Julie threads a long advancing wire through it and into the artery. Leaving the end of the wire waving in the air, she reaches for a fresh needle and syringe and repeats the steps with the femoral vein.

She uses a scalpel to nick the skin overlying where each of the two wires emerges from the groin after the needles have been withdrawn. As expected, blood oozes out of the arterial site. She calmly reaches for the smallest of the rubber dilators and runs it over the wire, creating a tunnel through the skin to the blood vessel. She enlarges the passage with three more dilators, each sequentially wider in diameter, and then threads a hose-sized cannula through the skin and into the artery. She repeats the procedure for the vein and then passes the ends of the cannulas to the perfusionist, who couples them to receiving tubes on the bypass machine. The perfusionist taps a few buttons and the ECMO machine whirs to life. The clear tubes fill with blood as the electronic pump assumes the role of Alexa's heart and lungs for her.

"Stop CPR," Julie says, and the paramedic pulls his hands from her chest.

"I feel a decent pulse," Sandy announces, holding her fingers against the patient's neck.

"And the blood pressure is fifty-five on thirty," Leandra adds.

Julie looks over her shoulder and sees the ICU fellow turning off the monitor above the Asian girl's mottled face.

"Maybe this one," Goran says as he rests a hand on her shoulder. But his tone isn't hopeful.

"Maybe," Julie says as she stares into Alexa's impassive eyes. She struggles, futilely, to stave off another mental image of Michael.

CHAPTER 2

Aiden Wilder stares at the spreadsheets that span the dual monitors on his desk. Hard as he tries to focus, he might as well be reading Latin or Sanskrit. Normally this is where Aiden thrives, doing what he's known for: making sense of the figures on such ambitious development projects. Not today. It's just one giant jumble. And, despite the perfectly comfortable seventy-degree temperature inside his thirty-second-floor air-conditioned corner office, sweat keeps dripping into his eyes. The intestinal cramps are almost unbearable.

Fuck you, Pete! he thinks again. It was a betrayal, no other way to look at it. Aiden had always thought of his family doctor, Peter McDonald, as a friend. And then, without any warning, not a proper one, anyway, Pete announced a few weeks ago that he couldn't continue to renew Aiden's oxycodone prescriptions, sputtering some lame excuse about how the College of Physicians and Surgeons is enforcing stricter rules on narcotic-prescribing practices because the risk of opioid dependence in chronic pain is too high. Or some such bullshit. Aiden couldn't even listen to the whole babbling spiel.

Is it my fault that I need these stupid painkillers? he thinks as another knifelike spasm racks his abdomen. *Did I deliberately blow out my knee playing ultimate Frisbee and then botch the goddamn surgery afterwards?*

Giving up, Aiden flings the desktop mouse away in frustration. He glances over to ensure the door is locked, even though he knows it is. He reaches his trembling hand into the drawer and pulls out the little baggie inside. He had no idea how difficult it would be to find legitimate prescriptions after Pete abandoned him. At first Aiden had some luck at the walk-in clinics and even, twice, at the ER. But for the last three days he hasn't been able to find a single physician in Vancouver willing to write him a prescription.

He stares at the little bag with disgust. It still makes Aiden sick that he had to resort to buying drugs off a smart-ass dirtbag dealer on the street, like he's some cliché of a junkie. For Christ's sake, he's now the second-highest-ranking partner in the development firm that he joined as an intern not fifteen years before.

But the cramps, the bone pains, the sweats, the diarrhea, and the constant threat of puking are too much. And the craving is like nothing he has ever known. Aiden honestly believes he would trade his own mother for a single pill. For the relief alone.

He grabs a tablet from inside the bag with damp trembling fingers, trying not to wet the other pills. He considers what the dealer had told him: "These fake oxys are badass. Could be too harsh for a preppy dude like you. Maybe just drop a half tab at a go?"

Screw that, Aiden thinks as he pops a whole pill in his mouth, swallowing it with his own saliva.

He rocks in his chair, as if the motion might speed up the pill's absorption.

Five minutes pass. Nothing. He bargains with a God he doesn't believe in. *This will be it. Just a few tablets to see me through. To wean me off. Then I'm done with it.*

And then, after what seems like forever, it happens. The fingers still. The stomach settles. The familiar tingles fill his belly. *Peace.* That's all he ever wanted.

But it doesn't just stop there. The most intense warmth floods over him. As if he were immersed in a hot spring. As if he had fallen into the arms of an angel. He's never known contentment like this. *Elation*. Even as his head bounces off the keyboard. Even as his fingers turn blue beside his face. Even as his eyes close, and his chest stills.

CHAPTER 3

I should be in my own bed, Julie thinks, craving the firm embrace of her memory-foam mattress, one of the few extravagances she owns. The past night was one of the most draining of her career. And the teenage overdose victims weren't the only patients who died on her shift.

No sooner had the resuscitation room been cleared than the paramedics rushed in a thirty-three-year-old man who was bleeding out from multiple stab wounds, after his delusional, crystal-meth-enraged girlfriend thrust a steak knife between his ribs while he was still sleeping. He was stabbed four more times before a neighbor, hearing the screams, broke in and wrestled the knife away. The patient had arrived at the ER without a pulse, but Julie resuscitated him enough—through massive blood transfusions and two large-caliber chest tubes—to get him to the operating room alive. But the surgeons couldn't stem the hemorrhage, and he died on the table. Yet another victim, indirectly at least, of drug abuse.

Though Julie has already discharged the last of her patients and finished her paperwork, she still hasn't left the hospital following her overnight shift. She dropped in on the ICU on her way out of the building, without intending to stay, but has lingered there for over ten minutes. She sits curled up on the chair beside Alexa O'Neill's bed, hoping to witness something she knows it's too early to see and might well never be possible: the sight of the girl rousing.

Julie has pulled the curtain open across the glass-walled partition that separates the rooms so she can keep an eye on Dylan Berg in the next stretcher over. The boy, whose whole body is pocked with distinct scaly patches of psoriasis, was the last of the teens from the party to reach the ER, and the only one whose heart was still beating on arrival. Dylan had stopped breathing, like the other kids on scene, and then suffered two seizures in the back of the ambulance. When he finally came to, he had been so delirious—thrashing and flailing on the stretcher and crying out nonsensically—that Julie had no choice but to stick a breathing tube down his trachea and paralyze him with anesthetic agents to protect him from hurting himself further.

Despite the heavy sedation of his medically induced coma, Dylan moves his head occasionally. Alexa, on the other hand, is totally still except for the ventilator-driven rhythmic rise and fall of her chest.

"Are you lost?" someone asks from over Julie's shoulder.

Julie looks over to Dr. Kamalpreet Singh standing in the room's doorway. "Hi, Kam." She flicks a finger from one bed to the other. "Both of these kids came in on my watch."

"So I heard. Some real fireworks downstairs last night." Kam smiles as she steps into Alexa's room. "Bold move opting to put the girl on ECMO."

Julie can't tell if there's judgment buried in the words. She has known Kam, an ICU specialist, or intensivist, since medical school, where she was one year behind her. Kam was always smiling back then, too, to the point where Julie, while always liking Kam, has never fully trusted her.

"She's off the pump now."

"Yeah, her heart has recovered well." Kam's smile vanishes.

But not her brain. Fatigue or not, Julie infers unspoken accusation. "Time will tell."

"You know the drill. It could take a couple days or more to figure out whether she's vegetative or not."

Kam is right. No fancy diagnostic testing, not even an MRI or an electroencephalogram, will predict for certain whether a patient's brain has survived a prolonged spell of oxygen deprivation like the one Alexa had suffered. Neurologists wait a minimum of forty-eight hours before declaring a patient brain-dead. Sometimes even longer.

Kam motions to the glass partition. "The boy is showing promising signs."

Julie glances over just as Dylan arches his neck again while a nurse suctions secretion from his ventilatory tube. "These kids are the only two to survive the night," she says.

"In a few years, my Chuni will be going to those same kind of parties." Kam rubs her temple. "Five of them. Dead. What the hell were they thinking?"

"They probably weren't. And I highly doubt they had any idea what they were taking."

"That's the way it is now. All drugs are cross-contaminated with this fentanyl crap. Good thing you . . ." Kam's words taper off.

"Got out when I did?"

"Ancient history, huh?" Kam clears her throat.

"Where are their families?" Julie asks, refusing to internalize her colleague's embarrassment.

"Alexa's parents have been here all night. They just stepped out to make some calls. Dylan's parents are flying in from Toronto. He was only out here visiting his friend from summer camp." Kam exhales. "His friend was pronounced dead at the scene."

Julie's gaze drifts back to Alexa. Her red hair is pulled back and away from the intravenous lines in her neck, and spills over the top of the stretcher. She looks even more childlike than she did in the ER. *She has no business being here.*

Kam rests a hand lightly on Julie's shoulder. "Listen, I understand why you chose to put the girl on ECMO."

"But?"

"Harold Mott came by earlier. He was making noises. Says this case will have to be reviewed at the quality-and-safety rounds."

"And so it should be." Julie folds her arms. "I was her attending physician. It was my call, Kam. I'd do it again, if I had to."

Kam lifts her hand off Julie's shoulder. "Just wanted to give you the heads-up."

Fuck Harold! Based on their history, Julie could never do right by him, anyway. But all she says is, "Duly noted. Thanks."

A petite woman with blond hair pulled back tightly in a bun flies into the room, followed by a slender man who trudges behind with his head hung low. Their body language alone tells Julie they must be the parents. As Alexa's mother squeezes past her, Julie inhales a whiff of rosemary and bergamot. The fragrance only seems to accentuate the woman's tangible desperation, the contrast like flowers at a crime scene.

Alexa's mother hovers over the bed and clings to her daughter's hand. "I just spoke to Liam, babe." Her voice quavers as she strokes Alexa's forehead. "You've got to wake up now. Your big brother is gonna fly home soon to see you." She snaps her head over her shoulder and locks eyes with Kam. "Any news, Dr. Singh?"

Kam offers a somber smile. "It's too early, Elaine."

Elaine O'Neill turns to Julie with a bewildered expression.

Kam motions from Julie to Elaine. "This is Dr. Rees, Elaine. She's the emergency doctor who—"

"The one who saved my baby!" Elaine's eyes well with tears, and she covers her mouth with her free hand.

"I . . . I . . ." Julie stammers. "It was a team effort."

Elaine reaches out and clutches Julie's wrist. "You were the one who put Lex on the heart pump. To keep her alive."

"It was the only option . . . left."

Elaine turns back to her daughter. "This is the doctor who saved you, babe. You need to wake up. To thank her." She chokes out a laugh between her sobs. "It's only polite, Lex." Julie wishes she would stop, but instead Elaine says to her husband, "We'll get Lex to make her one of those beautiful cards she designs. Right, Tom?"

"Yeah, sure," Tom O'Neill mutters.

The moment Julie meets Tom's gaze, she senses that behind his shell-shocked expression he's aware how grim his daughter's prognosis is, even if his wife doesn't seem to be.

"Drugs?" Elaine asks. "Are you certain, Dr. Singh?"

Kam nods.

"How can that be?" Elaine demands of her husband. "You know how she felt about them. Especially after Doug and all."

Kam's nose crinkles. "Doug?"

"My brother," Tom says with a slight shrug. "He's an alcoholic."

"It runs in Tom's family," Elaine says. "Their uncle and grandfather, too. Alexa is close to Doug. She's gone to Al Anon meetings and everything. She understands the risks. She's passionate about alcohol and drug issues. I don't think she's ever had a drink before. Has she, Tom?"

"She's a teen, Laine."

"Fentanyl or heroin?" Elaine cries. "My God! She'd never!"

Julie's throat thickens, watching the distraught woman. She carries the same genetic propensity for addiction as Alexa does, except in Julie's case it's on her mom's side of the family where alcoholism runs rampant. Julie, too, had been acutely aware of the dangers of substance abuse. She had never smoked weed and rarely touched alcohol until medical school, where she met Michael. But her own downward spiral was breathtakingly quick. "Alexa probably had no idea she was taking fentanyl," Julie says.

"Or maybe any drug," Kam points out.

Elaine gapes at them. "You mean someone could have just spiked her drink with it?"

"Possibly." Kam nods to Julie. "I'd defer to Dr. Rees on this one. She's not only an ER doctor, she's also a toxicologist."

"Dr. Singh is right," Julie says. "We're finding fentanyl derivatives everywhere nowadays. In cocaine, crystal meth, ketamine . . . even in some joints. Some of the newer derivatives are so potent you don't need to ingest them to overdose. Skin contact alone is enough."

Elaine stares desperately at her. "At a pre-grad party?"

Tom steps up to the bedside and drapes an arm over Elaine's shoulder. "Who'd do that to those kids?" he asks in a monotone that is somehow more moving than his wife's tears. "To my girl?"

CHAPTER 4

*G*round Zero. That's what Markku Saarinen calls the infamous Vancouver intersection at Main and Hastings. Markku has never been to New York. He was only nine years old when the Twin Towers fell. Besides, the intersection, with its turn-of-the-century brownstones and commercial brick buildings, one of which ironically is a legitimate drugstore, bears little resemblance to the apocalyptical devastation of 9/11. But the nickname has stuck for Markku ever since he came up with or, possibly, stole it. The busy corner does share at least one trait with the original Ground Zero site in terms of the suffering it has witnessed; except in New York the deaths happened in minutes, while in Vancouver it has taken years.

As Markku heads down Hastings Street, bitter rain spits down from the dusky charcoal skies and only compounds the misery around him. The businesses are barely closed and the storefronts shuttered in steel, but the usual array of sleeping bags, shopping carts, and spread-out pages of discarded newspapers has already claimed most of the sidewalk. The stenches of urine, body odor, and stale beer meld with the smell of cooking grease from a nearby Chinese restaurant in a toxic cloud. Despite his livelihood, Markku is appalled by the life-forms sprawled along the sidewalk before the spring sun has even set. *How many times do you have to tell them to pace themselves?*

Of course, Markku knows better than most how strong the temptation is. Every time his phone rings, a voice in his head tells him it could be about Elsa. She has already overdosed four times since they've been together. He has had to revive her twice himself with frantic injections of naloxone from the prepackaged antidote kits that the city hands out like candy to anyone who will carry one. The last time, Elsa turned so blue that he had to plunge the needle straight through her jeans and into her thigh.

Elsa. Markku wouldn't be mired in this pathetic world if it weren't for her. Or, at least, that's what he tells himself on days like today. He's never known anyone like her. Blue eyes that can break a heart from across the street. A laugh that can melt stone. When she's on, she's almost irresistible. But Elsa can't get through a day without a fix. And she's so reckless about it. "We're living on borrowed time, doll," she says. "That's what makes us so very beautiful." Elsa loves to tease Markku with words they both understand will, sooner or later, prove to be prophetic.

Markku slows as he passes a man crumpled in a doorway with his neck craned awkwardly back and to his right. Markku bends down to wave a hand in front of the man's face. The moment he feels his warm breath against his palm, he straightens up and moves on.

His first client, Zack Hollands, is already waiting for him at the corner of Hastings and Gore with hands stuffed in his pockets as he leans back against the faux-brick wall of the First United Church, which provides no real shelter from the relentless drizzle. Even from across the street, Markku can see Zack's weird tattoos. Or maybe Markku is just imagining he can, since he finds them so creepy.

"Dude, over here!" Zack calls, as though he weren't in plain sight.

Markku grits his teeth as he crosses the road to meet Zack. Even

though street-level dealing in the heart of the Downtown Eastside carries little risk—the Vancouver Police Department would have to quintuple the size of its force to properly crack down on it—Markku can't hide his annoyance. "We've talked about this, Zack, haven't we?"

"Yeah, yeah, discretion," Zack says, bobbing from foot to foot. "But what the fuck, man? Can't I call out to a friend?"

If we were friends, then maybe. But Markku lets it go. He can tell from Zack's jitteriness how dope-sick his customer already is. "You got enough for five?"

"Just four." Zack digs frantically in the pocket of his jeans and withdraws a mix of crumpled bills—twenties, tens, and fives—that are, fittingly, as dirty as his fingernails. Zack is too addicted to ever hold down a legitimate job, and with his androgynous good looks and nervous manner, he's too fragile to be breaking-and-entering or even dumpster-diving. That leaves only one likely source for his cash: hooking, or "gay for pay," as they call it. Markku never asks. Not only is it none of his business, but it helps him pretend he's not really part of the cycle of petty crime that drives this business.

Markku accepts the money, counting to eighty, and then reaches inside his own jacket and extracts a small clear baggie. He digs out one of the five gray pills—each marked with the distinctive "80" imprint on one side and "CDN" on the other—and slips it back into a larger bag in his pocket. As his fingers move, Markku does the math in his head. The margins are staggering. Twenty dollars per five-milligram tablet, which cost him five bucks apiece. His supplier might pay a dollar per pill, if that. And Markku doubts it costs the people running the factory in China more than a few cents to produce enough fentanyl to make one.

Zack darts a hand out toward the baggie, but Markku pulls it away, closing it inside his grip. "Show me your kit!"

"Not this again. Jesus, Markku!" Zack grabs the side of his own neck. "Every fucking time!"

"Exactly. Every time. Or find another hookup."

"OK, OK!" Zack stuffs a hand into his jacket pocket and extracts the black canvas kit that is emblazoned with a red cross and contains the opioid antidote naloxone inside. Markku still finds the packaging ironic. As if it's supposed to be some Red Cross humanitarian package intended for a Third World war zone. Then again, the analogy isn't so far-fetched.

"Open it," Markku instructs, knowing that as often as not, the lifesaving vial of naloxone and syringe is missing.

Zack fumbles with a shaky hand to jerk open the zipper and expose the clean syringe and intact vial inside. "Proper," Markku says, satisfied.

"Thanks, Mom," Zack huffs as he zips the kit shut. "Now . . . please?"

Markku extends his hand to Zack without opening his fist. "What's the other rule?"

"Never use alone."

"Exactly! But I know you do, you stupid fuck. I've seen you stumbling down the lane by yourself."

Markku opens his palm and Zack sweeps the pills from it.

"Christ, Zack, there are fix rooms all across the Downtown Eastside with people paid to watch you. Get off your ass and use one!"

"Yeah, yeah," Zack says as he pockets the supply and begins to turn away. "Why do you care, anyway?"

"Figure it out, dude," Markku tells Zack's already receding shadow. "Not so great for business to lose my regulars, is it?"

Markku wishes it were that simple. Despite his multiple warnings to clients, he's still lost two of them to overdoses in the past month alone. He tells himself he doesn't care. That it's not his problem. That there's an endless supply of new users. But all the rationalization in the world doesn't fully wash away the sense of responsibility. Not when Elsa could be next.

CHAPTER 5

Julie assumes, at first, that the pounding must be in her dream. Then her eyes pop open, and she's overcome with the panicky disorientation of being ripped from a deep nap. *Have I overslept? Did I miss my shift?* She consults her bedside clock and calms when she realizes it's only a few minutes before three p.m., and she's just been asleep for three hours.

She hops out of bed, throws on her sweatpants, and pads over to the door. She opens it to find Anson Chen, dressed in a slim-fitting navy suit with white shirt and open collar. She doesn't have to glance down to know that he's wearing polished brown Italian oxfords and socks with some colorful print. Nor does she bother to ask how he cleared the locked front door to her condo building.

"There you are," Anson says.

"Here I am," she says with a yawn. "Where was I supposed to be?"

"I dunno." He shrugs. "The hospital? Poison Control Center? Golf course? A bar? Anywhere but home in bed in the middle of the afternoon."

"Haven't you ever worked nights, Anson?"

"Not since I got my detective badge at twenty-eight. Some of us are upwardly mobile."

"Hmmm." She bites back a smile. "I guess that means you've already made inspector?"

"Nah, but can I help it if the VPD is rife with racism?"

"Sure." She can't help but laugh. "Why don't you complain to the chief of police? He might sympathize, being Asian himself and all."

"See, they've already met their quota." He ducks between her and the door, slipping inside the apartment.

Julie shuts the door and follows him over to the raised kitchen counter. He's already seated himself on one of the two barstools, his elbow resting on the countertop.

"Tea?" Julie offers as she lifts the kettle and fills it from the tap.

"No cab franc or Nebbiolo uncorked? What's the point of having rich doctor friends if you don't benefit from some of the perks?" His broad smile is infectious.

"Is that what we are, Anson, friends?" Julie asks, only half joking. Theirs is one of the most ill-defined relationships she's ever experienced. As far as she knows, he's still single. They've clicked since their first meeting, when Anson consulted her on an overdose death from a heart medication that he suspected—and later proved—to be intentional, the handiwork of an excessively greedy daughter-in-law. While Julie goes months without seeing Anson in person, they text often and in flirtatious fits that have yet to materialize into anything more.

"Tea works," he says, ignoring her question. "Can I at least trouble you for a splash of milk?"

"As high-maintenance as ever," Julie says with a mock sigh as she carries the kettle over to the stove and lights the gas element.

"Word is you had a memorable shift last night, Dr. Rees."

Julie feels her levity drain away. She pictures Alexa lying on the stretcher, with her frantic mother hovering over her while her father stares hopelessly at the floor. "Would rather not remember it at all. Are you investigating it?"

"Theo and I, yeah."

"It's a homicide?"

"We don't know what it is yet. The superintendent expects us to find out. There's already a ton of publicity." He exhales heavily. "Understandable. Five kids dead and all."

Julie pulls down two owl-faced ceramic mugs from a shelf and plunks a tea bag in each. "I've never seen one like this, Anson."

"I would've guessed you'd seen it all, in your line—or lines—of work."

"I've never had to pronounce three teens dead in one shift. With one other barely hanging on. And probably won't make it."

"I thought with these new fentanyl analogues it's incredibly easy to overdose."

"It is. Especially those drug-naïve users who have no inherent tolerance to opioids."

"Would it kill you to just say 'first-time users'?"

"But it's not only them. The ones at highest risk are former users who've been sober for a stretch. They lose the tolerance to opioids that they once had built up. What used to be their regular dose of down often turns lethal for them."

"Perfect. We're averaging, what? About four deaths a day in Vancouver?"

"Closer to three."

"OK, five in one go is a bad day. A very bad day. But it doesn't necessarily make it anything more than tragically bad luck . . . and wild stupidity." Anson leans over the counter toward her, almost as if challenging her. "Does it?"

"It might."

"Why? What's so different here, Doctor?"

Julie considers it for a moment, mentally switching gears from physician to toxicologist. "Did the crime scene technicians find any needles or other drug paraphernalia at the scene?"

"Not so far, no."

"Track marks on any of the victims?"

He shakes his head.

"So these kids didn't inject their drugs, which would have been the deadliest route. Did the techs find any evidence—pipes, hollowed pens, or even tinfoil—to suggest the kids had been smoking it?"

"They're still testing, but far as I know, they haven't found much of anything aside from a few bottles that were almost empty."

"So there are only three other possible routes of entry—insufflated, ingested, or transdermal."

"Holy! It's just like every time I call my grandma and have to remind her I don't speak Mandarin so good. And she's ninety-friggin'-two!" He groans. "So in English . . . those kids either snorted, swallowed, or absorbed the drug through their skin. Right?"

"You catch on . . . eventually." Julie grins. "And if they snorted or used through their skin, you'd think they would've found evidence of containers or patches. At least straws."

"So they must've swallowed pills? Makes sense. They could've been told it was anything—ketamine, meth, Ecstasy, whatever. Their dealer might not even have known what the hell he was even selling them."

"Sad that a bunch of preppy eleventh-graders would know where to buy those street drugs."

"C'mon, Julie. They're everywhere. Even in the junior schools. Besides, who said all of them went? Bet you one kid had the bright idea. Maybe the other kids didn't even know they were doing hard drugs."

"Makes sense, I suppose." The whistling of the kettle summons Julie. She takes it off the stove and fills both mugs with boiling water. "But there's a glaring problem with your theory."

"Which is?"

"You understand how people die of opioid overdoses, don't you?"

"Medically? They pass out and eventually stop breathing. Their hearts just give out, right?"

"Sort of. These opioids—heroin, oxy, fentanyl, whatever—are unique in how they kill. They suppress the centers in the brain stem responsible for the respiratory drive. Breathing."

"Like I said, they pass out and then stop breathing."

"Yeah, but sometimes they're still awake—groggy but awake— and they still won't breathe. Anyone who overdoses on an opioid will stop breathing."

"So they suffocate even though they're surrounded by oxygen?"

"Basically. But the treatment is so simple. The naloxone antidote that most addicts carry with them binds with the opioid receptors in the brain and works almost instantly to reverse the overdose. And even if they don't have those kits on them, someone can easily perform mouth-to-mouth until help arrives. Users revive each other all the time. So most fatal overdoses happen when someone is using alone and can't get help." *Except in Michael's case.*

"OK, so there was no one sober enough at that party to call for help."

"That's the thing, Anson. People do overdose together, occasionally." She fights off the memory of waking up wrapped in Michael's cool, lifeless arms. "But even then, the onset of the overdose is variable. They don't black out at the same moment. Especially if they swallowed the drug, because it always takes longer to kick in and it affects people at different rates."

"You're saying that seven of them wouldn't pass out at the exact same time?"

"Exactly. A few of them should've remained alert long enough to call for help."

Anson rubs his chin. "So what happened at that party, Julie?"

She only shrugs.

"There's no medical explanation?"

She hesitates. "Only one that I can think of."

"Out with it . . ."

"The opioid those kids took must have been so potent and so fast-acting that they didn't just take enough of it to overdose. They must have had enough in their systems to kill each of them many times over. And it had to be something that hit them almost immediately."

"Not fentanyl, then?"

"No."

"Carfentanil?"

"Possibly. Or alfentanil or sufentanil or any one of ten other fentanyl derivatives. New ones are popping up all the time, each more potent than the last. For some, just a few grains of the active ingredient can cause overdose."

"They're testing the blood and urine on the victims. We'll soon know what they took."

"Not necessarily."

"Why not?"

"These ultrapotent fentanyl derivatives are metabolized in the liver. Even though they start off as different drugs, they often get broken down to the same metabolite. And if the original or parent compound is no longer detectable—"

"You can't tell which drug they took."

"Not without very sophisticated toxicology testing, which can take days or longer."

"Perfect."

"But Anson, you've already told enough for me to know those kids didn't just get some dirty drug laced with a bit of fentanyl." She pauses, but he doesn't comment. "Deliberately or not, they must've been poisoned with a superpotent opioid. And if it happened to them . . ."

"There will be others." Anson leans back on his stool with his arms folded, digesting it all in silence for a few more moments. "OK. I'm convinced." His eyes lock onto hers. "I'm gonna need your help."

CHAPTER 6

The new Mercedes S 560 idles so quietly that Jian Li Wei—Wayne to his Canadian associates—barely senses it's running. It was a good buy, he thinks with satisfaction. Besides, its matte-black trim perfectly complements the fire-engine-red Porsche 911 and the silver Audi S5 when they're all lined up inside his four-car garage.

Li Wei and his little brother Hui, or Hugh, are parked at one a.m. in the lot across from the huge riverfront casino in Richmond, which is Vancouver's closest suburb, just across the Fraser River. For the Jian brothers, it's not an uncommon time or place to be doing business.

Li Wei turns to Hui, whose gaze is fixed on the neon sign towering over the casino. "They only call us at this time of night when they're losing," he says in English.

"This one always loses," Hui answers in Mandarin, without shifting his eyes from the sign. "And he's going to lose even more if he doesn't hurry."

"It's only been five minutes, brother. It's easier to wait for good news than for bad."

"What fortune cookie did you steal that from?"

Li Wei inhales slowly. Hui hasn't changed since they were children. He was always brooding, even then. He has only two moods: bad and worse. But Hui's the smartest business partner Li Wei could wish for. And, of course, being family, he would trust him with his life.

Hui finally turns away from the sign. "The Persians are a problem," he says, apropos of nothing.

"They have been for years."

"Yeah, but now they're a problem we need to solve."

Li Wei doesn't like this kind of talk. His throat burns from the acid reflux. He wishes he'd remembered to bring his ginger pills or even the Tums he usually keeps for emergencies. "Time will tell, brother," he says, hoping Hui will let it go but knowing better.

Before Hui can reply, the back door opens, and a man slips into the back seat, making little more noise than the car's engine.

Li Wei looks over his shoulder at Ping Zhang, a wisp of a man. Even in the dim interior light, Li Wei can see that Ping is already sweating under his oversized navy suit.

Ping wipes his brow and adjusts his wire-rimmed glasses as he nods to the brothers. "*Nǐ hǎo.*"

"Good evening to you, Ping," Li Wei says. "Were the tables good to you tonight?"

"No, no, not tonight," Ping answers in his nasal pitch, as if Li Wei were being serious. "But the tide is about to turn."

"Six hundred thousand more," Hui says without even looking back at him. "Is that what you need from us?"

"Yes, yes."

"On top of the five hundred thousand from last week?"

"You know me. Both of you." Ping's voice cracks. "I always pay. Next month. I will wire the money to your account in China. Like always."

Hui only grunts in response. He glances over to Li Wei, who nods his approval, and then reaches for the black leather knockoff briefcase—of which they have dozens more at home—at his feet. Hui rests it on his lap and clicks open the lid. He pulls the legal documents off the top, revealing the cash below, bundled in stacks of easily counted hundred-dollar bills. He shifts the briefcase closer to Ping until the glow of the interior reflects off the top layer of bills. But Hui only passes him the pages of the contract.

Ping flips through it, stopping on the third page. "Fifty-nine percent?" he cries, shaking the papers in his hand. "It was only fifty-two last week!"

Li Wei is still surprised that Ping can even read the terms of the contract. He's never heard the man utter a word in English. "The bigger the loan, the higher the risk. Therefore, the higher interest rate," Li Wei says with feigned helplessness. "It's simple economics. But if you can get a better rate elsewhere . . ."

Hui begins to slowly close the lid on the briefcase.

Ping holds up a hand. "I wish," he says with a resigned sigh. He reaches inside his suit pocket and withdraws a pen. He flips to the last page in the contract, rests it against his leg, and signs at the bottom with a quick flourish.

"You need to initial—" Li Wei begins, but Ping is already flipping back through the pages and initialing on all the appropriate spots.

Finished, Ping passes the contract over to Hui, who then hands him the briefcase.

"Good," Li Wei says, and means it. He knows the contract is totally legal and ironclad, since it's one point under the sixty percent interest rate that would make it criminal usury. Ping is again using his home in the heart of the affluent Shaughnessy neighborhood as collateral. On paper, the house is worth at least five million dollars. But Li Wei never fully trusts the assessments. He's driven past it twice in the past week to convince himself of the value. After all, he's confident it will soon be theirs.

CHAPTER 7

Goran bursts into the emergency doctors' private office with his usual raucousness. "I was too old for this job twenty years ago!" he thunders.

Julie glances up from the electronic medical records she's reviewing on her tablet. "Good evening to you, too, Gor," she says with a smile.

"You're working again?" He strides toward her, his salt-and-pepper hair askew and his stethoscope flung haphazardly over his rumpled scrub top. "Another night shift?"

"Back-to-back. Living the dream."

"On a weekend, no less! What's going on, Julija? Are you into a loan shark for some serious jack?"

"*Sarious yack.*" Julie parrots him, playfully exaggerating his accent. "Where do you come up with this stuff, Gor?"

"You know . . . through my peeps."

She chuckles. "How's the evening going?"

"Less dramatic than last night, praise be to God. The drunks are beginning to roll in, though."

"Them, I can deal with."

"How's the girl doing? From last night?"

"I haven't been up to the ICU since this morning to see Alexa." She neglects to mention that she has been texting Kam Singh for frequent updates. "She's off the heart-lung pump, but far as I know she hasn't come to."

"It's early, Julija."

"Yeah." But she knows as well as he does that it's still a poor sign.

He clasps her shoulder in his oversized grip. "And how about our ever-charming heart surgeon? Any more rumblings from Harold the Great?"

"I hear he's forwarding the case for formal review."

"Harold is too tall for short man's complex. So there's only one other possible explanation. SPS."

"SPS? I'm afraid to even ask."

Goran's eyes light up. "Small penis syndrome."

Julie pats the back of his hand and smiles her gratitude. "I don't care what Harold thinks. Honestly. I've dealt with far bigger pricks." When he opens his mouth to speak, she preempts his inevitable size joke with a shake of her finger. "Don't go there!"

"I wasn't . . . OK, perhaps."

She clears her throat. "Gor, I spoke to Alexa's parents this morning . . ."

She doesn't need to say anything else. He squeezes her shoulder again. "It really is too early to tell, Julija."

"Probably. And at least Dylan Berg—the kid who came in just as you were leaving—is beginning to come around. Looks like he's going to make it."

"Good. Good. That's something, is it not?"

"Yeah. Just not enough."

"My sons, they got up to some Olympic-level moronic shenanigans in their teens. Twin felons, I used to call them. One Halloween, Luka almost burnt down our house with illegal fireworks. Lada wanted to strangle him." His smile fades. "But those parents who have to bury their children now . . . I cannot even put myself there, Julija."

Julie can't help but think of Michael's funeral. It was the last time she saw his parents. She'll never forget the sight of them huddled together under a shared umbrella on the other side of the grave from her. His father stared blankly past her, but his mother's silent glare practically screamed: *You did this to us!*

The overhead speaker crackles to life. "Dr. Rees to resus one, stat!"

Grateful for the distraction, Julie hops to her feet. "See you Tuesday. Tell Maria I'm looking forward to catching up," she says as she rushes past him and out the door.

Julie races down the hallway and into the resuscitation room. The usual controlled chaos prevails, with nurses and paramedics swirling around the stretcher. People speak in clipped phrases. Monitors beep steadily. On the stretcher lies a cadaverous man with a dusky complexion and distinctive tattoos that run along the sides of his neck. His pupils are the size of pinholes—a consistent sign of an opioid overdose. The stench of his dirty socks permeates the room. Sally, a stocky respiratory therapist with long cornrow braids, leans over the head of the stretcher and "bags" the patient, pumping oxygen through a face mask that she keeps firmly sealed to his mouth with her other hand.

Julie views the monitor above the stretcher and sees that the heart rate and blood pressure are stable, but the patient's oxygen saturation reads only seventy-two percent, which is dangerously low for a man of his age. Her eyes find the balding paramedic who stands beside the respiratory therapist. "Talk to me, please."

"Twenty-something John Doe," the paramedic says. "No ID on the guy. He was shooting up at the safe injection site on Pender Street when he just stopped breathing."

"How much naloxone did he get?"

"Staff gave him three shots. We've given him three more. So he's already had a total of two-point-four milligrams."

"And he hasn't woken up after six doses?" Julie slips on her glove and steps up to the stretcher across from Gwen, one of her favorite ER nurses.

Gwen leans over the patient while she pokes an intravenous catheter through the skin at the bend of his elbow. The dark red flash at the end of the catheter indicates she has hit the vein.

"He kind of woke up after the fifth shot of naloxone, but he drifted off a minute or two later," the paramedic says. "Stopped breathing, and we had to bag him again. The dude must've taken some strong stuff."

No shit. "Gwen, can you give him two more milligrams of naloxone and start an IV drip as soon as it's in?"

The androgynous nurse blows her an air kiss. "Anything for you, babe."

The mock flirtation barely registers. Gwen has been teasing her for years in the same affectionate, innocuous way. Still, Julie makes a mental note to have a quiet word with her later. In this post–Me Too era, outsiders might not appreciate the harmless playfulness of it.

"Can we also get blood work, a drug screen, and a stat chest X-ray on him?"

"Check, check, and check," Gwen says. "I'm way ahead of you."

Julie studies the patient, waiting for him to stir after the massive dose of opioid antidote Gwen just injected into him. But there's no response. Not even a minimal attempt to breathe on his own. *"Strong stuff" is a colossal understatement. Is this the same crap that killed those kids?* "Repeat the naloxone, please, Gwen."

"Another two milligrams? For real?"

"For very real. And he might need a lot more after that."

Julie plugs in her stethoscope's ear tips and applies the flat diaphragm to the man's sunken chest. She thinks of the cocky young resident who had proclaimed earlier in the week, "We won't even be carrying these obsolete contraptions in ten years." She didn't disagree—bedside ultrasound has replaced much of the stethoscope's function—but right now hers allows her to hear the coarse crackles in the bases of both lungs. It tells her that the patient has already choked on his own secretions and has developed what is known as aspiration pneumonia.

"We need to intubate him," she says.

"Thought you'd never ask." Gwen lifts up a curved endotracheal, or breathing, tube in one hand and a syringe filled with white anesthetic agent in another. "Ketamine OK for sedation?"

"Yeah. A hundred milligrams. And seventy milligrams of rocuronium, too," Julie says, calling for the medicine that will temporarily paralyze the patient and relax his jaw enough for her to thread the endotracheal tube down his throat, through his vocal cords, and into his windpipe.

"Given and given," Gwen announces seconds later.

Julie reaches for the handle of the scythe-shaped laryngoscope. She slides the curved blade along the patient's tongue and then pulls the handle upward, lifting his whole jaw. All she sees is the thick yellowish-white mucus obscuring the anatomy in his throat. At one time, when she was more junior, the total lack of visibility would've tightened her own throat with panic—once a patient is paralyzed, the clock is always ticking on the time remaining to secure an airway before brain damage or worse can occur—but not anymore. "Suction, please, Sally," she calmly instructs.

The respiratory therapist passes her the long and narrow handheld vacuum tube. With a steady hand, Julie inserts it over the laryngoscope's blade. Snorting loudly, it suctions away the gobs of mucus. The vocal cords pop into sight. Julie easily slips the tip of the endotracheal tube between them and into his trachea. "I'm in," she says as she straightens.

Sally connects the tube to the bag and pumps oxygen through it as she listens with her own stethoscope to either side of the patient's chest. "Tube placement is good," she confirms.

"Let's start broad-spectrum IV antibiotics—doses of pip-tazo and vancomycin," Julie says. "And can someone please page ICU for me? We got to move him. It's Saturday night. We're going to need this stretcher soon."

Ten minutes later, the patient is packaged for transport to the ICU with the tubes and lines hanging from a pole attached to his stretcher and a portable monitor on the mattress beside him. Gwen begins to wheel the stretcher toward the elevator.

"I'm coming, too," Julie says as she follows them out of the room.

"You sure, babe?" Gwen asks. "I got this."

"Like there was any doubt." Julie grins. "But I want to give handover to the ICU doc in person." She knows it's just an excuse to check in on Alexa again.

As they ride the secure elevator three floors up to the ICU, Gwen says, "The paralytic should have worn off by now, right?"

"Yeah. And he's still not breathing."

"Even after all that naloxone. What did he take, do you figure?"

"Must be some superpotent fentanyl derivative. Maybe even a new one?"

"Where the hell would he have gotten that?"

"Whatever it was, I think we're going to be seeing a whole lot more of it," Julie says, chilled by her own words.

"Wonderful," Gwen groans, shoving the stretcher out of the elevator as the doors open, toward the ICU.

"Room Twelve," barks the older clerk behind the main desk inside the ICU without even looking up from her computer screen.

Gwen rolls the stretcher into the room, where an ICU nurse is already waiting. Julie peels off in the opposite direction. She pauses outside Dylan Berg's room, inside of which she notices a middle-aged couple leaning over either side of his bedside and talking to him. The head of the bed is propped at a forty-five-degree angle and Dylan is breathing on his own, but his eyes are shut, and he doesn't appear to respond to his parents.

Julie moves to the next room, where Alexa lies flat on the stretcher with the ventilator tubing still in place. Her mother is asleep on the bedside chair with her head flopped forward, resting on the edge of Alexa's mattress, while her father leans against the glass partition in the corner. Alexa's hair is tied neatly behind her head now, but no matter how hard Julie searches for evidence of improvement, the girl's mannequin-like appearance is unchanged. Despite having never known Alexa, Julie's heart aches, as if she's watching her own relative barely cling to life.

Not wanting to wake Alexa's mother, Julie beckons her father outside of the room with a small wave.

"How are you and Elaine holding up?" Julie asks as Tom joins her.

He shrugs. "First time Elaine has slept in the past two days."

"Any change?"

"Lex was flapping her arms and legs earlier. Elaine was so excited, she cried. Until Dr. Singh told us it was only a seizure. From the brain damage."

Julie doubts Kam would have phrased it so harshly, but she doesn't argue. "Seizures are pretty common in these situations."

Tom motions to Dylan's room. "The kid beside her woke up earlier this evening. They pulled the breathing tube out of his throat and everything."

"Comas are highly unpredictable." She struggles to find words that reflect realism without stealing his hope. "Some patients rouse within hours, while others don't wake for weeks, months, or . . . more."

Tom's expression remains blank. "They still don't know where or how Lex got the drugs, do they?"

"Honestly, Tom, we still don't even know which specific drug was involved."

"You're going to find out?"

"We will. I work for Poison Control, too. I'll make sure we run every analysis. No stone left unturned. Promise."

Tom nods robotically.

"I also know the detective leading the investigation. Anson Chen. He's good. Really good. I'd trust him with my own . . . um . . ." She regrets the comment, regarding a detective who works in Homicide, before she's even finished making it. "Loved ones."

"If I were a detective, I'd start with Joshua."

"Who?"

"One of the kids at the party. He'd been hanging out with Alexa's friends lately."

"Why Joshua?"

"The others in her gang, they were—I don't know—so young. For sixteen-year-olds, anyway. Way more so than our son and his buddies used to act at this age. The other boys Alexa hung out with—Nick and Grayson—were kind of shy and a bit awkward around Elaine and me. Not this Joshua kid. He was always so talkative, so friendly. Too much so. I thought he might be sweet on Lex." He clears his throat. "If any of them did bring drugs to this party, he'd be my prime suspect."

"I'll let Detective Chen know."

"OK, thanks."

They lapse into an awkward silence. Julie shifts from foot to foot, trying to conjure a crumb of reassurance before she leaves, but nothing comes to mind.

"When Alexa was barely six months old, she had this terrible chest infection," Tom says. "Bronchiolitis. She ended up on a ventilator in the children's ICU for three days." He nods toward his wife.

"Almost like déjà vu. Elaine was glued to her bedside back then, too. So worried about her baby. Somehow, though, I knew Lex was going to pull through that time." When he looks up, his expression is still impassive, but his tired eyes burn with despair. "Lex isn't going to wake up this time, is she, Dr. Rees?" he asks, but Julie knows it isn't really a question.

CHAPTER 8

Huang Chonglin—Charlie, to his Canadian friends—feels nauseous as he approaches the young officer in her crisp navy Canada Customs uniform. But it has nothing to do with nerves. The flight from Shanghai had been one of the most turbulent Charlie, a seasoned transpacific traveler, has ever endured. He read somewhere that multiple factors—including sudden changes in wind temperature and jet streams—all contribute to turbulence. But he blames the pilots and vows to never again fly on the same airline. Even as he voices the thought to himself, though, he realizes it's an empty promise, since that airline has by far the most convenient flight times for his usual route.

"Are you all right, sir?" the stern-faced young woman asks with typical Canadian politeness.

I could kill those pilots for making me look guilty. "Airsickness," Charlie explains with a sheepish grin. "Very, very bumpy. My stomach is still not right. But much better since when we landed."

"I see," she says as she takes the Canadian passport from his hand and studies it. "How long have you been out of the country?"

"Six days." *Three longer than necessary*. But the very short turn-around times tend to draw more attention.

"You were in China the whole time?"

"Yes, all the time," he says, emphasizing his accent as he always does with customs officers. "Shenzhen and then Shanghai. My family live there."

"And the purpose of your trip?"

"I look at laptop screen suppliers."

"Computer hardware? That's your business?"

Charlie nods. "I own a store." Which is true. He does import computer equipment from China—primarily portable storage drives and laptop clones—to sell in the shop he co-owns with his older sister. And while running the store still consumes most of his time, it accounts for only a fraction of his income.

"You have no checked bags?"

"Always fly carry-on." He lifts the compact roller bag beside him. "Lose too many suitcase in the baggage claim."

The officer nods at the bag. "May I please see your bag, Mr. Huang?"

"Of course." He hoists it up toward her.

"Over here, sir."

She leads him over to an office and, once inside, motions for him to rest his bag on the long metal table. She slips on a pair of disposable gloves and then unzips the bag. She sifts through the shoes, clothes, and dirty laundry inside. Then she opens the outer compartment and extracts his laptop computer. She examines it from both sides, before passing it to him. "Can you please open it, sir?"

Charlie takes it and pops the lid open. The screen glows with the Windows log-on graphic.

If this were a year earlier—on one of his first return trips—he might have suffered a panic attack. But aside from the persistent flip-flopping of his stomach, he couldn't feel much calmer. The officer could study the laptop from every possible angle. She could

X-ray it with their most sophisticated machinery. She could swab it with the most sensitive drug-testing strips or have the search dogs sniff it. But unless she smashes it open with a hammer and disassembles the hard drive, she will never find the kilogram of powder packed inside it.

CHAPTER 9

By any standard, it was a brutal flight. Not only did they land at YVR over two hours late, but the passengers were miserable and the flight crew despondent. Numerous drinks and dinner trays had spilled during the violent turbulence. Two or three of the passengers hadn't reached their airsickness bags in time and the faint stench of vomit permeated the cockpit for the last half of the transpacific flight. The bickering inside the cockpit among the three pilots was worse than Justin Bowles had experienced in a long while. He had argued that they should be increasing, not decreasing, altitude to escape the relentlessly choppy air. The first officer had sided with him, but Captain Yvette Harding had insisted on flying lower, and she outranked Justin as the senior pilot onboard.

In retrospect, Justin realizes that maybe if he'd been a bit more tactful, less insistent, Yvette wouldn't have dug her heels in so firmly. *Screw that,* he thinks. *She doesn't have to be so goddamned stubborn. And why, in this day and age, does gender politics have to factor into every professional disagreement?*

Justin checks his watch, which reads a few minutes before eleven, and realizes it's far too late to call home. Both his girls would be sleeping, and, in all probability, Jen would've fallen asleep in bed with them while reading bedtime stories. He envies his wife. Reading to his kids is one of the activities he misses most when he's away working the layover flight.

As Justin stares at his tired reflection in the bathroom mirror of the trendy downtown bistro, he wonders again why he isn't already tucked into bed in his hotel room. Even before their flight took off from Shanghai, Justin had agreed to attend the thirtieth birthday dinner for Mandy, one of his favorite flight attendants, along with most of the crew and some of her local friends. If he's being honest with himself, the only reason he came is because of Yvette. Months earlier, the two pilots had agreed to end their affair and focus on their respective marriages, but his resolve has already cracked, and he senses that hers is teetering, too—one evening out socializing together might be enough to get her back into his bed.

But if Justin expects to make it through the dinner and the inevitable party in the flight attendants' room afterward, he's going to need a little pick-me-up. He reaches into his pocket and pulls out the thin glass vial that the bellman, Vince, had dropped off in his room shortly after check-in. Vince assured him that this blow was even better than what he supplied him with last month.

Justin glances at the door to ensure no one's coming—*as if it would matter in downtown Vancouver*—and then sprinkles half the vial's powder onto the crook of his thumb and forefinger. He hesitates a moment. He doesn't do coke that often, but it's another vice he had vowed to cut out when he ended his affair with Yvette. *Just one bump*, he tells himself, as he snorts the powder off the back of his hand and immediately experiences the heady nasal rush.

Justin can't believe how quickly it hits him. The jolt of alertness feels somewhere between an electric shock and a bucket of ice water dumped over his head. Vince was right. This stuff is powerful.

Before Justin can even turn away from the sink, he's overcome by a foreign sensation. There's burning heat in the center of his chest. His head begins to float. And the euphoria is like practically nothing he's ever known—as intense as the time he first held Layla seconds after she was born, as exhilarating as his first solo landing. His expression in the mirror is so goofy, he can't help but laugh. The eyes staring back at him begin to flicker, but there's nothing he can do about it, since his feet refuse to cooperate and his arms just hang limply at his sides.

As he watches his reflection drop like a detonated building, his only thought is how odd it is to see someone collapse while grinning from ear to ear.

CHAPTER 10

The loud knocking at her door recurs at ten-thirty in the morning, but this time Julie is already awake. She's been flip-flopping in bed, trying to read herself back to sleep on her tablet, alternating between the boring chick lit e-novel she's been working on for weeks and online articles about the teenagers' deaths. The latter had only undermined her pursuit of sleep, but she couldn't pull herself away from all the news and social media coverage. She might have bagged two hours of sleep, in total, since coming home from her night shift.

Julie gets out of bed, throws on a long T-shirt, and heads out to answer the door. As she expected, Anson is waiting on the other side. "You probably should get yourself a phone at some point," he says by way of greeting, even though she reminded him only yesterday that she switches her phone off after a night shift.

"They sell those?"

"So I'm told. No time for coffee or wine, Julie. Get dressed. We've got a busy morning."

"On a Sunday?" She yawns into her wrist. "What happened? Did your partner file for a divorce?"

"Nah, we're in divide-and-conquer mode this morning. Theo's gone to see the pathologist who's doing the postmortems today."

Julie doesn't argue. "Give me five minutes to change."

"Take seven," he says as he slides in. "I'm feeling generous."

Smiling to herself, Julie picks out a white shirt and indigo skirt from her closet and steps into the bathroom. She jumps into the shower for a quick rinse, and out again. As she stands at the mirror brushing back her straight brown hair, and wishing it had a little more body, she assesses her reflection. The bags under her eyes aren't too deep and the crow's-feet at the corners are still faint, but to her, she looks every one of her thirty-five years this morning. She doesn't mind that her age is beginning to show. She enjoys that patients and colleagues seem to take her more seriously now, that she's not routinely mistaken for a nurse anymore, and that the young residents from other services hit on her less frequently than they used to. But at moments like these, she can also hear her mother's voice in her head, repeating a familiar refrain. "Lord knows Cameron isn't planning on kids. You're my last hope, Jules. If you don't settle down and start soon . . ."

Julie has never shared her mom's urgency. She finds it difficult to imagine herself married, let alone as a parent. She hasn't dated much since Michael's death. And in the few relationships that did start to develop—all of them with decent, caring guys—she always found, or invented, a reason to end them. At times the loneliness gnaws at her, but the fear of losing everything all over again is worse than the thought of being alone.

As she lowers the brush, Julie considers applying a dab or two of makeup before rejoining Anson, but in the end she opts only to run lip gloss over her mouth.

"That was nine minutes, but who's counting?" Anson says as she emerges from the bathroom. "And major points for the outfit. It screams: *Fun and educated professional, but not one to be trifled with.*"

She chuckles. "A Zara's shirt and skirt can say all that?"

"The right one can, sure. Kind of depends on the choice of bag, though."

"Let me try you." She eyes him up and down, feigning a careful assessment of his slim-fitting gray suit and pale blue shirt. "OK. How's this? *Wildly confident metrosexual who spends way too much on brand names.*"

If he's the least bit insulted by the dig, Anson doesn't show it. "Not that far off. Except you can't spend too much on the right brands." He holds open the door for her. "Shall we?"

"Where to? The crime scene?"

"Theo and I've already been there," he says as they walk down the hallway to the elevator.

"And?"

"Not a lot to see. Big old house on the West Side. The seven kids OD'd together in the downstairs den. No one else was in the room at the time. No drug paraphernalia. A couple of empty wine coolers and a half-finished bottle of some jungle-juice-type mixed drink. Forensics is testing them all."

"Did you interview the kid who hosted the party?"

"Yeah. Sydney Evanston. Her parents, too. They were home the whole time, chaperoning. They even had a no-booze policy. They didn't have a clue what was happening in their own basement. They're devastated."

"Hard not to be," she says, as they step into the opening elevator. "Why did these kids keep to themselves like that?"

"None of them went to the same school as Sydney. She was friends with Taylor and Alexa through field hockey, but Sydney didn't know the others. Those seven kids traveled in a tight pack and didn't even try to mix with anyone else at the party."

"So the other guests aren't going to be much help?"

"Doubtful."

"What about the kids' phones? You've got those, I assume."

"Yeah, but we still have to wait on the warrants to access them."

"You need a warrant?"

"Absolutely. Privacy laws are a bitch. You need one warrant to access the texts, emails, and photos on the phones. And, since most kids only communicate over social media, you need another warrant to get the passwords for those sites, because they're all third-party apps."

"The parents can't just give them to us?"

"Parents usually don't know them. Besides, they don't have consent from the owners."

"Who happen to be dead."

"The law doesn't discriminate." He shakes his head. "It'll take days to get the warrants, if we're lucky."

The elevator doors open to the lobby. "So where are we going now, then?" she asks.

"The epicenter of this crisis. Need to talk to the folks at street-level."

Julie doesn't need to ask to know that he means the Downtown Eastside. "I should check in with Poison Control on the way," she says.

"Good idea."

They step out of her building and into the bright sunshine. The temperature teeters somewhere between comfortably warm spring and the more intense heat of summer. Anson's black sedan is parked with flashers blinking in the loading zone directly in front of the building. The exterior is spotless and gleams as if it has just been driven off the sales lot. Julie climbs into the passenger seat and isn't the least surprised to discover the interior is equally as immaculate.

As Anson pulls out into the street, Julie says, "I had a case last night that could be related to yours."

His eyes dart over to her with a look of concern. "Not another kid?"

"No. A hard-core IVDU—a regular intravenous drug user—for sure."

"Did he die?"

"Almost. He took massive doses of naloxone, and we still had to put him on the ventilator. If he hadn't been using at a supervised injection site, he'd be dead for sure."

"But you think he took the same stuff as the kids?"

"If not the same, at least something as potent. That's why I want to call Poison Control."

"If only you had a phone."

She digs around in her purse and, miming surprise, holds her cell up. "Look what we have here."

She taps the number listed on her speed dial and, after two rings, hears Glen Swinney's familiar Yorkshire accent over her speakerphone. "Poison Control. How may I be of assistance?"

"Hi, Glen, it's Julie."

"Ah, Julie, miss you, luv!" Glen says with his usual affection. "Where have you been of late?"

"I've been on nights. But I'll be into the office for meetings next week."

"Brilliant! We'll have a tea and a catch up. Meantime, what can I do you for today?"

"Thanks, Glen. I wanted to ask you about those teenagers."

"So tragic, in't it?"

"Terrible. I saw four of them in the ER. And then last night I had another case that behaved much the same. In a seasoned user, this time. I was wondering—"

"Oh, you heard about the pilot, then?"

"What pilot?"

"Thirty-nine-year-old from Toronto. Found dead early this morning in the bathroom of some chichi restaurant in Yaletown."

"What happened?"

"Powder still caked on his nostrils. We assume he thought he was snorting coke. He was quite dead by the time the paramedics got to him."

Julie looks over to Anson, who shakes his head in bewilderment. "Do we know what was in the powder?"

"They've sent off samples. Of course, the cocaine must have been tainted with one of the fentanyls or other. Probably won't know until tomorrow or later. We only found out here at Poison Control because the paramedics were worried about handling the body. Potential hazardous material and all. They've heard horror stories about being poisoned through skin contact."

"Any word on other unusual overdoses over the weekend?"

"Not this morning. But if I were you, I'd check in with the ambulance service. If there were a rash of overdoses, they'll have heard. Maybe the morgue, too. As you know, they don't usually call us about the corpses."

"OK, Glen, thanks. See you soon. Tea, definitely," she says as she ends the call.

"Teenagers, a pilot, a junkie . . ." Anson glances at her expectantly. "This stuff is crossing a lot of demographics."

"If it's all the same stuff."

"True." He nods as he turns off Seymour onto West Hastings, passing the building that houses the downtown campus of Simon Fraser University. "I'll do a bit more digging on that pilot. But if he thought he was snorting blow, then maybe those kids did, too."

"Then why didn't you find any powder in the den or on the victims?" She sighs. "Speaking of, have you spoken to the parents yet?"

"Not yet. They've been hard to pin down." He stops at a red light and turns his head to look out the driver's-side window. "Guess making funeral arrangements for your child can preoccupy a person. Tomorrow, for sure."

"I've gotten to know one set of parents, a little. Alexa O'Neill, the girl in the coma. If it's OK with you, I'd like to be there when you speak to the other families."

Anson frowns. "That might cross the bounds. Go beyond expert consultation."

"Maybe. But what if they drop a toxicological clue that you don't even pick up on?"

"Such as?"

"Could be anything," she says, scouring her brain for a convincing argument. "Something as innocuous as a prescription one of the kids was taking that could've affected things."

He eyes her skeptically but doesn't comment.

"Also, Alexa's dad told me that he thinks that if any of Alexa's friends brought drugs to the party, it would've probably been the kid named Joshua."

He glances over again. "Why him?"

"Nothing specific, really. He just made Joshua sound more—I don't know—badass than the others."

"OK. We'll check it out." He pauses and then adds, "And yes, you can join us for the interviews with the other parents."

The light turns green and they cross Carrall Street, heading east on Hastings. Even though Julie has driven past the same intersection numerous times before, she's struck by the sudden change in ambience. Trendy gentrified downtown abruptly gives way to the heart of the Downtown Eastside. It's packed with people. Several are passed out on the sidewalks, while others wheel their worldly possessions in stolen shopping carts. One middle-aged woman lies on a piece of cardboard while suntanning in a flimsy neon-green bikini.

Anson swerves suddenly to his right, and one side of the car hops the curb before coming to a stop. Without a word, he opens the driver's door and jumps out. Julie follows him toward an abandoned building, where a scrawny woman leans against the boarded door smoking a cigarette. She wears a short leather skirt and a stained yellow crop top frayed at the collar, with knee-high white boots. Her dirty blond hair is pulled tightly back in a ponytail. Her half-shut eyelids are caked with liner, and a thick layer of foundation only partially covers the sores on both cheeks. As rough as the woman looks, Julie doesn't recognize her, which means she is not a regular at St. Michael's.

"Hiya, Suzie," Anson says.

Suzie crosses her arms defiantly, wobbling slightly. "I'm not tricking here, Anson."

He offers her a big grin. "None of my business if you were, Suzie."

"Right," she grumbles, and then points suspiciously to Julie. "Who's she?"

"A doctor."

Suzie nods to Julie. "You a family doctor? 'Cause mine retired. Or maybe died. The dude was old. Haven't seen him in years. Either way, I need a new one."

Julie shakes her head. "Sorry. Emergency medicine only."

Suzie looks past her. "Haven't see any emergencies around here today."

"That's the thing, Suzie," Anson says. "I was hoping you could tell us about the local supply on the street."

"Sure. Why not? Then maybe I'll cut my own fingers off and save the boys the trouble."

"No, Suzie. No names or anything. I just mean the stuff itself."

"What about it?"

"Have you heard about any bad down circulating recently?"

"Are you fucking kidding me?" Suzie shakes her cigarette at him. "It's all fucking bad, these days! Can't count how many friends I've lost over the past two years. Not to mention a husband." She blows out her cheeks. "Died on his third OD. The lovable son of a bitch never got anything in his life right the first couple tries."

"I'm sorry, Suzie. Really." Anson's tone softens. "What's gone on down here is practically genocide."

"So what are you asking for, then?"

"The really bad stuff," Julie pipes up. "The kind that does the toughest user in with one hit."

Suzie takes a long drag off her cigarette. "I keep to myself, mainly."

Anson pulls his wallet out of his back pocket and withdraws some folded white slips the shape of dollar bills. He holds them out to her between his index and middle fingers.

"Detective Chen! Big spender!" She howls. "You and your McDonald's gift certificates."

"Will get you twenty bucks' worth of food, under the Golden Arches." Anson waves them to her. "Go ahead. Take 'em. Whether you can give us anything or not."

She hesitates a moment and then snatches them from his hand.

"Can't imagine how many people you've lost already, Suzie," Julie says. "But if the stuff circulating is what we think it is, then you're going to lose a lot more."

Suzie's lips curve downward. "Don't have that many left to lose."

"You sure?"

She only shrugs. "Like I said. I keep to myself these days."

Anson eyes her for a long moment. "OK, Suzie. Be careful. We'll see you around."

Anson and Julie turn back toward the car. When they're halfway there, Suzie calls out to them. "Heard a rumor this morning up the block. Don't know. Might be bullshit."

Julie and Anson pivot at the same time. "What did you hear?" Anson asks.

"Heard Zack went down last night. Hard," Suzie says. "And that clown is indestructible."

"Hard?" Anson grimaces. "What do you mean?"

"The guy never ODs. I've seen him walk away like nothing after three hits, when one would've put me on a cold slab."

"But he did last night?"

"Word is he OD'd while at one of the fix rooms. Even though he did it right in front of staff, they couldn't get him back with all their kits. He must've taken something special."

"Who's Zack's plug?" Anson asks.

"Yeah, right, as if I'd say even if I knew." Suzie wiggles her fingers. "Like I told you, I want to hang on to these."

"Same guy as yours?"

"Doubt it."

Julie thinks of the John Doe from her shift. She reaches for Suzie's arm, but the other woman recoils. "What's Zack's last name?"

"No idea. But you can't miss the freak." Suzie laughs bitterly. "He's got a fucking tree growing out of his neck!"

CHAPTER 11

Sometimes Markku Saarinen scares himself a little when standing on the balcony of his thirty-sixth-floor, northwest-facing condo. He thinks of his friend who will not step foot on a balcony because he experiences an irrational urge to jump, even though he's not suicidal. His buddy swears it's a real condition. Markku wonders if he suffers from a low-grade version of the same thing. He often considers what it would be like to jump, though he doesn't experience any real urge to do so.

The balcony is still Markku's favorite feature in his home. He can't get enough of the view. Especially on sunny cloudless afternoons like this one, with the hint of brine floating on the light breeze. Perched high above the Granville Street Bridge, he looks down on False Creek as it expands into English Bay and kisses the shores of Stanley Park before it flows into Burrard Inlet at the base of the towering North Shore Mountains. He can spot the arches of the iconic Lions Gate Bridge, which connects downtown Vancouver to the North Shore, peeking over the treetops in Stanley Park. He can even see the gondola as it runs up Grouse Mountain, where a few patches of snow remain as a testament to what was a long, successful ski season.

Markku doesn't even have to move his head to drink in beach, ocean, mountain, and vast swaths of greenery. He can do it with a quick sweep of his eyes alone. No wonder the price of real estate is so out of control in this stunning city, which, despite the heavy annual rainfall, boasts the mildest and most livable climate in all of Canada. But he knows too well, through his daily dealings, that beneath Vancouver's beautiful veneer lies a lot of ugliness. He would rather be doing almost anything else, but how else is he supposed to afford his nearly two-million-dollar condo and its thousand-dollar-a-month property tax bill?

The buzzing of his phone pulls him from his thoughts. Markku steps back inside the living room to read the text from Elsa, which says: "Only an elevator separates us now, doll." As usual, a kissy-face emoji stands in place of a period. But this time, she adds an eggplant phallic symbol, the sight of which turns him on.

Markku hurries over to the table and gathers up the different bags of pills and powder lying on it. He tosses them, along with the tied stacks of bills and two business phones, inside his worn brown briefcase and carries it into the closet of the spare bedroom. He moves the winter coats out of the way and slides back the false panel in the shelving unit behind the clothes. He types in the six-digit electronic combination on the safe, and after a metallic growl, the door clicks open. He stuffs the case on top of the handgun inside, and then locks the door with a single tap of the screen.

Markku can hear the front door open just as he replaces the panel. Elsa bounces over to meet him near the doorway of the spare bedroom. She jumps into his arms and straddles his waist with her skinny legs. She kisses him full on the mouth as he spins her around. "Did I just catch someone with his hand in the cookie jar?" She giggles as she kisses him again on the tip of his nose.

He doesn't bother to deny it. After all, Elsa knows where the safe is. But he changes the combination regularly and prefers not to open it when she's home, concerned she will somehow spy out the code. "It's been a good week, El," is all he says.

She lets out an exaggerated squeal. "Good weeks are my favorite kind!"

As soon as he lowers her to the floor, Elsa asks, "Hey, Markie, did you hear about the kids?"

"What kids?"

"I saw it on Facebook."

"How old are you?" Markku says, recycling an old joke between them. "Who uses Facebook anymore?"

"Ah, my mom and my nana, for starters. Love Nana's posts! Look close enough at her photos, and you'll always find a finger somewhere in the corner."

Markku loves seeing Elsa like this. She's undoubtedly high, but the carefree light mood and the infectiousness of her perfectly lopsided smile makes everything better.

Her smile suddenly disappears. "Seven kids OD'd the other day."

"It happens, El." He shifts from one foot to the other. "No matter what you tell them. You of all people know that."

"Yeah, but these weren't regulars. Five high schoolers at a party. All dead."

His shoulders tense. "Where?"

"Some swellegant digs on the West Side. But still, Markie, a bunch of sixteen-year-olds who didn't know better. You think they got adulterated stuff?"

"More likely they got stronger stuff than they could handle. And then just took too much."

"Novices. Those poor parents . . ."

"And everyone else who loved them." He eyes her steadily. "This kind of stuff is happening every day to regulars, too."

"I'm more careful now, silly." She grabs his elbow and jerks him toward the bedroom, her gravity gone as quickly as it came. "I need a little cuddle time."

The thought of Elsa's bare legs and the piercing in the center of her abdomen pushes aside Markku's concerns about the teens, and he willingly complies. Before they even clear to the door to the bedroom, Elsa pulls off her top and slips out of her shorts without seemingly breaking her stride. She turns to him, naked beside the bed. Her small breasts, narrow thighs, and the trimmed tuft of hair between her legs make him hard in a glance. He begins to strip off his clothes.

"Markie, did I mention I was late?" Elsa says casually as she flops down on top of the covers.

"Late?" He lets his shirt fall back down in place.

"Yeah, a week or so, maybe."

"El, you're not . . . ?"

"Not sure yet." She beckons him over with a wave of her hand. "Don't worry. I'll handle it if I am. Not the end of the world."

He doesn't budge. "Handle it," he mutters.

"Yeah. My bad. Missed a few pills."

"Hold on." The sudden rush of exhilaration takes him by surprise. "Who says you have to handle it?"

Her nose crinkles in surprise. "What are you on about, doll?"

He motions to the room around them. "This is a huge pad, El. Two bedrooms and everything . . ."

"Wait, are you saying . . ."

"I'm crazy for you, El. Want to be with you forever," he says, floored by the depth of his own sincerity. "I make good money. I could support us. Why not have a baby?"

Elsa stares at him for a long, still moment before she breaks into a heartfelt laugh. "Markie, we couldn't." She stops laughing abruptly and sits up. "Could we?"

CHAPTER 12

"It's the same guy!" Julie tells Anson as soon as they get back into his sedan. "From my night shift."

"Zack?" Anson asks as he pulls out into traffic. "The OD that Suzie was going on about?"

"Has to be! How many guys with tree branches tattooed up their neck could've OD'd last night?"

"Who knows? This is Vancouver, after all."

"Shouldn't we go see him? Find out where he got his drugs?"

"Didn't you say he was on a ventilator in the ICU?"

"He might be off it now. I can check."

"We'll go soon. But while we're down here, I want to talk to a few more of the usual suspects."

Julie's phone vibrates in her lap. She glances down to see the screen lit up with a one-word text from her mother: "Hi." Rightly or wrongly, Julie immediately infers the text to mean: *Why haven't you called me lately?*

Julie loves her mother, but their relationship has always been complicated. She's aware of her penchant for assuming the worst about her mom, but she can't help herself. When she was seven, she blamed her mom for making her dad leave home. Years later, Julie viewed her opioid addiction as a natural by-product of her mother's years of closet alcoholism. Still, her mom did visit her every day in rehab.

"Something up?" Anson asks.

"Nothing urgent. Work stuff." Julie looks away sheepishly and makes a mental note to respond to her mom later, aware there's no guarantee she will.

Anson pulls over again three blocks farther east, just past the intersection of Hastings and Gore. The streetscape looks much the same as it did a few blocks west, except here an ambulance is parked in the middle of the sidewalk with its lights still flashing. The locals stroll and stagger past, taking little more notice of the ambulance than if it were a parking meter. Two paramedics attend to a bearded man who lies on the stretcher behind their vehicle, with IV tubing running from his arm to a bag that one of the paramedics holds above the stretcher.

Julie recognizes both the crew and the patient from the ER. She heads toward them with Anson in tow. "Hey, Walt," she says to the older paramedic who's attaching the IV bag to a pole at the end of the stretcher.

"Dr. Rees, you're coming to us now? How convenient!" the older paramedic jokes, while his young partner, Katie, focuses on measuring the patient's blood pressure.

"Just happen to be in the neighborhood. What've you got here?"

"Another OD. What else do we get called for these days?"

"Hey, I am a tax-paying citizen," says the wide-awake patient, whose name Julie can't place. "I got my rights."

Walt tsks. "You haven't paid taxes since the war."

"Which war?"

"Name one, Mitchell."

Mitchell. Julie leans down closer to the stretcher. "Hey, I've seen you before at St. Michael's."

Mitchell grins at her, exposing the gap where one of his upper teeth should be. "You're the hot doc! Worth the ambulance ride to the ER alone."

"Behave, Mitchell," Walt cautions.

Unperturbed, Julie asks, "So did you smoke or shoot it?"

"Bought a point. Shot a point."

"Was it way stronger than your usual stuff?"

"I dunno about that."

"Don't think so, either," Walt says. "Old Mitch is a frequent flier. He came around with a single dose of naloxone this time. I've had to give him way more on previous calls."

"Not like the other ones we heard about," Katie pipes up as she pulls the stethoscope out of her ears.

"Which ones?" Anson asks.

"The night crews back at the station were talking about a couple ODs they responded to last night. Convinced they were going to run out of naloxone, they used so much."

"I was on last night," Julie says. "I think I saw one of those patients in the ER. Do you happen to know where they took the others?"

"One died and the other ended up at St. Mike's," Walt says. "Must've been the guy you saw."

"Heard three others went straight to the morgue," Katie says.

"Christ! If this keeps up, our hood's gonna be a ghost town soon enough," Mitchell says with total lack of irony or insight.

Anson shakes his head, turns, and walks off.

"Stop using alone, Mitchell, OK?" Julie says as she follows Anson, throwing a quick wave behind her head to the paramedics. "See you later, Walt, Katie."

"Inevitably," Walt calls after her.

Anson and Julie spend the next hour canvassing the block, questioning several people. Julie recognizes many as former patients but struggles to remember names. She's impressed by how many of their first names Anson can recall. The locals range in age from teenager to septuagenarian, and their genders span male, female, trans, and one person who identifies as gender-neutral. Some are guarded, evasive, or outright hostile, while others are more forthcoming. But none of them seem to know much about the bad dope.

As they're heading back to the car, Anson stops a twentyish kid in a bandanna who tries to roll past on a skateboard.

"Zack," Anson says. "The guy with the branches on his neck. You know him?"

"A little. He's OK," the skittish kid admits, holding his skateboard in both arms.

"You and Zack do fentanyl together?"

"No way! I don't touch down!" he insists, as if he were being charged.

"What's your name?"

"They call me Roller."

"So, Roller, you just hang out here—in the heart of the dope world—because you like the fresh air and wildlife?"

"Look, OK, mainly I'm a weed guy." Roller backpedals from Anson, gripping his skateboard even tighter. "Maybe, a bit of up— some crystal, here and there. Never fenny!"

"Sure." Anson snorts. "So who does Zack buy from?"

"Never met his connect. Swear to God."

"His name?"

Roller shakes his head helplessly.

"What does Zack say about the dealer?"

"Says the dude is always up in his grille about safety."

"Safety?"

"Zack calls him 'mom' . . . says he's always lecturing about keeping his naloxone nearby and telling him not to use alone."

Anson presses Roller for other details but it's evident that the kid has little else to offer, or at least that he's willing to share. After watching Roller skate off, Anson and Julie return to the car.

As soon as they pull away from the curb, Julie says, "A dealer with a conscience, huh?"

"Not much of one, if he's peddling guaranteed death."

"Maybe he doesn't realize he is. Trust me. I know from my gig at Poison Control that the quality control of the stuff on the street doesn't exactly meet FDA standards."

"Maybe." Anson glances in the rearview mirror and adjusts the collar of his shirt. "Besides, no proof Zack got the same stuff as those teenagers."

"We might be able to establish that with IMS."

"Which is?"

"Ion mobility spectrometry."

"Yet another one of your mouthfuls. Who saw that coming?"

"It's a very expensive machine that maps out the chemical components of an opioid sample. Basically, it's like DNA testing for fentanyl derivatives."

"I thought you said they all get broken down to the same by-product. And that's what makes them so hard to identify."

She grins. "Aw, Detective Chen, you do listen to me sometimes."

"It's unavoidable. You talk an awful lot."

She rolls her eyes at him but can't hold back a laugh. "IMS is extremely sensitive. Even to a tiny sample. What's more, we have access to it through Poison Control."

"Warm up the machine that goes ping, then, Doc." The smile leaves his lips. "Before we go question Zack at the hospital, there's someone else I have to talk to."

She raises an eyebrow. "Just you?"

"Probably best. This one is bad news, Julie."

"I'm familiar with bad news. Think I can handle it."

He looks over to her as if he might argue but then turns his gaze back to the road. "This guy, he's smart—well, sly, at least. Knows how to read people. You don't get to where he has without a killer instinct and a gift for spotting weakness."

"Sounds like some of the surgeons I work with."

"Just be . . . on your guard. You know?"

Julie smiles to herself, appreciating his protectiveness. "I'll be all right, Anson."

They head west in silence for several blocks, leaving the Downtown Eastside and driving through Vancouver's Financial District, which is lined with bank towers and other high-rises. Between the buildings, Julie catches glimpses of the row of snow-dusted mountain peaks looming across Burrard Inlet, their spectacular beauty somehow accentuated by the human misery she and Anson have just left behind.

On Alberni Street, in the heart of the downtown nightclub scene, Anson pulls up to the valet parking in front of a row of restaurants. He flashes his ID at the approaching red-jacketed parking attendant. The young man grimaces at the lost tip and spins away from the car.

They step under a black and blue neon sign that reads CENA and into the dark restaurant. Julie has been to the trendy spot before, albeit reluctantly, once on a work-related function and another time on a tepid date, but she has yet to have a decent meal or even a good cocktail there.

They ride the elevator up to the fourth-floor rooftop deck. The doors open to a sunlit lounge that's covered by a translucent roof and decorated with funky glow tables and freestanding gas fireplaces. Anson strides across the floor to the table in the far corner, where two men sit at a booth, both facing outward. One is a swarthy Goliath with a thick neck and shaven head who has a half-finished beer in front of him, while the other, with perfectly gelled hair and a light suit that almost matches Anson's, drinks from an espresso cup.

"Farhad Hashemi! I heard you were here," Anson says as he plops down in the booth beside the man with the glistening hair. "Guess the Gang Squad can't chase you and your associates out of here anymore now that you own the place."

The bodyguard appears disinterested, but Farhad offers an ivory-white smile. "I don't own it, Officer Chen," he says. "I just happen to be friends with the owners."

"Friends. Sure. I'm guessing the 'owner' on the title is probably your driver or your gardener or something. And, technically, it's Detective Constable Chen, but seeing as we're old pals, Farhad, you can just call me Detective Chen."

Farhad motions to Julie. "Your old partner finally got the transfer he begged for, did he?"

Anson feigns a laugh. "You drug-trafficking murderers are such cards."

"If I'm either of those, why haven't I ever been charged?"

"You will. Or, more likely, just bumped off," Anson says as if he were just making casual banter. "Always takes a bit longer with someone who's so talented at silencing witnesses."

"Your mind is strange, Detective Chen." Farhad smiles again. "It's good to see that you're batting out of your league, though." He turns to Julie. "Can I get you a drink? Detective . . . ?"

"No," Julie says, not bothering to correct his misassumption as she slips into the booth beside the bodyguard and is immediately hit by a whiff of his woody fragrance.

"Listen, Farhad, I think you need to have a word with your wholesaler," Anson says.

"My wholesaler of what?"

"Coffee? Rugs? Tampons? Whatever it is you"—his fingers form air quotes—"'import-export types' pretend to sell these days."

"What's wrong with my tampons?"

Anson's smile vanishes. "They're killing even more people than usual. Including a whole bunch of innocent teenagers."

The bodyguard is stone-faced, but Farhad's mouth creases in disgust. "I heard that on the news. So senseless."

"Odds are, directly or indirectly, you supplied the fentanyl that killed those kids."

Farhad takes a sip from his cup. "No. Not me."

"Those teens aren't the only ones. There's some really nasty shit on the street right now."

Farhad shrugs without looking up.

"And since you supply a huge percentage of the fentanyl to the East Side . . ."

Farhad is quiet for a while. "Listen, Detective, you won't believe a word I say, but I hate hearing these stories. I've got kids near that age."

"Stalin had kids, too. Didn't raise his compassion level much. Don't see you winning any father-of-the-year competitions any time soon."

Farhad doesn't rise to the provocation. "The gangbangers, the street runners, the dialers, the addicts . . . they understand the game. The risks. This? With the kids? That's not right."

"Spare me!" Anson says as he leans in so close that his head and Farhad's nearly touch. "If not you, then where is this bad dope coming from?"

Farhad doesn't flinch. "How would I know? This city . . . it's the Wild West, Detective. You've got the Viets, the Indians, the natives, the Hondurans, the bikers, and every other mixed gang. Even the cartels are getting in on the act, way up here in Canada. And your people—those Chinese Triads—the worst of the worst. Could be any one of the above." He pauses. "But it's not coming through me. This much I promise you."

Anson leans back. "Farhad Hashemi promises . . ." He sighs.

"Farhad." Julie speaks up. "Do you know of an IVDU who goes by the name of Zack? Tree branches tattooed along his neck?"

"I don't know the users." Farhad motions to Anson. "Even the great Detective Chen would concede that much."

Anson doesn't respond.

"How about a local dealer who insists his clients carry naloxone kits before he will sell to them?" Julie asks. "Does that ring any bells?"

"Worried about losing repeat customers, is he?" Farhad turns to his bodyguard, who cracks a slight grin. "Not a bad strategy, I suppose. About as useful as wearing a helmet in a plane crash, but at least he's trying."

"So that's a no?"

"That's a no."

Julie stands up, but Anson remains seated. His intense gaze shifts from Farhad to the bodyguard and back. "Someone's gone way too far this time. The sky is going to drop on whoever's behind this. Even on the off chance you're not involved, Farhad, the collateral damage could devastate you. If you hear so much as a whisper about bad dope, I better hear from you in a hurry."

Farhad's smile verges on a smirk. "You'll be my very first call, Detective Chen."

Julie and Anson drive to St. Michael's and make their way to the fifth-floor ICU. Inside, she spots Kamalpreet Singh sitting behind a computer screen at the nursing station. Julie introduces Anson to Kam—whose smile seems to have extra wattage for the cute detective, or maybe Julie just imagines it does.

"Is the John Doe from last night off the ventilator, Kam?" Julie asks.

"Yup."

"Can we talk to him?"

"If you can find him."

"Find him?"

"He absconded. About ten minutes ago. As soon as we pulled his endotracheal tube, he yanked out his IV and just took off. We never even got his real name."

"And you just let him go?" Anson asks.

"Patients walk out AMA—against medical advice—all the time," Julie explains, even though she's as frustrated as he is. "Especially the IVDUs after they go into opioid withdrawal. We've got no grounds to stop them."

"True," Kam says. "Plus, he can't be the hardest guy to find with those neck tattoos of his. Why are you looking for him, anyway?"

"He might've taken the same stuff as those teens," Julie says.

Kam's smile grows. "And if you could find his supplier . . ."

"It'd be a start," Anson says.

Julie nods toward Alexa's room. The glass door is pulled closed. One look at her despondent parents, sitting silently on either side of the bed, tells Julie that it's not a good time for them to interview her family. "No change?"

Kam shakes her head. "The neurologist will reassess again tomorrow."

Julie understands that the neurologist's only role, in this case, will be to confirm whether Alexa is brain-dead.

"How about the other boy, Dylan Berg?" Anson asks.

"He's doing well," Kam says. "We're transferring him out of critical care to a ward bed. Anytime now."

"Can we speak to him?"

"Don't see why not," Kam says, and turns her attention back to the computer.

As they walk past Alexa's room, Tom looks up and offers Julie a grim smile and Julie nods solemnly to him. His daughter lies immobile on the stretcher. Her doll-like expression only reinforces Julie's guilt. *Maybe Harold was right. Maybe I did just prolong the whole family's suffering.*

Julie and Anson enter the room beside Alexa's where Dylan Berg is sitting up in his bed and drinking apple juice though a straw. Dylan's otherwise pale face is marked with a few scaly red blotches, typical of psoriasis. All the tubing that was there before is gone, except for a single IV line attached to his arm.

Julie makes the introductions, and then asks, "Where are your parents?"

"Downstairs getting food," he says in a low mumble.

"You're not from here, are you, Dylan?" Anson asks as he steps closer to the bed.

Dylan breaks off the eye contact. "Toronto. Oakville, actually. Kind of the same."

"And you were in town visiting your friend Grayson?"

"Gray, yeah. We went to camp together. Lake Huron. The past four summers."

"You didn't know the other kids, then?"

"No. I just met 'em a couple days before. They were superfriendly. Really welcoming. Especially Alexa." He thumbs to the room beside him without looking over. "I'm not always, um, great with new people and all. But . . ."

"The night of the party," Anson says. "Who brought the drugs?"

"I . . . I don't know," Dylan sputters, wiggling on the bed as if in pain.

Julie moves closer to him. "You're not in trouble, Dylan. Honest. We're just trying to piece together what happened."

"I don't remember! I swear."

"Did anyone talk about bringing drugs? Joshua, maybe?"

Dylan holds up a shaky hand. "You don't understand. I don't remember *any* of it. Don't remember going to the party. Don't remember taking anything. Nothing from the whole day." His voice cracks and tears begin to drip down his cheeks. "I don't know how it all happened." His voice quiets to a whisper. "And I don't understand why . . . why I was the only one who woke up."

CHAPTER 13

———————/\———————•

Bunsen always feels edgier, almost claustrophobic, under the bulky gas mask. Plus, his face gets so warm and itchy. But it's better than the alternative. One good whiff of all the powder floating around him might be enough to kill him, despite the powerful ventilation system. Sometimes he finds it funny when he catches glimpses in the mirror of himself in his mask. Like he's living under chemical attack in Syria or something, instead of working in a kitchen that has been converted into a makeshift lab inside a run-down house on Vancouver's East Side. Fortunately, his landlords are understanding. After all, they also own the drugs he is processing.

Three years ago, Bunsen was a student at the University of British Columbia, struggling to pay off student loans while slaving away on an undergrad chemistry degree that might or might not have helped him land a job as barista. He wasn't "Bunsen" back then. He didn't become known by the nickname until the same asshole who got him into the trade made a joke about him being glued to a Bunsen burner. Not only was the quip not funny, it wasn't even accurate. Bunsen doesn't synthesize the fentanyl, or "fenny," as most users call it. It comes to him in the form of concentrated fentanyl powder from Guangdong or wherever the hell in China they pump the stuff out like salt. He only cuts it with the proper proportion of active ingredients and additives to get the dosage right before pressing it into the "fake oxy" pills, as they're known on the street. His favorite additives include baking soda, starch, crushed ibuprofen and acetaminophen tablets, and, of course, coloring, but never the talcum powder or rat poison that some of the other dicks use while cooking up fenny.

Still, the nickname has stuck. And most of his associates don't even know his real name. For that reason alone, he's grateful.

Bunsen has already made more money in the past two years than he expected to make in twenty. But the demands never end. It's almost two in the morning and he's way behind schedule. He's been working all day without a break, and he has only just now finished cutting the last batch. He views all the containers stacked with pre-cut powders, unable to even calculate their enormous street value in his head.

Bunsen's back throbs and he craves coffee and a cigarette. But all he has time for is a little bump off the raw powder. He steps out of the kitchen, lifts his mask, and takes such a small snort that he doesn't even consider it getting high—just something to settle the nerves and lessen the back pain before he sits down at the elaborate pill-press machine to crank out the rest of the roughly one hundred thousand fake oxys they're expecting by morning.

What would the Workers' Compensation Board make of such inhumane conditions? Bunsen wonders, only half jokingly. The WCB couldn't protect him from his employer. No one could. If he ever let those sharks down, he would find himself floating in pieces in the Fraser River or however the hell else the Triad prefers to send their messages these days.

The fenny kicks in. His backache is gone. And he feels pleasantly grounded again, ready, almost eager, to get back to work. Besides, *Time is wasting,* Bunsen reminds himself as he lifts the nearest container, which feels hardly heavier than a bowl of popcorn. He's constantly amazed how so little powder can make so many pills, which in turn, will give countless users the high they crave. And probably kill a few along the way. But Bunsen doesn't like to dwell on those thoughts. Besides, it's not his responsibility. He's neither a dealer nor a supplier. He's merely the cook.

CHAPTER 14

What's the old expression? Zack Hollands struggles to conjure it. His granddad had so many of those hokey sayings. *Never look a gift horse in the mouth.* That's the one.

Zack woke in the hospital, dope-sick from withdrawal and with the rest of his stash gone. The doctors and nurses refused to substitute morphine or methadone for him, no matter how much he begged. He had to get out!

Without a dime in his pocket, Zack had no idea how he was going to get the fix he so badly needed. But luck smiled on him—as his granddad would say—when a new client texted him via his online ad. He would've done anything to, or for, the pudgy Persian dude whom he met in the cheap hotel room. But the client got cold feet and wouldn't even take off his pants. Before Zack could even demand to be paid for his time, the guy pulled out a dime bag of fenny and asked him if it would suffice. *Oh, would it ever!*

As Zack now sits on the bed in his room inside the low-income housing complex and carefully dissolves the powder onto the spoon, he remembers his promise to Markku to never use alone. Abiding by it probably did save his life the night before, inside the fix room, where the staff pumped him full of naloxone after his overdose. But the fuckers also tipped him into the worst case of withdrawal he'd ever suffered.

His skin has been crawling ever since he left the hospital. And after the whole ordeal there, with a tube rammed down his throat and multiple needle pokes to find one of his few unscarred veins to draw blood, he's not about to drag his ass a mile away to some fix room now, only so they can fill him up with more of that naloxone crap and package him into another ambulance.

Zack levels the lighter's flame below the spoon. He lets the mixture cook for just a few seconds until the first bubbles appear. He draws up the golden liquid with a used syringe. He moves his fingers along his neck until he finds the hardened jugular vein. Willing his hand to still, he inserts the tiny needle into the vessel by feel alone. He can tell it's in the right spot by how little resistance his thumb meets while depressing the plunger.

The drug hits him in seconds. He giggles. *This is going to be one hell of a ride!*

His fingers involuntarily relax. And everything goes dark even before he topples off the mattress and slams face-first into the floor.

CHAPTER 15

Julie is already rubbing her eyes as she steps into the doctors' private office inside the ER. She's exhausted from the day of running around with Anson, after catching only a couple hours of sleep following her second night shift in a row. The ambiguity of her relationship with Anson only compounds her fatigue.

Julie reflects on the first time she met him, almost three years before. He and his partner, Theo, showed up unannounced at Poison Control seeking advice on a victim who had allegedly overdosed unintentionally on his own cardiac medications. Anson intrigued her from the start. It was more than just his breezy wit and laissez-faire approach; she also picked up on a detachment, an inaccessibility, that she could relate to. Long after they established his victim had been murdered, he continued to consult her in person. But he never asked her out. And she wasn't about to make the first move. It's been maddening but also exhilarating ever since—like one long pursuit.

Julie still can't believe she has to work another evening shift, having just worked the previous overnight. There's no way the group's scheduler, Joe Rickard, would've put her on shift again with less than twelve hours of turnaround time in between. Crusty as Joe is, he's not that cruel. *I must've traded into this weeks ago*, she thinks, wanting to kick herself. She vaguely remembers agreeing to swap shifts with Goran—he had some family event, possibly one of his grown kids' birthdays, to attend—but after her marathon day, she regrets her generosity.

Still muttering to herself, Julie grabs her stethoscope from her locker and then heads out into the department.

She only makes it a few feet down the hallway when the voice on the overhead speaker calls, "Dr. Rees to Bay Three. *Stat!*"

The rush of adrenaline washes away the fatigue. She sprints down the hallway to the third bay, separated from the neighboring ones by curtains on either side. A young woman lies on the stretcher with an oxygen mask covering her mouth. Her complexion is sickly and pale, despite her African ethnicity. Her breathing is labored, and her chest gurgles with each inspiration. Her expression is calm, but her wide eyes betray her fear.

Sandy, the charge nurse, glances at Julie while her bony fingers fiddle with the blood pressure cuff above the patient's elbow. "Dr. Rees, this is Chloe Lincoln. Chloe has postpartum cardiomyopathy. She's on the transplant wait list," Sandy says, meaning that the patient's heart had been attacked by her own immune system during pregnancy and has been damaged so badly that it has to be replaced. "Chloe had worsening dizziness and shortness of breath this evening."

Julie pulls the curtain closed behind her and then steps up to the other side of the stretcher from Sandy. "Chloe, is the oxygen helping?"

Chloe shakes her head slightly.

"Any chest pains?"

"Not really. The breathing is hard . . . and I feel so light-headed."

Julie glances to the monitor above the stretcher, where the heart rate reads a hundred and thirty while the systolic blood pressure sits critically low at sixty and the oxygen saturation is only eighty-one percent. It's information enough for Julie to diagnose Chloe with cardiogenic shock and florid heart failure. Her lungs must have filled with fluid and she's drowning in her own secretions, which have backed up because of a heart that's too damaged to pump blood properly. The syndrome is one of emergency medicine's most feared Catch-22s—a patient who desperately needs to have her breathing supported, ideally with a ventilator, but can't afford any intervention that will drop her blood pressure by even a single point, including intubation or the forced air of positive pressure ventilation.

"Please call cardiac surgery," Julie calmly says to Sandy. "Meantime, can you prep a norepinephrine drip?" she asks, requesting the powerful inotrope—or pump-enhancing—medication that will help regulate the blood pressure.

Sandy's forehead creases as she steps away from the stretcher. "You're thinking ECMO?"

Julie's neck tightens, remembering the last time she called for the heart-lung bypass machine, and the disaster that followed. But there's no other option. "Yes."

"What is that, Doctor?" Chloe pants.

Julie squeezes her shoulder. "A machine to help support your blood pressure. Like a backup pump."

"I see." Chloe closes her eyes. "Could you call . . . my husband . . . Maxwell? He's with our baby. The waiting room."

"We will bring them in soon, Chloe."

"I want to see them . . . once more." Chloe reaches up and takes Julie's hand in her weak and worrisomely cool grip. "I'm not . . . going to make it, am I?"

Julie never gets used to these moments, where the delicate balance between comfort and truth do not always align. "First step is to get you on the pump, and then we'll go from there."

Chloe only has the strength to nod.

Just as Julie is slipping her stethoscope in her ears, the curtain flies open and Harold Mott stands in the gap. His glare for Julie gives way to concern as soon as he recognizes the patient. He hurries over to the space beside the stretcher that Sandy just vacated. "Chloe! Are you misbehaving?"

"Dr. Mott!" Chloe cries with genuine relief.

"She's in cardiogenic shock," Julie says.

"I can see. We'll take her up to the ICU and start the ECMO there." Harold turns to Chloe, and his tone softens as he cups her cheek. "You just need to hang in there now, Chloe. You're at the top of our transplant wait list. We'll find you that new heart. Promise."

Two other nurses join Sandy to help prepare Chloe for urgent transfer. Julie slips away from the bedside to allow them space to work. As she's heading back to the nursing station, a slight man, whom she assumes to be Chloe's husband, rushes past her while clutching a baby to his chest.

"A word, Dr. Rees?" Harold calls from behind her.

"Yeah, OK," Julie says without turning around.

She leads him into the ER doctors' office, which is vacant, but still smells of coffee and someone's sweaty bike gear. Though there are plenty of chairs in the room, they both opt to stand, an arm's length apart.

"Now, Chloe is an example of a very appropriate use of ECMO," he says.

"Which is why I paged you," Julie says evenly.

Harold's eyes narrow. "Your overdose the other night clearly was not."

"You couldn't have known that for certain at the time."

"I could, and I did. Now the poor girl is lying upstairs, brain-dead. Tying up essential resources. And making it that much harder on her family."

"She's sixteen years old, Harold," Julie says, struck already by the futility of her argument but unable to help herself. "There were no options left for her. What would you have had me do?"

"The kind thing. The ethical thing. The medically *appropriate* thing. You should've let her go, Julie." He shakes his head and exhales with uncontained disappointment. "But your judgment was too clouded for that, wasn't it?"

The hairs on her neck bristle. "What does that mean?"

"You know perfectly well what it means. You can't separate the personal from the professional in these particular circumstances."

"This wasn't about me or my past!"

"Wasn't it?"

"It's been nine fucking years!"

"Wouldn't matter if it were twenty-nine." He tosses up his hands. "I was there when they wheeled Michael away."

"That's what this is really about, isn't it, Harold? How I stole Michael from the family?"

Harold snorts. "I'll never forget the look on your face. The utter remorse in your eyes."

Julie feels her cheeks heating. She's so tired and flustered that she can't even find the right words.

"Perhaps you overcame addiction, Julie. Perhaps. But the guilt? No one would ever overcome that. That's the reason why I didn't want you to work here. I knew it would forever affect your judgment."

Julie struggles to fight off the tears, but she can't. She's mortified as she feels them flow down her cheeks. She wants to crawl into a hole. She wishes she could just disappear.

A voice crackles on the overhead speaker. "Dr. Mott, the patient is ready for transfer."

"I have to go tend to Chloe now." Harold wags a finger at her. "But we will be reviewing your actions at the quality-and-safety rounds."

CHAPTER 16

———————————∧——————————•

Sister Theresa loves the warmth. Thrilled as she is to call Vancouver home now, her adopted city's temperate climate has never been warm enough for the native of San Antonio. It's only when June arrives that Theresa begins to feel comfortable. Especially in the early evening when the nun does her rounds, patrolling the alleyways of Gastown, looking for the hungry, the scared, the wayward, and—most of all—the overdosed.

Two years ago, she had never administered an injection. Now she can't even recall the number of naloxone kits she has spent, injecting the lifesaving antidote into the users who pass out unseen in the many nooks and crannies of the Downtown Eastside. Too often, she arrives too late. *Why do these poor souls use alone?* It's a death wish she cannot even fathom.

Theresa pads down the lane between East Cordova and Powell. She inhales a slight whiff of marijuana, but she can't identify the source. As she passes the spire of St. James Church, she thinks fondly of its rector, her good friend Reverend Polson. He's as committed as any of her Catholic brothers and sisters to easing the rampant suffering of the Downtown Eastside. So many good people—community support workers, nurses, doctors, and volunteers—are trying so hard. And yet so little progress is being made.

A voice draws her attention. "Hiya, Sis!"

She stops and looks over to see the chubby young man with frizzy hair, sitting on a flattened cardboard box and propped against a metal door of the old building. Curled up beside him lies a long-haired shepherd-retriever cross. The scent of marijuana intensifies, and she spots the burning joint between his fingers. "Benjamin, what are you and Gracie doing back here?"

"Wanted a bit of peace and quiet." Ben taps his temple. "It's noisy up here."

Theresa has known Ben for years. He doesn't use hard drugs. And he doesn't have to live on the street, since he has supportive parents who live in the city. But the chronic schizophrenic gravitates to homelessness, preferring to live outside with his always perky and well-groomed dog. Theresa has given up trying to get Ben and Gracie into a shelter.

Gracie's tail begins to wag as Theresa extends a hand toward her. She rolls over on her back, encouraging the nun to scratch her exposed belly.

"Are you hungry, Benjamin?" Theresa asks as she kneels beside them, lowering her knapsack to the ground while she strokes Gracie's side.

"Not really," Ben says. "But who would say no to one of your tuna salad sandwiches?"

"Such a charmer." She extracts from her pack one of the wrapped sandwiches that she prepared just before she headed out. "I think I have something for Gracie, too."

He takes the sandwich in one hand and offers her the joint with the other. "Want a drag?"

Theresa feeds Gracie one of the dog treats she always carries with her on her nightly rounds. "Not my thing, Benjamin."

"You should try. Calming. Dulls the voices."

Theresa only nods. She has seen many psychiatric patients self-medicate themselves over the years. And Ben's strategy of using only marijuana is more benign than most.

As he chews a mouthful of sandwich, Ben motions with the joint down the lane. "Did you check out the girl down there already?"

"What girl?"

"The one behind the dumpster. She was singing a few minutes ago. And then it just stopped."

Sensing trouble, Theresa jumps up. Her dysplastic hip, deformed from birth, throbs as she snatches the backpack and bounds down the lane. She rushes over to the bright orange dumpster but doesn't see anything at first. Then she spots a foot sticking out from behind the dumpster. She races around back, where she sees the scrawny young woman in a black tank top, wedged against the wall. Her complexion is dusky, and saliva is frothed across her mouth and nose.

Theresa sees slight bubbling between the girl's lips as she fumbles for a naloxone kit inside her backpack. She pulls out a pre-loaded syringe, realizing she has no time to slip on her disposable gloves. She squeezes into the space between the dumpster and the fallen girl and drops to her knees. Theresa jabs the needle into the girl's exposed shoulder and plunges down on the syringe.

Theresa reaches out to feel for a pulse at the girl's cold wrist but detects nothing. She runs her hand up to the elbow, as she's been taught, searching for a bigger artery. She doesn't even notice the discarded syringe sticking up between the girl's arm and chest until the needle pricks her little finger. Her heart goes cold, thinking of the communicable diseases—especially HIV—she might've just been exposed to. But there's no time to worry about the needlestick. She'll have to deal with that later.

Theresa holds her fingers against the crook of the girl's elbow until she feels the slight pulse underneath them. *She's still alive!* But she's not breathing.

Theresa knows what she has to do. She reaches behind her and sticks a hand blindly into her backpack until her fingers wrap around the plastic airway device meant for safer mouth-to-mouth resuscitation. She yanks it out of the bag and sticks it through the saliva filling the girl's mouth.

Theresa leans forward and exhales through the device with all her might into the girl's mouth. She feels dizzy from the effort. She takes a breath to prepare for another exhalation, but the wooziness comes out of nowhere. So does the floating sensation. It's the strangest feeling. As if she has just nodded off in the middle of a storm. She has to will herself to breathe, but her body is so slow to respond.

Even in her dense haze, she understands what must have happened. *How could I overdose on a poke from a discarded needle?* She wants to reach for another naloxone kit. But her hands feel so useless. *Just keep breathing, Theresa*, she coaches herself as she has done for so many others. *Help will come.*

As she begins to drift off, she hears the muffled sound of barking.

CHAPTER 17

Markku studies the gentle curve of Elsa's slender neck, resisting the urge to run his tongue along it, when she suddenly stirs. She stretches her neck and then rolls sleepily over to face him. "Morning," she murmurs. "Time is it?"

"About five."

Elsa shuffles closer and wraps him in a naked hug. Her breath warms his cheek. "You try the sleeping pill?"

"Yeah, they don't do much," he says of the medication his family doctor prescribed.

She rubs his thigh as she turns her head away to yawn. "You always such a terrible sleeper?"

"Only the last couple years."

"It's the business, huh?"

"I dunno. There's so much shit going on right now. Lots of rumors."

"Such as?"

"They're nervous on the street. There's talk of some killer fenny that's circulating."

"Like those kids got?"

"Maybe." *This fucking business*. "Listen, El, you can't be careful enough with the stuff right now."

"It's been ages since my last naloxone low."

"Two months."

"See!" She laughs and kisses him on the cheek. "That's ages in my book. Besides, you're going to get even less sleep if there's a baby rolling around here."

He cocks his head expectantly.

"I said *if*, Markie," she says as she snuggles in even tighter.

"You'd be a great mom, El."

"I think so, too." She giggles.

"Provided you stop using."

"I know."

He slips out of her embrace and sits up. "I'm serious, El. It's one or the other, you don't get to do both. That's way too fucking selfish."

She rolls over to face the wall. His eyes drift, almost involuntarily, back to the curve of her neck.

"I know it has to be one or the other," Elsa says quietly to the wall. "Maybe it's time for the other."

His heart fills. He's never heard her speak in those terms. "Could you stop, El?"

She hesitates a moment, then says, "I could try."

CHAPTER 18

"Not that I mind being your dedicated Uber driver, but how come you don't own a car?" Anson asks without taking his eyes off the road.

Julie shrugs. "Get more exercise without one."

"Do you even have a driver's license?"

"Last time I checked."

They lapse back into the silence that has filled the car since he picked her up minutes earlier. Julie can't stop thinking about the run-in with Harold yesterday evening. The heart surgeon had always been resentful after Michael's death, but she had no idea how much he blamed her for what had happened. The altercation re-opened the wounds as effectively as a scalpel. Despite her exhaustion, she had a fitful night. It was the first time in years that she had cried herself to sleep.

Stopping at another red light, Anson turns to her. "What's up with you this morning?"

"Tired."

"Is that all? You haven't taken one potshot at me since I picked you up." There's concern behind his amused grin. "Was your shift that bad?"

Julie considers unloading to him. To admit that no matter how many lives she helps to save in the ER, none of it compensates for the role she played in her fiancé's death. *Harold is right, you don't get over that kind of guilt*, she thinks. But at times like these, she finds that talking only makes it worse. Besides, she's not ready for Anson to see this side of her, so she forces a smile. "It was just an exhausting weekend between working nights and covering for your missing partner in the daytime. Man, you must have pissed Theo off something fierce this time, huh?"

"And . . . she's back." Anson chuckles, looking back to the road. "My grandma says I'm a great listener. Of course, she's stone-cold deaf and barely speaks English, so what choice do I have? Still." He clears his throat. "If you ever want to talk about stuff . . ."

"I'll let you know, Anson. Thanks." She touches his arm briefly in appreciation. "So where is Theo?"

"Why does everyone keep asking? It's not like I plastered him inside my wall—tempting as the thought is. We just decided to split up the interviews of the victims' parents this morning."

"I guess there are enough of them, right?"

"Ten too many." He nods despondently. "I've arranged interviews with two of the kids' parents. Theo is seeing others. It's going to be a long day for all of us."

She tries not to think of Michael's family. "We're still in the dark here, Anson. Until we know exactly what killed those kids."

"Agreed. I already checked with Forensics on my way over to get you. Toxicology reports aren't complete yet."

Julie reaches for her phone. "There might be another way to find out. Indirectly, at least."

She hits the speed dial key for Poison Control and, after two rings, hears Glen Swinney's broad accent over the speakerphone.

"You're working again, Glen?" Julie asks.

"Feels like twenty-four seven, luv. But it's only my fourth day in a row. What can I do you for?"

"Wanted to check in on the opioid overdoses—" she says.

"You heard about the nun, then, did you?"

"What nun?"

"We got the call last night. Good Samaritan, the poor dear is. Was trying to revive an overdosed user she came across, and poked herself on the girl's discarded needle. Wouldn't you know it, the sister overdoses herself. Might've died if a local and his mutt didn't find her and administer a shot of naloxone."

"The nun overdosed from a needlestick alone?"

"Apparently."

"Incredible," she says, floored by the implication. "Did you get the name of the user?"

"No. The lass didn't make it. But I do have the name of the nun . . ." Julie hears papers rustling. "Sister Theresa Garcia. She's already been discharged from the hospital."

"Thanks," Julie says, making a mental note to try to track down more information on the nun and the user. "Glen, have you seen any of the tox reports on the other overdose victims?"

"You'll have to be way more specific, luv."

"My patients Alexa O'Neill and Dylan Berg, from Friday night. Also, ideally, the John Doe known as Zack from early Sunday."

"Righto. Hang on. Let me check."

As soon as the hold music sounds on her speakerphone, Anson asks Julie, "What's so incredible about the nun?"

"She stabbed herself on a discarded needle. Means all she would've been exposed to is whatever active drug was left inside the lumen of the used needle. Micrograms, at most. Do you know how potent the opioid would have to be to overdose her at that tiny amount?"

"I'm beginning to think I do."

The music stops abruptly, and Glen comes back to the line. "Nothing on the John Doe yet, but I have Berg and O'Neill here. Dear me. Both of them are negative for everything, except carfentanil."

Julie sits up straighter. "Only carfentanil? No fentanyl, heroin, nothing?"

"According to the screen, just carfentanil. Of course, this is all preliminary. We haven't seen the IMS report yet. Could be much smaller dose of other opioids on board, I suppose."

"*Jesus Christ!* OK, thanks, Glen. If you hear anything else on my John Doe or the other recent cases . . ."

"Will ring you straight off!"

After she hangs up, Anson glances over to her. "Hasn't carfentanil been on the street for a few years now?"

"It has. Some dealers cut it into heroin or fentanyl to offer a harder-hitting, longer-lasting high. But never pure carfentanil. That's insanity."

"Why?"

"All these opioids—whether you're talking morphine, heroin, or the fentanyls—basically work the same way." She knows it's an oversimplification, but she doesn't want to get bogged down in the insignificant differences in the drugs' actions. "It boils down to potency that separates one from the other. Fentanyl is about a hundred times more potent than heroin. But carfentanil? It's a hundred times more powerful than fentanyl . . ."

"So we're talking *ten thousand* times as strong as heroin?"

"Exactly. The stuff was developed for tranquilizing elephants. Literally. A single grain of it can kill a person."

"Seriously?"

"Seriously. And even if you get to someone in time, it still takes massive doses of naloxone to reverse. In the early 2000s, the Russian army used aerosolized carfentanil to take down Chechen terrorists who'd captured a theater full of hostages. Problem was they ran out of naloxone and ended up killing hundreds of hostages, too."

Anson shakes his head. "So if someone is selling pure carfentanil on the streets . . ."

"They're either guilty of the worst criminal negligence imaginable . . ." She locks eyes with him. "Or mass murder."

"Just when you thought these douchebags couldn't get any worse." His voice turns businesslike. "We need to confirm if Zack, the pilot, the nun, and any of the other ODs this weekend got the same ultrapotent stuff."

"We also better issue a public advisory. I can arrange that through the communications point person at Poison Control."

"Those don't work, Julie. Even if you could reach the people most at risk—and that's a huge if—they wouldn't listen. They've heard it all before. They've seen so many friends die. Those warnings are white noise to them now."

"If pure carfentanil is circulating on the street, we don't have a choice."

"Doesn't seem like there's much *if* about it."

Julie turns to look out the passenger window, where the weather reflects her mood. The skies have darkened, and as they cross the Burrard Street Bridge, the first drops of rain hit the windshield. A wall of angry clouds hides the wall of mountains and dulls the normally stunning view of English Bay and False Creek below them. She thinks again how fully the rain clouds transform her city. *Or maybe they just expose Vancouver for the six-dressed-up-as-nine that she really is,* she thinks miserably.

They head along Cornwall Avenue passing the popular Kitsilano Beach with its huge saltwater swimming pool and sandy cove, which would be packed this morning with suntanners and more than a few weed smokers were it not for the weather. The farther west they drive, the more luxury cars dominate the road. Range Rovers—the chosen vehicle of West Side stay-at-home moms—are everywhere. They climb the hill toward the UBC campus, the westernmost point of the peninsular-shaped city. Anson turns toward the ocean at Belmont Street, which would arguably replace Boardwalk if Monopoly were to be reset in Vancouver.

They drive past wide lots with massive houses perched up on the southwest side of the sloping street to capitalize on the unobstructed panoramic views of the ocean, mountains, and the downtown core. Anson slows the car and turns into the driveway of a dark green house built in Julie's favorite craftsman style.

"This is the home of the Xies," he says. "As in Gary Xie."

"Who?"

"Gary, or Gao, Xie. Probably one of the top two or three realtors in Vancouver. Must pull down a couple mill in commissions every year."

"And that's related how?"

"It's not, I suppose. But his daughter, Rachel, was one of the victims."

Julie thinks of the girl with the blue-streaked hair, remembering how overwhelmed she felt the moment the paramedics burst into the room with Rachel on their stretcher—the third cardiac arrest to arrive in ten minutes. Julie had been so focused on resuscitating Alexa that she hadn't even learned Rachel's name until much later.

They walk to the door, where they're met by a man and a woman who are, physically, complete mismatches. The wife is tall and lean and wears an elegant black dress with carefully applied makeup, while the husband is squat and balding and dressed in a tracksuit. He looks to be in his sixties and at least twenty years older than his wife.

"*Nǐmén hǎo*," Anson says with a bow of his head. He spouts several more clipped words in Mandarin, surprising Julie with his fluid Chinese.

Gary Xie shows him a stoic smile. "Thank you, Detective," he replies in English with a singsong accent.

Anson makes introductions. The wife, Lucy, says nothing as her husband leads the guests into the expansive living room that is decorated in the Chinese style with elaborately carved wood furniture and marble sculptures. A faint scent of burned incense floats in the air.

Anson and Julie both decline Gary's offer of tea as they sit down across from the couple on matching white sofas.

"I can't imagine what a difficult time this must be for you," Anson begins. "We're sorry to have to disturb you, but we're trying to figure out how this tragedy could have occurred."

Gary nods. "We so want to know how this happened to our Rachel." He looks over at his wife, who remains so blank-faced and still that she could pass for one of the sculptures in the room. "How can we help?"

"For starters, can you tell us a little about your daughter?"

"Rachel was our middle child," Gary says. "She would have turned seventeen next week. Always such a good girl. Much less willful than her older sister, Peggy. Her piano teacher said she was the most disciplined student." His voice cracks, and he pauses to swallow. "The way she played Bach . . ."

"She was supposed to study at the conservatory next year," Lucy says in almost a whisper.

Anson glances from mother to father. "Do either of you know if your daughter ever experimented with drugs?"

"Experimented? With drugs?" Gary shakes his head adamantly. "She was an A student. She didn't have time for alcohol or drugs. Or boys."

Julie clears her throat. "Mr. Xie, what about the . . . haircut?"

"We didn't like it." Gary shakes his head. "But after she won the physics prize at her school . . . it was all she asked for."

"And her friends? The ones at the party. Do you know much about them?"

"The girls—Alexa and Taylor—have been close with Rachel since the eighth grade. We never allowed Rachel to go on sleepovers, but they stayed here many nights. They loved to play in our pool. I never met the boys before. Rachel never spoke of them."

Lucy mutters something in Mandarin. Gary winces and Anson raises an eyebrow, but neither comments.

"There's no one you can think of who might've sold them drugs?" Julie asks. "Or brought drugs to the party?"

"No. No one." Gary glances helplessly at his wife, who stares vacantly at the marble coffee table in front of her. Her heartbreak is palpable.

Julie makes eye contact with Anson, who wordlessly conveys that they've delved far enough. They rise from the couch together. Anson reiterates their condolences and thanks the couple for their time.

Once they get back in the car, Julie says, "I thought your Mandarin wasn't any good."

"How would you know if it was?"

"Right," she says. "That poor woman. What did she say?"

"Nothing good ever comes from spending time with boys. Or men." He shrugs. "She's just in shock."

"I can't imagine," she says, although that's not entirely true.

He looks at her with a sad smile. "Ready to go visit the next victim's family?"

"No."

"Me neither," he says, as he pulls out of the driveway. "But Joshua's mom is expecting us."

They head back toward the city center. Anson slows the car once they reach the neighborhood known as Douglas Park. He pulls up to the curb in front of a mid-century bungalow with peeling yellow paint and damaged roof shingles. "Not quite the mansion we just left, is it?" Julie says.

"Still way outta my price range."

Julie appreciates that the joke isn't much of an exaggeration. Like many Vancouverites, she's dismayed by the city's stratospheric real estate prices, which threaten to squeeze all but the wealthiest out of the market.

A woman opens the front door with a lit cigarette in her hand.

Fiftyish, she wears a loose gray T-shirt, baggy jeans, and no makeup. Her thick curly hair is unruly and the bags beneath her eyes are dark hollows.

"Mrs. Weir?" Anson says.

"Sheila."

"I'm Detective Chen, Sheila. This is Dr. Rees. Is now still a good time to speak?"

"There are no good times." She turns and trudges away from the door.

Anson and Julie follow her into the untidy kitchen that stinks of stale smoke and rotting produce.

"I just wanted to tell you how sorry we are for your—"

Sheila cuts him off with a wave of her hand. "No more 'sorry'! I've heard way, way too much of that useless fucking word already."

"Of course," Anson says. "We were hoping to learn a bit more about Joshua."

"Why?"

"To try to piece together how the overdose—"

The hand shoots up again. "*Poisoned!* My son was poisoned, OK?"

"No question, Sheila," Julie says. "*Poisoned* is the right word. But do you happen to know if your son ever experimented with drugs?"

"What the fuck?" Sheila cries as she wraps her arms around her chest. "How dare you accuse Josh of being somehow responsible!"

"Not at all, Sheila. I'm not." Julie holds up her hands. "I'm a toxicologist—a poisoning expert—and I know that almost any drug—even marijuana—can be laced with anything."

Sheila calms visibly and takes a heavy drag off her cigarette. "I guess he smoked weed sometimes. Used to smell it on his clothes when I'd do his laundry." Her voice cracks. "He totally admitted it. Just weed and some booze—like vodka coolers and that kinda crap. Nothing more! He'd tell me if he did. He used to tell me everything."

"That's helpful. Thank you."

Sheila's eyes bore into Julie's. "How could this happen? This fentanyl shit. It's supposed to kill the no-good junkies and parasites in the Downtown Eastside, right? Like natural selection or something. Not good kids like my Josh."

Despite her sympathy for the woman, Julie can't help but be offended. But she bites her tongue and, instead, says, "Sheila, did Joshua mention if any of his friends might have—"

"As if. They were lightweights, those kids. I think Josh only hung out with them because he was sweet on the little redhead." She frowns and then waves the cigarette toward them. "How about the Chinese kid with the silly blue hair? Her dad is a big deal. Real estate, right? Isn't he in tight with that crowd?"

"Which crowd?" Anson asks.

"Come on, you know exactly who I am talking about, Detective. All the big money from mainland China. The super-high-end real estate. Christ, they've bought up most of this town. Made it unaffordable for the rest of us. I heard something on the radio about how much dirty money there is. Organized crime and shit. Have you looked into that yet or are you too busy harassing people who've lost everything?"

Julie can't contain herself any longer. "Sheila, I know you're grieving, but there's no need to—"

Anson grabs Julie's elbow and gives it a small squeeze. "Sheila, I promise, we will look into every angle," he says gently. "We won't stop until we find how your son was poisoned. And who did it."

Sheila nods. "Guess it doesn't matter much anyway, I suppose." She looks away, as if talking to herself now. "I got nothing left. He was all I had. The lousy ex took off when Josh was a couple years old. Getting me knocked up was the only good thing that deadbeat bastard ever did. And that was enough." Her voice falters again. "When my Josh was still here."

CHAPTER 19

The flies, the stench, the human clutter—the cardboard cutouts that pass for homes and shopping carts that stand in for furniture—none of it bothers Wade Patterson. He enjoys his strolls down East Hastings. At least the clients are respectful there. They understand their place.

But here on Georgia Street, it's a different world. Wade has no time for these spoiled downtown pricks—the entitled rich to whom life has just handed the cushiest of jobs with law firms, brokerage houses, and real estate companies. Wade sees how these lawyers, accountants, and brokers look down on him. As if he couldn't be doing as well or better than them if he'd had the same breaks they did—the doting parents, the private schools, and the instant membership to the boys' club—instead of having to grow up in Princeton, that shithole of a small town, to neglectful parents who couldn't even make rent half of the time. Wade probably earns more money than most of these professionals, but that's not the point. They still treat him like something stuck on their shoes.

As Wade walks into the food court of the Pacific Center, he spots Jarrod Nader waiting for him beside the Japanese noodle place. As usual, Jarrod is wearing a suit and tie that comes straight out of a Nordstrom's ad. And, as always, the young lawyer is pacing anxiously.

Wade appreciates the value of discretion, though. He's no stranger to dressing for success himself when visiting this neighborhood. He's wearing a Boss blazer and dress jeans for today's meeting. Clean-cut and tattoo-free, Wade could fit right in at any of those snotty firms on a casual Friday.

Wade meets Jarrod with a small smile and a quick fist bump. "Love the threads, bro," he says, motioning to Jarrod's jacket. "Forget about law, you should be modeling in Milan or wherever they do that shit."

"Thanks, dude," Jarrod says stiffly. "It's Armani."

"Let's hoof it somewhere a bit quieter," Wade suggests.

Jarrod nods and follows him out of the food court and into the main mall. They head through one of the exits into the underground parking. Standing between two parked cars at the back end of the second parking level, Wade has a quick scan around to ensure they're alone and then asks, "How much you looking for today, bro?"

"Thirty grams," Jarrod says in a hush.

Wade whistles. *"Thirty?* You throwing a major bash I should know about?"

Jarrod laughs nervously. "Yeah. Something like that."

Wade gets a kick out of the lawyer's discomfort. "At those kind of Costco sizes, I can cut you a sweet deal, bro."

"Which is?"

Wade doesn't even need to calculate in his head. "Eighteen honeys."

Jarrod nods. He glances over both shoulders and then reaches inside his jacket and pulls out an envelope. He counts out a stack of hundred-dollar bills.

Wade accepts the money without double-checking it. If there's one thing he's learned, it's that you can rely on lawyers to never lose track of a penny. He reaches inside his own jacket and extracts three ten-gram bags of cocaine. He passes them to Jarrod, who stuffs them into his jacket so quickly it's as if they were burning his hand.

"You heard about those teenagers?" Jarrod asks. "The ones who died at the party?"

Wade tilts his head. Jarrod isn't usually chatty. Especially once a transaction is complete. "Yeah, so?"

"They obviously didn't know what they were getting into, right? To overdose together like they did?"

"Hard to say, bro. Sometimes their eyes are just bigger than their stomachs. You know?"

"But all of them?"

Wade frowns. "What's with you today, man?"

"Nothing." Jarrod holds up his hands. "Don't want to take chances. I hear horror stories about the supply out there these days. That it gets cut with all kinds of stuff. That fentanyl is showing up in the blow."

Wade smiles. "How long have you known me, bro? Close to a year, right?"

"About that."

"When have I sold you anything but the best and purest stuff?"

"You haven't. It's just that—"

"I get it," Wade says, suppressing the urge to smack Jarrod. "Everyone's freaked out on the streets. But you've got a huge advantage over most of the others. You stick with one very reliable supplier." He taps his own chest. "Yours truly."

Jarrod hesitates and then says, "Yeah. OK." He turns and heads back into the mall without saying goodbye or arranging another meeting, although Wade knows he'll be getting another text from him within a week or so. This lawyer really has a hungry nose.

As Wade walks down the long slope to the next level where his car is parked, he laughs to himself. The truth is, he has no idea what is or isn't in the coke he just sold Jarrod.

CHAPTER 20

Julie chose the funky pizzeria, in the heart of the trendy downtown entertainment district known as Yaletown, hoping they would be able to sit out on the street-level deck. But the rain chased them inside to a high-top table. Her phone buzzes again and, after scanning the message, she begins to type her reply.

Anson waves a hand in front of her face, pulling her attention from the screen. "First you tell me you don't have a phone—"

"You came up with that gem of detective work on your own."

"Let's not point fingers." He grins. "Either way, now I can't get you off the thing."

"I'm going back and forth with Poison Control, working on the wording of the advisory."

"How about keeping it simple: 'Drugs are bad, don't do 'em'?"

"Wish I'd thought of that," she mutters, as she returns her attention to the screen and finishes the text. Once she's hit send, she slips her phone back into her bag.

"So, Dracula, you working again tonight?" Anson asks.

"No. I'm actually off now for a couple days. I'm on call for Poison Control tomorrow, though."

"Why do you work two jobs? Is there some issue with the ER docs' union?"

"The issue is we don't have one." She laughs. "I don't work full-time ER. A lot of us at St. Mike's have secondary interests. We have two docs who do ICU part-time. And two others who also work palliative care on the side. One guy even writes books—medical thrillers—they're not half bad. I happen to have specialized training in toxicology. It's a nice balance, actually."

"Balance, huh? All that work can't leave a ton of time for a social life."

"It's not so bad. We tend to work our shifts in clusters. Then we have lots of time off in between. And you know what the best part of being an ER doctor is?"

"The great cocktail party stories?"

"Them, too." She smiles. "No. When we're off shift, nobody misses us. There's always another ER physician to take our place. We're the most anonymous of doctors. In fact, being a good ER doc is like being a good ref in sports."

"How so?"

"We're doing our job best when no one notices us."

"And I thought I was the cynical one!"

"What about your work? Must impact your life, too."

"Not really."

"So what do you do for fun? Aside from clothes-shopping."

"Maintaining this level of fashion excellence does chew up a lot of time." He indicates his shirt and blazer with a sweep of his hand, before his smile gives way to a more pensive look. "My grandma taught me from a young age that the little details matter. How you keep your room, how you present yourself to the world, and so on. I can't help but focus on the details. It's probably because of her that I ended up a detective."

"Your grandma sounds cool. I like her already."

"Not sure she'd like you. She doesn't trust doctors. Especially the Western kind." He blows out his cheeks. "Not at all."

"I don't always, either." Julie laughs. "But you didn't answer my question, Detective. What do you do outside of work?"

"You know. Usual stuff." He clears his throat. "Hang out with family and friends—not too many cops, though, I get enough of them at work. Ski in the winter. Mountain-bike in summer. Got a bit of a travel bug. Been to Asia and Africa in the past year." He chuckles self-consciously. "Jesus, I'm beginning to sound like a walking Tinder profile."

She smiles. "Speaking of, have you done the online dating thing?"

"Nah. Not a fan. You?"

"My friend Goran forced me to give it a try a couple years back. Not really my thing, either."

"Aren't we just a couple of millennial losers?"

"Fair." She tucks the loose strands of her hair behind her ear. "Last month you mentioned something about showing me that pub with all the different Belgian beers on tap."

"Maybe later in the week if we—"

"Finally, lunchtime," a voice interrupts from behind him. "I'm famished."

Julie looks over as Theo Kostas sits down beside her. She's struck again by what physical contrasts Theo and Anson are. With his baggy suit, slouched shoulders, and thick paunch, the olive-skinned detective looks more like an accountant than a cop. But as Anson has told her, there's a lot more to his partner than meets the eye. Not only is Theo a decorated officer, happily married, and a devoted father of five, but he was almost killed fifteen years earlier in a high-speed chase that ended in a fiery crash that killed his then-partner as well as the suspect. Theo still has the limp to show for it. He could've retired on long-term disability but instead returned to work within three months of his discharge from the hospital.

"Hi, Theo," Julie says with a wry smile.

"Good to see you again, Julie," Theo says, and then nods to Anson.

"Hey, pal." Anson juts out his chin. "How did your interviews go this morning?"

"OK, I suppose." Theo rubs his eye. "Spoke to the folks of Nick, Grayson, and Taylor. Three sets of heartbroken parents. That's a *long* morning."

Julie shakes her head sympathetically. "They don't get much longer."

"So what did you learn?" Anson asks.

"Little of use," Theo says. "All of them are shocked about the drugs. Honestly, these kids sound so goody-two-shoes. More like chess club than fight club, if you ask me."

"On the other hand, if they were only half as good at hiding shit from their parents as I was at their age . . ." Anson says. "Still, from what we've seen so far, I got to agree."

"Except maybe for Joshua Weir."

"What about him?" Anson asks.

"Nothing specific. It's just that none of the other parents trusted him."

"I heard that, too," Julie says. "From Alexa's dad."

"Maybe that's because he's from the wrong side of the tracks," Anson says. "Joshua's mom is crushed. Lashing out like some people do. Josh told her he only ever used weed. She swears she would've known if her son had been into the hard stuff."

Theo nods. "Still, I got the name of a couple of Joshua's other friends. Ones who weren't at the party. We should talk to them."

"Definitely. Would also help to finally get access to those kids' phones."

"The warrant should come through today or tomorrow. You'd think, anyway." Theo looks from Anson to Julie and back. "You learn anything else this morning?"

"Not much from the family interviews, no." Anson nods at Julie. "Looks like we found out what killed them, though."

"Carfentanil. The pure stuff." She explains to Theo how unusual it is to see the lethal drug sold in its pure form.

"That could explain the spike in overdose deaths this weekend," Theo says.

Julie taps the table. "And if there's more of it on the street . . ."

"There must be," Theo says as he slips off his jacket. "I got a call this morning about a high-powered real estate developer who was found dead in his office over the weekend. Wilder, Avery? No . . . Aiden. Yeah, Aiden Wilder. Ring any bells?"

"Never heard of him," Anson says. "Probably a coincidence, but one of the victims' dads, Gary Xie, is a big-time realtor himself."

"I recognize that name. Half the palaces for sale in Shaughnessy have his signs out front. Worth following up on." Theo nods. "The good news—for us, anyway—is they found some fake oxy pills inside Wilder's desk."

"That is good," Julie says. "If it's the same stuff that killed those kids, then we can test to see if it really is pure carfentanil."

"Plus, the markings on those pills are like fingerprints. They could lead us right back to the source."

"Especially if the pills were pressed locally," Anson adds.

Their discussion is interrupted by the server who arrives to take their order. Theo and Julie order individual pizzas, but Anson opts for the lunch salad without the feta.

"Counting every precious calorie, are we?" Julie says, and then turns to Theo. "This one must get teased a lot back at the station house?"

"No." Theo grins. "He's too delicate. Like a little flower."

"Yeah, yeah." Anson says, suppressing a smile. "This flower is about to rain some serious pollen down on your ass. Besides, if anyone should be counting calories at this table . . ."

The server returns with their drinks, an orange juice for Julie and coffees for the detectives. After she leaves, Theo turns to Anson. "You'll never guess who I ran into out front."

"You're absolutely right. I'm not gonna guess."

"Nicole's mom. She said to say hi."

Anson's gaze drops to his coffee cup.

"Who's Nicole?" Julie asks.

"An ex," Anson says with a slight roll of his shoulders.

One look at his face tells Julie's there's far more to the story. But it's not the time or place to ask.

"How did Janet look?" Anson asks.

"Pretty good, actually. Way better than the last time I saw her." Theo shakes his head. "I mean, obviously. That was at the funeral."

Julie glances at Anson, hoping he might offer more, but he only sips his coffee.

"You know what?" Theo says. "We should go see Hoops."

Anson lifts his chin. "That's not a half-bad idea."

"Hoops?" Julie says in confusion. "As in basketball?"

"No. You'll see." Theo smiles. "Hoops has worked in the Gang Crime Unit forever. An undercover cop. A good one, too. Then again, in that line of work, you're dead if you're not."

Anson shakes his head. "Don't know how those undercover guys sleep at night. I couldn't do it."

Theo's eyes light up. "Maybe if we were trying to bust up an overpriced clothing ring?"

Anson snorts. "Just because you're a fashion-blind slob . . ."

Theo promises to arrange a meeting with Hoops, and the conversation meanders off in other directions until lunch arrives. As the light banter flows over their meal, Julie is even able to put the overdose deaths out of mind for a short while. She realizes, too, how much she enjoys their company, especially Anson's, but she's almost embarrassed at how often her thoughts drift back to his ex and what might have happened to her. And them.

Her phone rings while the server is clearing their dishes. She digs it out of her bag and hears Glen's distinctive voice in her ear. "Just wanted to let you know that I've got the toxicology results on your John Doe lad. Zack Hollands."

"And?"

"Same as the kids. Pure carfentanil."

Even though Julie expected nothing else, she still feels deflated. "Thanks, Glen. Let me know if you hear anything on the pilot, the nun, or any of the others."

"Aye. I'm at your beck and call."

Julie updates Anson and Theo, who seem to take the news for granted.

"Find Zack, and maybe we find who's dealing this carfentanil," Anson says.

"Agreed. Maybe Hoops can help with that." Theo pulls his phone out of his jacket and makes a short call. As soon as he hangs up, he says, "He can see us now."

Julie frowns. "Isn't he supposed to be undercover?"

"Not anymore. He's at a desk now. Though you'd never know it by looking at him."

Theo rides with them in Anson's car as they head over the Cambie Street Bridge to VPD headquarters, situated at the foot of the bridge. Inside, they pass numerous uniformed officers on their way to the fourth floor and a modest office halfway down the hall with a placard on the door that reads SERGEANT TIMOTHY ROBB.

The moment Julie lays eyes on Hoops, she understands what Theo meant. In his mid-forties, Hoops is buffed and good-looking in a bad-boy way, with closely cropped hair, a hoop in each ear. Only the police uniform looks out of place, especially with the sleeves of tattoos that cover his exposed forearms.

"If it isn't Cagney and Lacey!" Hoops bellows.

"That reference is probably hysterical to you old-timers," Anson says.

Hoops greets Anson and Theo with big hugs. "Good to see you two sons of bitches," he says, and Julie picks up on the remnants of a southern twang.

After they all sit down around his desk, Hoops turns to Julie with a warm smile. "Who are you? And why are you slumming with these clowns?"

"I've been around worse," she says with a laugh.

"Julie's a doctor," Theo explains. "A toxicologist. She's helping us with the investigation into those kids who OD'd."

"That clusterfuck." Hoops sighs.

"To put it mildly. But Julie's been a bit of a godsend." Anson gives her an appreciative nod. "We'd be lost in the weeds without her expertise."

Embarrassed, Julie looks for a way to change the subject. "Are you from Texas, Hoops?"

"Not even close. Nashville, originally. Made the mistake of falling for a Canadian back in college."

"Think we all know that Karen is the one who made the big mistake there," Anson says.

"True enough."

"About those kids, Hoops . . ." Theo says, and goes on to give him a quick summary of their investigation to date.

"Pure carfentanil? Those fucking morons! There's just no bottom to their greed or stupidity."

"Surely it's a mistake, though?" Julie says. "Makes no business sense to peddle pure carfentanil."

"Wouldn't be too sure about that. Could be one of these idiots' way of sending a message to the others."

"A message?"

"Turf war. Whatever."

"By killing teenagers?"

"They don't give a rat's ass, Julie," Hoops says. "I worked undercover for twenty years. You meet these guys, and most of them seem regular. Friendly, often. I was working this one operation for three months on this one dealer. Got to know him pretty good. I'd go to his place for beers and to watch games. One day we're driving along and he's telling me all excited-like how his one-year-old son just took his first steps. I thought the dude was going to break into tears. And then, not five minutes later, he tells me he's got the dead bodies of some rival plug and his seventeen-year-old girlfriend in the trunk of the fucking car! I shit you not."

"Ah, the old days. Good times." Anson rolls his eyes, clearly having heard the story before. "Hoops, who would you be looking at as being behind this?"

Hoops leans back in his chair and squeezes a rubber stress-relief ball in his hand. "All the gangs are in the fentanyl trade these days. Heroin is dead. No money in it. Whereas fentanyl . . ." He whistles. "They can turn one kilo of fentanyl—a twelve-thousand-dollar investment—into a million. Of course, coke is still king, but fenny is catching up in a hurry."

"Who are the biggest players?" Theo asks.

"Let's start with who probably isn't. Most of the World Soldiers gang have been killed or incarcerated. Same with the Baxter brothers. The Hondurans have been depleted, too—these guys knock each other off at an impressive clip. And the Hells Angels are way less active since their 'hotels' were converted to social housing by the city."

"Who does that leave?"

"The Persians still control a ton of the drugs that run through Vancouver."

"We already spoke to Farhad Hashemi," Anson says. "Swears he's not involved."

"And if you can't trust Farhad Hashemi . . ." Hoops grunts as he crushes the ball in his grip. "And the East Indian gangs—the Choudaries, the Sharmas, and the like—are still active, too. Another very good bet, of course, is the Triad. They've got direct access to the biggest fentanyl supplier, aka China. They deal right down to street level, but they also wholesale a ton to the other gangs."

"So we could be looking at multiple gangs?" Theo asks.

"Or none."

"How so?"

"Fenny gets to Vancouver about a hundred different ways. Sure, the gangs bring it here in bulk. From China, mainly, but Mexico, too. Some bring it in as premade pills, while others import the raw fentanyl and do the cutting and processing here. But you or I could go on the dark web right now and order the drug directly to some random post office box. It'll show up in under a week and, long as it's under twelve grams, no one will even check it at the border. The joke around here is that the courier companies are bigger drug dealers than all of the cartels."

Julie's heart sinks. "You mean these lethal pills could be showing up through the mail?"

"Maybe," Hoops says. "If it were just the kids, I'd say it's very possible. But your IVDU—Zack or whatever his name is—probably isn't ordering drugs online. Doubt he has a home, let alone a PO box. No, that's probably gang distribution."

"So that's where we'll focus." Anson motions in Hoops's direction. "You'll help us, right, Hoops?"

"Course, bro. As we say down South, you detectives couldn't find your asses with both hands in your back pockets."

CHAPTER 21

Less than five minutes after Charlie Huang has pulled down the blinds and turned the sign in the window of his electronics store to CLOSED, the door opens. The Jian brothers are nothing if not punctual. As usual, Li Wei is smiling, while his brother, Hui, is not.

Neither of them appear physically imposing. Charlie figures he's taller than both. Weighs more, too. The brothers have never been anything like what he expected. Growing up in his hometown of Gaozhou—before he moved to Vancouver to study computer science at Simon Fraser University—Charlie had heard so many legends about the Triad gangs. How the Triad had defied the Communist authorities for years, and how they dispensed their own form of justice through the blade of a meat cleaver. He'd seen the gangster films that romanticized their exotic code names, distinctive tattoos, and secret signs. He used to assume the gang members could hold entire conversations through only eye movements and the repositioning of their cigarettes.

But, aside from Hui's orneriness, the Jians are disappointingly ordinary. They have no visible tattoos and never speak in code. They look and behave like most other businessmen Charlie has dealt with over the years. Only their product is different.

"Li Wei, Hui, welcome, welcome!" Charlie greets them in Mandarin from behind the counter, where he stands in front of piles of boxes holding printers, laptops, and screens.

"I trust you are well, Chonglin," Li Wei says as he approaches with a leather briefcase in hand.

"Where is your sister?" Hui asks in lieu of a greeting.

"Not to worry," Charlie says. "She left hours ago to take her daughter to violin lessons."

"Good," Li Wei says. "How was the trip to China?"

"Productive."

"An uneventful flight home, I trust?"

"No! It was terrible. I've never been through worse."

Hui's eyes narrow. "What went wrong?"

"Everything."

"Tell us, please, Chonglin." Li Wei glances over his shoulder as though there might be someone sneaking up behind him as he speaks. "What do we need to hear about your trip?"

"Six hours of nonstop turbulence! Like we were flying inside a spinning dryer. No food, no drink. Such terrible flight sickness. Those useless pilots!"

"This is what you mean by terrible?" Li Wei laughs with relief. "The turbulence?"

"Of course."

Hui wrinkles his nose as if inhaling an unpleasant odor. "You brought our laptop home safely, then?"

"I did." Charlie smiles slyly. "With the upgraded hard drive. I picked it up myself from the factory. Very, very busy factory. Lots and lots of hard drives. And this one weighs exactly one kilogram. I installed it—"

Li Wei waves a hand. "We don't need to know the details, Charlie." His tone is friendly, but there's warning behind it. "As long the laptop is in working order."

"Can we have it now?" Hui asks impatiently.

"Of course." Charlie leans down under the counter and types the code—his niece's six-digit birthday—into the safe's digital lock. The thick door pops open and Charlie extracts the laptop.

As soon as he straightens up, Charlie sees that Li Wei has rested the briefcase on the counter with the lid open. He pulls out a thick envelope before closing it. Even though the envelope is sealed, Charlie's heart thumps as he pictures the stacks of bills inside. It takes all his restraint not to reach for it.

"The computer?" Li Wei says, extending the envelope toward him.

Charlie pulls the laptop tighter against his chest. "It really was such a terrible flight," he says. "I was so nauseous, I almost wished for the plane to crash."

Li Wei's smile disappears. "Not all flights are smooth, Chonglin."

"Yes, but this flight keeps getting rougher, Li Wei. And the lines at the customs desk only get longer. You never know when they're going to go through all your bags. It really is very stressful."

"You intend to raise the price of your laptops?"

Charlie holds up his free hand. "At some point, I have to pass the added cost on to my customers."

"How much, Chonglin?"

"Unfortunately, given the circumstances, it will have to be double."

Li Wei glances at his brother, who has remained still during the conversation. He nods once and then says, "All right."

As Lie Wei opens the briefcase again and reaches inside, Charlie struggles to contain his excitement. He can't believe the brothers have accepted his first offer. He would have settled for twenty percent. Double is beyond his wildest dreams. *How wrong the movies are! These guys are pushovers!*

Charlie doesn't even notice Hui's hand move until it's against his neck. He has no idea where the long blade came from. He doesn't even feel it slicing into his skin until he hears a strange whoosh and feels a warm gush against his upper chest.

CHAPTER 22

"We should drop in on Babar," Theo suggests as soon as they reach the fourth-floor elevator.

Anson nods. "Might as well."

"Babar?" Julie looks from one detective to the other. "Is he one of the gangsters Hoops mentioned?"

Anson folds his arms across his chest. "Just because the guy's name isn't Wesley or Philip doesn't automatically make him a criminal."

Her face heats. "No. Of course not. It's just that after what Hoops was saying . . ."

Anson flashes a mischievous grin, while Theo looks skyward and says, "You can be such an ass, partner."

"Sorry," Anson says. "Just couldn't resist."

Simultaneously miffed and amused, Julie bites back her smile. "So, who's Babar, then?"

"Babar Khan, our guy in Tech Crime," Theo explains. "He's supposed to analyze the kids' phones."

As they ride the elevator down to the basement, Theo checks his phone. After a moment he turns it toward Julie. "Looks like your health alert bulletin is already catching on. Andreas, my second old-est, just re-posted it on Facebook."

Julie reads the headline that she helped to craft: "Poison Con-trol Warns of Ultra-Deadly New Fentanyl Circulating on Vancouver Streets."

"You opted for subtle, then?" Anson says with a half smile.

Still annoyed with him for embarrassing her earlier, she ignores the remark.

When they reach the basement, they head down the hallway and through the door under a sign that reads VANCOUVER TECHNICAL CRIME UNIT. Julie's never been inside the dark office before, but she's not surprised to see cubicles furnished wall-to-wall with computer screens.

Theo leads the way to the corner cubicle where a thin, bearded man types madly at his keyboard. He doesn't even notice them, until Theo says, "Hey, Babar, good to see you."

"What is it that you need now?" Babar asks without looking away from the code that is filling his central screen. His accent is a cross between British and South Asian.

"No new requests." Theo holds up his hands in surrender. "We're just checking on your progress with those teenagers' cell phones."

"The progress is nonexistent without proper warrants."

"Fair enough. But can you tell how difficult they will be to crack once we do have the warrants?"

Babar looks at them with an expression of mild disdain. "They are children's phones," he says, leaving Julie unsure if it means they will be more or less difficult to access, but she assumes the latter.

"We're hoping to have the warrants by tomorrow," Theo says.

"Tomorrow will not work. Or Wednesday. I have cases that have been waiting much longer than yours."

Anson spins Babar's chair away from the keyboard. "Five kids are dead and one is barely hanging on," he snaps. "Their phones could help tell us why. And who's responsible. What the fuck could be a bigger priority than that?"

Babar wriggles his chair free and spins it back to where it was. "I have two gang murders in East Van. A rapist in Kerrisdale who's still on the loose. At least these teenagers are no longer in danger." He shakes his head. "Every one of you thinks your case is the only one that matters."

"I hear you, Babar," Theo says to soothe him. "You get it from all sides."

Babar only stares at his screen. "You do realize, Detectives, the good cop–bad cop routine is less effective when applied to another cop."

Anson opens his mouth to speak, but Julie cuts him off. "Babar, I'm Julie Rees. Not VPD. I'm with Poison Control. No doubt you're swamped with important cases, but the reason this case is so vital is that whatever killed these kids is still on the street. If we can't get to the source, others could die. A lot of them."

Babar slowly turns his chair toward Julie. "Once I have a warrant, I can make the phones a priority."

"Thank you. Is there anything you can tell us about them in the meantime?"

"The phones, no. The teenagers, perhaps." He turns back to his keyboard and begins to type.

"Like what?"

"I've reviewed their social media pages. Most of them had theirs set to private. However, Rachel Xie's Facebook page was not, nor was Grayson Driscoll's Twitter account."

"And?" Anson asks.

"Rachel seems to have used Facebook only to post family pictures and communicate in Chinese. With relatives, I assume. Grayson used his page as somewhat of a political platform for his left-wing leanings. But I didn't find any photos of himself or any references to his social life."

"And that's it so far?" Theo asks.

"I did run some behind-the-scenes analytics and was able to discern that none of the teens were very active users, in terms of posts or on-line friends, on any of the big sites—Facebook, Instagram, or Twitter."

"Isn't that unusual for teenagers?"

"Not necessarily. It suggests they were probably using alternate platforms to communicate, which could be problematic if their site of choice was Snapchat."

"I'm the Luddite here," Julie says. "I'll bite. Why's that?"

"Because all conversations are automatically erased on Snap-chat," Anson says.

"It is more complicated than that," Babar says. "But for all intents and purposes, probably true. If they had been communicating via group snaps—as they call those chats—we wouldn't be able to read them even if we had access to their accounts, unless they were saving the threads."

Anson exhales. "So we might never know what those kids were up to leading up to their overdoses?"

"It's possible, yes."

"Thanks, Babar," Theo says. "We'll be in touch after we secure the warrants."

None of them speak on their way out of the VPD building. After they climb back into the car, Anson punches the steering wheel, honking the horn and drawing the attention of two nearby uni-formed cops. "This is so fucked!"

Theo leans forward from the back seat and pats him on the shoul-der. "We just have to figure out who's dealing this poison. Track back through all the overdoses in the past seventy-two hours—the pilot, the developer, the dead user the nun found. And all the oth-ers. Then we'll find him."

"Or her," Julie suggests.

"Rarely."

Anson shakes his head. "But the only victim who's still alive—

aside from the nun who pricked herself on a discarded needle and isn't going to know jack—is Zack. He's the key."

"We can't discount any of them," Theo says.

"Time to divide up again?" Anson suggests. "You follow up on the other ODs, while I"—he glances over to Julie with a contrite smile—"*we* track down Zack?"

Theo nods.

They drop Theo off at his car outside the pizzeria and head east from there. The skies are still dull and overcast, but the threat of rain has receded. Anson clears his throat. "Sorry about . . . back there."

"No big deal. Everyone loses it once a while. It's cathartic."

"Yeah, I can be a bit of a hothead. Especially on the cases that really get to me. Like this one." His gaze falls to the floor. "But what I meant is I'm sorry for teasing you. That was offside."

She says nothing for a moment. "Actually, it was kind of funny."

He reaches over and squeezes her hand. "You're kind of cool for a doctor." He grins. "Slash toxicologist."

"And you're all right for a cop-slash-clotheshorse." She holds on to his hand. "So . . . Nicole?"

"That was a . . . lifetime ago." He slips free of her grip.

They drive in silence for a while, but Julie's determined not to let it go so easily. "I lost someone, too, Anson."

He glances at her but says nothing as he turns onto East Hastings. He slows the car but doesn't stop as he scans the bustling sidewalk.

"I met Michael in med school," she continues. "We were only friends for the first couple of years. Never wanted to date a classmate. But, man, was he persistent. Finally charmed me into it. We were together for three years. We were engaged when he . . ." Anson still doesn't comment, so she adds, "Don't know what was worse, losing my partner or my best friend."

Anson suddenly points out his window to where a woman in

a crop-top writhes so jerkily on her feet that it appears as if she's dancing through a seizure.

"That's Suzie, isn't it?" Julie says.

"Yeah. She's not going to be a lot of help today."

Seconds later he slams on the brake and hops out of the car without even pulling over to the curb. He races over to an arched alcove, where a man with his hair in a bun stands shoulder-to-shoulder with a willowy woman.

Julie reaches the alcove just as Anson grasps the man by the collar of his jean jacket and yanks him backward.

"What the fuck, man?" the guy cries as he shakes free of the grip. The woman freezes on the spot.

"VPD!" Anson growls without showing identification. "What did you just sell her?"

"Nothing, man. She's my friend."

Anson pivots toward the frightened-looking woman. "Show me what's in your hand!"

The woman turns wide-eyed to the man for help.

"Now!" Anson barks.

She slowly opens her fist to reveal a small clear bag full of whitish gray crystals.

"Meth!" Anson snatches it from her hand and swivels back to the guy. He shoves him against the glass window, pinning him by his shirtfront. "You dealing fenny, too?"

"No, man. I'm no plug. I just had extra."

"Bullshit! Show me what else you're carrying."

The man digs inside the pocket of his jean jacket and pulls out three or four more bags of the same size with a similar amount of crystal meth in each. Anson grabs them from him. "OK, look, I move a few bags here and there," the guy says. "To pay for my own stash. But I don't trade fenny. Swear to God! Don't want to be killing no one."

The woman nods. "It's true. Smokey is meth-only, for sure."

Anson releases him. "I'm looking for a Zack. Tattoos on his neck. You know him?"

"Seen him around, yeah," Smokey says.

"Where does he live?" Julie asks.

"No clue," Smokey says. The woman only shakes her head.

"His plug is some guy who insists his customers carry naloxone kits," Anson says. "Ring any bells? I need a name. Otherwise, you'll just have to do."

Smokey's face crumples, and he looks on the verge of tears. "I might've seen the dealer. If it's him. Clean-cut. Good-looking dude. No idea what his name is. I swear!"

"But you're going to find out for me by day's end, aren't you?"

Smokey nods frantically. "Sure. OK."

"Get out your phone," Anson says, and Smokey complies. "Type in my number and send me a blank text."

After Smokey sends the text, Anson stuffs the bags of drugs in his own pocket and turns away. "By day's end . . . or I'll be back for you, Smokey," he says without looking back.

As they're heading back to the car, Julie hears a slight rumble behind her. She looks over to see the kid with the bandanna skateboarding toward them. As soon as he sees them, Roller screeches to a stop, grabs the board, and pivots in the other direction.

"Hey, Roller!" Anson shouts.

Roller freezes and then slowly turns to face them, looking as nervous as ever.

"Where's Zack?" Anson demands.

"Haven't seen him. Not since you grilled me last time."

"You know where he lives, though?" As soon as Roller hesitates, Anson grips him by the upper arm. "You're taking us there. Right now!"

Roller reluctantly gets into the back of the car. As they drive, he directs them through the streets of the Downtown Eastside to a run-down brick building on Powell Street with a faded sign that reads THE EMPEROR. Julie recognizes it for one of the many low-rent single-room-occupancy hotels—or SROs, as they're better known—that the city subsidizes for welfare recipients. She wonders how much the Downtown Eastside must have changed over the years for all these rooming houses to have started off with such grand-sounding names.

They walk into the dark, muggy lobby, where no one is manning the front desk. A vague stench of decay wafts through the room as Roller leads them up a flight of steps to the second floor. The stink only intensifies as they walk down the narrow corridor to a door near the end.

Anson nods to Roller, who knocks on the door. "Dude, it's me, Roller."

No answer. Anson pounds on the door. Still nothing. He reaches down and jiggles the doorknob, which turns in his hand. He pushes the door open.

Someone is lying facing down, crumpled in the tight space between the bed and the near wall.

"Oh, damn, Zack! I can't deal!" Roller cries as he swivels away and rushes out the door.

Julie hurries over to the body and kneels beside it. Careful to ensure there are no visible needles near his exposed arm, she runs the back of her hand along it. It's as cool as the room. She can't help but think of Michael again. "He's been dead for several hours," she says.

When she looks up, Anson is slipping his hands into latex gloves. "Excuse me," he says, and she moves out of the way to let him take her spot.

He leans forward and rolls Zack over by the shoulder. A syringe falls from his neck to the floor.

"Be *careful*, Anson!"

He nods as he crouches over the corpse. Zack's face is dusky and waxy, and his eyes are so glazed they're almost milky. Anson carefully pats down Zack's pockets. He gingerly reaches inside and pulls out a mobile phone with a cracked screen.

He presses the home button and a picture of a forest appears through the cracks. "It's locked," he says.

"Who doesn't lock their phones these days?"

"My grandma. 'Cause she can't remember the password." He reaches for Zack's arm and pulls it toward him. "He's really stiff already."

"What are you doing?"

Anson straightens Zack's index finger and holds it against the sensor at the bottom of the phone. After a moment the forest is suddenly replaced by a bunch of icons on the screen.

"Is this . . . legit?" she asks.

"You saw what happened at Tech Crime?" He straightens up with the phone in hand. "All those hoops and barrels. You think we can wait another week to maybe get 'proper' access?"

Julie shakes her head.

"Me neither." He scrolls through the texts on the screen. "Markku . . ."

"Who's that?"

"One of the last people to text Zack. Looks like his dealer. Lots of meeting dates and times. Amounts, too." With his other hand, Anson pulls his own phone out of his inner pocket and snaps photos of Zack's screens.

"Anything else?"

Anson scrolls back through the texts. "Lots of numbers without names assigned." He opens a few of the texts. One photo is a full-frontal nude shot of Zack from the neck down, identifiable by the distinctive tattoos at the top of the screen. "They're from various johns." He scrolls down to another text. "This is the last text Zack sent. Arranged a meeting with one of the johns at a dump of a hotel nearby called the Ambassador." He checks the time. "It's from yesterday afternoon. Must have been right after he took off from the hospital."

Anson clicks more photos of the phone numbers and texts on the screen. Finished, he slips the phone back into Zack's pocket. "Time to find Markku."

CHAPTER 23

Li Wei sits across from his brother, each of them perched on a stack of printer boxes. Li Wei replies to messages on his phone using, as always, the PGP-encrypted texting platform through which he conducts all his business, while Hui uses a screwdriver to take apart the laptop in his hands.

From where he sits, Li Wei can't see Charlie's body, which has fallen back behind the counter. But, even five minutes after he died, blood is still dripping down from the top of the counter and leaking out under its base. *So disgusting.* Li Wei is just grateful his favorite Gucci loafers weren't ruined.

"How much longer?" Hui growls, as he smashes open the hard drive casing and extracts the sealed block of drugs.

"Any minute now, brother," Li Wei says, having just received a message from the leader of the cleanup crew saying they were driving into the lane behind the store.

Hui looks up at him with a sneer. "Are they aware of just how big the mess is?"

You mean how big your mess is. Li Wei sighs to himself. *He's so much like Father.* Jian Wang Wei was a notorious lieutenant and enforcer for one of the most powerful Triads in Guangdong. Their father might've risen all the way to the top, as the dragon head, if his quick temper and jealous streak hadn't led him to strangle a fellow lieutenant—the nephew of the then-current dragon head—whom he suspected of having an affair with his mistress. The bullet to the back of Wang Wei's head rapidly ended any hope of further career advancement, but his teenage sons were still absorbed into the Triad family. The gang even covered the cost of Li Wei's exclusive private English school, though Hui dropped out of his state-run school and went to work for the Triad almost immediately.

Li Wei's phone buzzes, alerting him that the team is waiting out back. He opens the back door and the three black-clad young men enter, each offering the brothers a quick head bow as they pass.

Hui waves to the counter. "Wipe all prints. Three times, at least."

"Yes, sir," the first one says.

Hui hands Li Wei the brick of fentanyl, and he places it inside his briefcase. The brothers leave together through the same door. As it closes behind them, Li Wei doesn't give the situation inside another thought. He trusts his crew. Charlie will never be found.

They walk down the lane to the side street where Li Wei has parked his brand-new white BMW 760Li—a spontaneous birthday present to himself that he had only picked up this morning.

As they drive across town toward the lower-middle-class neighborhood in the southeast corner of Vancouver, Hui tunes the radio in to the local Chinese news station. It reminds Li Wei how his little brother has never even tried to leave the old country behind. He's not alone. After more than ten years of living in Vancouver, Li Wei is still amazed at how entrenched Chinese culture is in the city. He knows several compatriots who have lived in Canada for even longer than he has without speaking a word of English. And he's aware of others who spend their days in the city eating only Asian food, shopping exclusively at Chinese stores and consuming all their news and entertainment in Mandarin. Sometimes Li Wei wishes that Vancouver were a little less like home.

As soon as the announcer mentions the health alert that the city has issued over tainted fentanyl, Hui turns up the volume. The woman goes on to speculate about whether the warning might be related to the teenagers who overdosed over the weekend, although, she says, no one has officially confirmed it.

What passes for a smile crosses Hui's lips. "Remember what Uncle used to tell us? Every crisis brings new opportunities."

At moments like these, Li Wei wonders if Hui and he really are truly related by blood.

They reach the residential neighborhood known as Champlain Heights, which, despite the grandiose name, offers some of the lowest-priced real estate in the city. Li Wei turns onto a nondescript side street and parks in front of the drab little bungalow that still holds sentimental value for him, because it was one of the first homes they had repossessed on a mortgage default.

At the front door, Li Wei has to knock twice before the young man with the foolish nickname answers, wearing a gas mask pulled up over his forehead.

"What you do if stranger at door?" Hui demands in his guttural English, pointing to the mask.

"I checked the cameras, Mr. Jian," Bunsen says. "I would've never answered if it was anyone else."

"Good to see you again, Bunsen." Li Wei uses a finger to gesture a circle around his mouth and nose. "Is it safe for us to enter?"

Bunsen nods. "I've closed all the bins. And the ventilation is on high."

The brothers follow Bunsen back inside the kitchen that he has converted into a lab. With each step, the hum of the powerful fans grows louder. Clear bins with pills and powders are stacked on the countertop beside the stainless-steel pill press Li Wei had ordered from Germany. At the end of the counter sit two black briefcases identical to the one in Li Wei's hand. The first case is closed, but the second one is wide open and packed with neatly bundled baggies of grayish pills.

"One hundred thousand?" Hui asks.

"Yes. Fifty thousand in each."

"Good," Hui grunts, though he doesn't stop scowling.

Li Wei lays his own briefcase on the countertop and opens it. He removes the same envelope he offered Charlie. As he's holding it out to him, Bunsen's eyes flicker with concern. It's only then that Li Wei spots the blood splatter on the corner of the envelope. Rather than try to explain it away, he just smiles, realizing it can only help to deter any unreasonable last-minute contract renegotiations such as Charlie attempted.

After Bunsen hurriedly slips the envelope into one of the top drawers, Li Wei passes him the brick that Hui extracted from the laptop. "And the carfentanil?" Bunsen asks.

"We delivered it two weeks ago," Li Wei says. "Enough for a month or more."

"Yeah, course." Bunsen's eyes crease momentarily, before he breaks into a nervous chuckle. "Long couple of nights. With these bigger orders and all." He raises the block in his hand. "Speaking of, when will you need these?"

"Tomorrow," Hui says.

"Guess the girlfriend's not getting the birthday dinner she was counting on tonight. And Holly doesn't do disappointment well. Or quietly."

Bunsen laughs again, but neither of the brothers so much as cracks a smile.

CHAPTER 24

On the way home, Julie asks Anson to drop her off at the hospital, claiming that she needs to finish her dictations and follow up on the results of lab tests from her weekend ER shifts. But the truth masks a small lie. She can't resist checking in on Alexa again, though she dreads what she expects to learn.

Julie also feels frustrated that—four hours after the crime scene technicians bundled up Zack's body—they still haven't tracked down his dealer. They've made some progress, though. A few locals in the Downtown Eastside recognized Markku, saying that he comes around regularly. And the terrified Smokey texted Anson back to confirm that Markku was, in fact, Zack's regular "plug."

Since it's already ten minutes after nine p.m., Julie has to use her hospital ID to unlock the electric doors at the entrance to St. Michael's. As she walks down the main hallway of the historic old building, she spots Dr. Tanya Dutton approaching. Julie considers veering off in another direction, but her plan is thwarted by the other woman's welcoming wave.

"Julie, hello," Tanya calls.

"Hi, Tanya." Julie stops and waits for the chief of staff to catch

up with her. Even though Tanya is well over sixty, the fit and always stylish neurologist still moves as lithely as the national middle-
distance running champion she once was.

"This is somewhat fortuitous. I was hoping to chat with you."

There's no mystery behind her request. "Regarding the ECMO
case? Alexa O'Neill?"

"Yes." Tanya glances from side to side. "We don't have to talk
now, of course."

"It's as good a time as any," Julie says. "Harold lodged a complaint, I take it?"

"Not exactly." Tanya clears her throat. "Harold did make his concerns known to me. But I'm also on call for Neurology this week. I
assessed Alexa's brain function earlier."

"What did you find?"

"She only has brain-stem function. And her EEG is not . . .
promising."

"Is she brain-dead, Tanya?"

She hesitates. "We need another twenty-four hours to say with
certainty, but it's not looking good. Regardless, the parents—the
mother, anyway—aren't ready to let her go."

Julie can tell Tanya is just hedging her bets, as any thorough neurologist would, but she recognizes the certainty in her colleague's
eyes. "I see."

"As I'm sure you know, Harold is concerned that you . . . devi-
ated from protocol in this case."

"He's right," Julie mumbles, still digesting the finality of Tanya's
assessment.

"Why, Julie?"

"There was nothing else to do. I thought she might have an outside shot on ECMO."

Tanya clears her throat. "Harold seems to think that your judgment might've been clouded in this particular instance."

"Because of Michael."

Tanya squeezes Julie's elbow. "What you went through, Julie . . . No one else can understand. But—"

"I'm not the only one whose judgment might be clouded." Julie's rising indignation edges out her sadness as she pulls her arm free of Tanya's grip. "Harold was Michael's uncle. He's never forgiven me for what happened. He never will."

"I understand. And I hate being put in the middle of this, between two doctors whom I genuinely respect. It's the worst part of being chief of staff. Still, I do have to forward this case for review at the quality-and-safety rounds."

"I wouldn't expect anything less," Julie says as she stalks away.

"Julie!" Tanya calls after her, but Julie is too incensed to discuss it further. She won't let Harold provoke any more tears than he already has. She tells herself that she's done enough crying for a lifetime, but she knows her newfound resolve is born of anger and might not last.

Julie doesn't calm until she reaches the elevator. She thinks of Alexa and all the other lives ruined by the pure carfentanil those kids inadvertently consumed. She tries to console herself with the thought of Dylan Berg. At least one of them is going to pull through. If only he had some memory of the hours leading up to the party, then they wouldn't need to crack the other teenagers' phones to figure out what happened that night.

His phone! It's hits her like a jolt.

Julie bounds up the stairs to the medical ward and flashes her ID to the bewildered clerk behind the nursing desk. "Dylan Berg!" she says. "Which room is he in?"

The clerk checks her computer screen. "It's 8018," she says.

"Thanks," Julie says as she rushes down the corridor to the private room.

Dylan is lying on the bed in a blue hospital gown, propped up by pillows. His earbuds are plugged in, and he's watching a video on the tablet that rests against his thighs. A large bouquet of balloons stands on the window ledge with four or five get-well cards resting against it.

"Hi, Dylan," Julie says as she steps up to the bedside. "How are you feeling?"

"Oh, hey." He pulls out his earbuds and puts the tablet on the bedside table. "OK, I think. Might be discharged tomorrow. They say I can fly home in a couple days."

"That's great news," she says genuinely. "I just wanted to ask you a couple more questions. About the party."

He lowers his head warily. "Like I told you yesterday, I can't remember anything about the party or that whole day."

"No, what I wanted to ask you was how your group of friends communicated."

"Communicated?"

"You've got a phone, right?"

He looks at her if she might be simple. "Yeah." He pauses. "I mean, I haven't got it back since the . . ."

"So how did your friends chat? Through text? Or WhatsApp? And did you have any group chats going?"

"I only ever texted with Gray."

"None of the others?"

"I didn't have anyone else's digits."

Julie fights to keep the disappointment off her face. She'd been hoping Dylan's phone would give them access to the teens' group conversations. "Do you know how the rest of them chatted with each other?"

"Not sure. I'd see Gray get a lot of Snaps on his screen."

His answer saps the last of her brief gust of optimism. Anson was right. *This is fucked.* If the kids were communicating through Snapchat, the investigators might never piece together what happened at the party.

"Dr. Rees . . ." Dylan swallows. "How is Alexa?"

Julie doesn't see the point in hiding something that he's bound to soon find out. "Not good, Dylan."

His chin drops to his chest. "Oh," he gulps.

Julie thanks Dylan and wishes him a safe trip home. She heads back to the elevator and, as she waits for it, considers just heading home herself. She has no doubt visiting Alexa will only dishearten her further. But she feels compelled to see her again, perhaps for the last time.

That suspicion is confirmed the moment she steps into the ICU. Elaine and Tom sit at their daughter's bedside. Elaine's head is buried in her husband's shoulder as Julie enters the room. Alexa's expression is placid. Aside from the endotracheal tube between her lips, she looks as though she could wake up at any moment. But Julie realizes how cruelly misleading the appearance is.

Tom nods to her. His face is blank, his eyes as sad as ever. Elaine lifts her head up and sniffles several times. "They don't think Lex's gonna wake up," she manages.

"I just spoke to Dr. Dutton," is all Julie says.

"They're wrong sometimes, aren't they, Dr. Rees?" Elaine implores her. "I've seen it on TV where people wake up from comas after years!"

Julie appreciates that it's not the time for false hope. "Those are different situations, Elaine. Not like what happened to Alexa."

"Dr. Dutton says she can't be certain until tomorrow."

"You should listen to her. She's an excellent physician."

Elaine holds her gaze for one desperate moment, before her face crumples and drops back onto Tom's shoulder. Muffled sobs soon follow.

Julie reaches down and gives Alexa's limp hand a squeeze. It feels so deceptively warm. She never knew the conscious Alexa, but she intuits that she would've really liked the girl. Her heart cracks a little as she lets her hand go.

Julie looks over at Tom and suddenly feels at a loss for words. All she can muster as she leaves the room is a grim smile and a small nod.

CHAPTER 25

As Li Wei drives downtown with his brother, he doesn't want to hear any more talk of tainted drugs, so he switches off the radio and they travel in blissful silence. He slows the car to a stop out front of the restaurant on Alberni Street where a valet attendant is waiting for him.

"Welcome to Cena, sir," the young man with the red hair and freckles says in an accent that Li Wei can't place but thinks must be British.

"It's brand-new. Too soon for scratches," Li Wei says to the boy, whose eyes light up at the sight of the fifty-dollar bill wrapped around the car key.

Another man with greased hair in a form-fitting suit greets them with a massive smile at the front door. "Welcome, Mr. Jian and Mr. Jian. Mr. Hashemi is expecting you. Please, follow me."

The man leads them up an elevator to the third floor. He guides them down a dark hallway, past an empty private dining room, and into a bright contemporary office. It's decorated with splashy prints, a taupe leather sofa and matching love seat, and a sleek white desk. Farhad Hashemi sits behind the desk, across from his brawny bodyguard. The man who guided them upstairs backpedals out of the room and closes the door behind him.

Farhad rises to greet the brothers with his usual smug smile.

These oily Iranians think they own this city. Li Wei can only imagine what his brother must be thinking.

"Hugh, Wayne, good to see you." Farhad extends a hand to them. "Thank you for coming."

"It is good to see you, too, Farhad," Li Wei says as he meets the man's firm handshake.

Ignoring the Persian's hand, Hui bows his head and offers only a terse, "Good day."

"Come, sit." Farhad leads them back to the desk, where they sit down across from him. "Business must really be booming, Wayne. I heard about your new house on Marine Drive. I should say mansion. Estate, really. I drive by it all the time. I'm wildly jealous."

"If there's anyone to be jealous of, it is the realtors in this city. In Vancouver, real estate is even more profitable than our business."

Farhad laughs. "Especially if you can get favorable interest rates."

"Very true." Li Wei isn't sure whether Farhad is referencing their high-interest loans or not. But he can see by how straight Hui is sitting that his brother has taken umbrage at the comment. The burning in his throat intensifies. The last thing he needs is for Hui to overreact. Li Wei reaches down and grabs the briefcase full of pills at his feet and lifts it up to the desk. "We have filled your prescription."

Farhad laughs. "I hope your pharmacy still accept cash," he says as he produces a stainless-steel briefcase of his own from behind his desk.

They exchange the cases without opening them, each aware how shortsighted it would be to shortchange the other—a recipe for guaranteed war.

Just as Li Wei is about to stand, Farhad asks, "Have the VPD interviewed either one of you yet?"

"Interviewed?" Hui grimaces. "Why?"

"The dead teenagers," Farhad says with a small shrug. "The health advisory. They say there is bad product on the street."

"No," Li Wei says. "They have come to see you?"

"They did. Asking all sorts of questions, leveling all kinds of accusations. They were particularly interested in one junkie and his dealer."

"Why?" Li Wei leans forward. He can practically taste the stomach acid now. "Is he the one selling the bad dope?"

"The cops didn't share much with me."

"Do you know who this dealer is?"

"I do." Farhad's lips part into a self-satisfied smirk. "They don't."

CHAPTER 26

As Julie is walking out of the ICU, she sees Chloe, one of her patients from the evening before, through the glass wall inside the last room before the exit. Chloe holds her baby pressed to her breast. Julie takes the young mother's smile as invitation to enter.

Julie hears the whir of the heart-lung bypass machine even before she sees the bulky device at the head of Chloe's bed. The two garden hose–sized tubes leading from the front of it are engorged with blood that pumps to and from Chloe. Her waxen complexion is no better than the last time Julie saw her, but her eyes are brighter, and her welcoming grin is reassuring.

"It's good you can still breastfeed," Julie says.

"I try," Chloe replies in a weak voice. "Not making much milk. We have to supplement her all the time. But I'll keep doing it. As long as I can."

"Good for you."

Chloe's gaze drops down to her baby. "I would do it again, Dr. Rees."

"Do what?"

"Have Maya. Even if I knew it was going to wreck my heart. I wouldn't change anything."

Julie has no doubt of her sincerity. "No word yet on a donor heart?"

"Dr. Mott checks all the time. He says it will be available any day." Chloe looks back up at Julie and nods to the ECMO machine. "Not sure how much longer this pump can keep me going."

Julie only shrugs. "That's beyond my expertise."

"But if they don't find another heart soon . . ."

"There must be other options. Like VAD, for example," Julie says, citing the initials for a ventricle assist device, which is a portable external pump that connects tubes directly to and from the main chambers of the heart through the chest wall.

"Dr. Mott mentioned it. I just know in my heart"—Chloe laughs sadly—"my broken heart, that if they don't find a donor organ soon . . ."

Julie has a sudden, hopeful thought, but she knows better than to share it now. "It will happen. Just hang in there, Chloe. That little bundle needs you."

Julie says goodbye, heads back downstairs, and leaves through the main doors. As she passes the parking lot, trying to decide whether to walk home or use the car-sharing app to book a ride, she hears a familiar voice.

"I didn't see your name on the schedule, Julija," Goran says from where he stands beside the driver's door of his beat-up old Volvo station wagon. "Please, Lord, do not tell me you picked up another night shift. You will just lose your marbles."

Without saying a word, Julie rushes over to Goran and throws her arms around him. He wraps her up in a big warm hug. "It has been a tough few days, Julija?"

Without lifting her head from his chest, she murmurs, "You have no idea, Gor."

He strokes her hair. "Is Harold still on your case?"

"He's the least of my troubles," she says, as she eases out of his embrace.

"What else? Tell old Goran. He's a good listener. Or, at the very least, he knows how to fake it."

She tells him everything, without reservation. She describes the investigation into the poisoned fentanyl. She tells him about Alexa's dismal prognosis and her devastated family. And then she finishes by saying, "On top of it all, I can't stop thinking about Michael. It's like the door to the vault where I locked away those memories has just been blown off."

"It's natural, Julija. It's the same for me with Lada. Any occasion—birthday, holiday, favorite movie—I can't even predict what will trigger the memories. Maria—Lord love her—she's so understanding, but it never changes."

"That's very different, Gor."

"How so?"

"Because you didn't kill Lada."

He grabs her firmly by the shoulders. "We stopped this sort of talk years ago, Julija! Remember?"

"Maybe I stopped talking about it. But I never stopped thinking it."

Goran exhales loudly and then pulls her in for another hug. "You're just exhausted. You've been through so much these past few days. It's only natural the trauma resurfaces."

Julie lingers in his embrace for a while, feeling incredibly grateful to have him in her life. The father figure she never had—at least not since she was seven years old.

Julie had been close to her dad when she was little. Her memories of him are still those of a gentle and loving father, one who could make her laugh no matter how sad, sick, or hurt she felt. He was a family doctor, and she has always credited her choice of career to him. But her parents' bitter, bruising divorce had come out of nowhere, or so it seemed to Julie, the way it probably always does to seven-year-olds. She wouldn't learn of her dad's affair with his office receptionist for another ten years. And, when Julie was only nine years old, her dad was killed in an avalanche while backcountry skiing.

Julie shakes off the memory and pulls back to view Goran. "Hey, about tomorrow's dinner . . ."

Goran raises an eyebrow. "Yes, what of it?"

"Is it too late for me to bring someone?"

His eyes twinkle as he breaks into a hearty chuckle. "Julija, when is it ever too late for a miracle?"

CHAPTER 27

Wade Patterson sits in his home office and sorts through his inventory. He picks up the sealed bag of fake oxys and weighs it in his hand, estimating he still has at least two hundred of the grayish fentanyl pills left. As he holds it up to the light, Wade again notices the differences in color and markings, especially the bluer-tinted ones from his last buy.

Wade deliberately mixes his purchases together. No two batches are ever the same, in terms of dose or even content, and by blending them from the start, he assures that his clients don't come to depend on the same potency. Besides, he doesn't always rely on one supplier, so variations—big ones sometimes—are to be expected. He prides himself on getting the best wholesale prices on the market. He even jokes about developing an app for dealers, similar to one of those sites that show which service station has the lowest gas prices. But the last thing he needs is another business. He can barely keep up with the demands of his dial-a-dope service. The referrals and random connects from it used to only account for a small percentage of his deals, but now it generates more income than his regular clientele. But since the dial-a-dope callers aren't loyal customers,

Wade does most of his experimenting and substituting with them. Sometimes he'll cut a little fenny into the coke. A smidge of it is helpful to bring clients back to the table without them even knowing they've crossed the line into the opes. He isn't even averse to switching up tablets from time to time, substituting one type of drug for another when he's running low. It's good for these preppy snots to be exposed to the full rainbow of the substance experience. *Builds character*—he smiles to himself—*and God knows those assholes could use some.*

Wade puts the fentanyl away and lifts the clear plastic container where he stores his coke. Supply is running low, after the big sale to Jarrod. He could crush a few more fake oxys into the mix, but it wouldn't get him far enough. *I'm out of Ecstasy, too*, he reminds himself. Not a huge demand for E tabs these days, but still, he's overdue for restocking. And there aren't many other buyers to whom he'd be able to pass off fake oxys as E.

Wade mentally calculates what the supplies will cost and then counts out the money from his hiding spot in the false bottom below his dryer. As he slips the cash into his billfold, he stuffs an extra grand in the wallet as a bonus for himself—*thank you, Jarrod, you arrogant prick*—unsure if it will take the form of a new pair of boots or, possibly, a night with two honeys. Maybe both. He can pay the girls off in product; the cash is only for the cost of a hotel room and room service.

Wade doesn't feel like driving. Instead, he throws on his backpack, heads down the elevator, and unlocks the state-of-the-art titanium lock on his cruiser bike. *You can never be too careful with all the rats crawling around downtown and stealing anything they can get their filthy mitts on.*

It's a short ride under the warm and clear evening skies from his condo in Coal Harbor to Yaletown. Besides, as some woman on Facebook put it: "Vancouver is not only bike-friendly, it's openly hostile to cars." Wade could tell from her profile that the woman was, as expected, fat and bitter, but her point was still valid. The city's misguided mayor is so busy turning the streets and bridges into biking thoroughfares that he has made downtown driving a nightmare for the other ninety-eight percent of commuters.

Wade cruises into the alley off Homer Street and down the ramp to the underground garage. He types the code at the gate and ducks beneath as it rises. He cycles down to the second level, to the same stall as usual, number seventy-eight, where Jamie Maddox is waiting.

Jamie leans against his Harley and chews gum noisily. The tree trunks that pass for his arms are folded across his chest. "You're a biker, too, now, Wade-O?" He scoffs.

"I try, bro." Wade grins, reminding himself that it won't be too long before the Persians or the East Indians or some other gang-bangers put a bullet in Jamie's smug face. His squad of "World Soldiers" have already passed their best-before date. "That's an impressive ride!"

"If only it came with training wheels, huh? Then you could take her out, too."

"Now you're talking my speed, bro," Wade says, promising himself that he'll do a grade-A shot of tequila the moment he hears that this douchebag has been killed.

"Time is cash. What do you need?"

"Three hundred g's of blow. And a hundred tabs of E."

The skin around Jamie's eyes creases. "No fenny?"

"Nah. I'm good there."

Jamie unfolds his arms and stands up straight, hovering a full head above Wade. "Why not, Wade-O? You got a better supplier for that?"

"I'm just flush," Wade says, scrambling to come up with an alternate explanation. "And demand has been down this week."

"Yeah, right!" Jamie leans close enough for Wade to pick up a whiff of spearmint. "No one's doing fenny anymore now that weed is legal. That it?"

"No, Jamie, it's all the bad down out there. The warnings and all. People are scared."

"Like that would stop them."

"Probably not. You could tell them the fenny was laced with cyanide for an extra boost and they'd gobble it up." The biker says nothing and, still unnerved by his looming presence, Wade feels compelled to fill in the void. "A client of mine even asked for that stuff."

"What stuff?"

"The stuff they're warning about. The dead teens and all. He even had a name for it: 'The Last High.'"

Jamie only snorts.

"Could be a good market." Wade points to the side pouch on the Harley. "You're not selling any of The Last High, are you?"

Jamie lunges so fast that Wade doesn't react until he's dangling in the air, hanging by the collar of his own jacket.

"What did I say?" Wade pleads.

"You little fuck!" Jamie sprays him with spittle. "Are you telling people I sell that shit?"

"No!"

"That's why you're not buying fenny today? Is that it?"

"No, bro! Nothing like that. Was just a terrible joke."

Jamie hurls Wade backward and he lands on his ass with an agonizing thud. His head and elbow follow, hitting the concrete simultaneously. It's all he can do not to cry out.

"If I find out you've breathed one word linking me to that shit . . ." Jamie makes a snapping motion with his fists, as if breaking an imaginary branch between them. "I'm going to rip your limbs off and bury you alive!"

CHAPTER 28

Holding the warm container of urine in her hand, Julie wonders yet again what could be more humiliating than stepping out of a bathroom stall and handing your own pee sample over to a nurse who has just watched you produce it.

Nine years. She has been coping that whole time with the monthly drug screens that were mandated by the College of Physicians and Surgeons. In eleven more months, she will reach the ten-year mark and the end of her compulsory screening. But after what she's been through the past three days, this morning's testing seems harder to endure than usual.

As the nurse labels her sample, Julie reflects again on how she reached this point. If someone had suggested to her during medical school that she would soon become addicted to opioids, she would have laughed it off. Sure, Julie had a few blindingly drunk nights during undergrad, but she paid for each with a punishing day after, largely spent hovering over a toilet bowl and vomiting intractably. Besides, her mom's battle with the bottle that she tried so hard, but failed, to conceal from her kids—the bruises from "Mommy's clumsiness," the long mornings in bed with "migraines," and the random men who came and went from their lives—had been deterrent enough for Julie. At least until Julie got involved with Michael.

Michael began using opioids before she did. He claimed to have developed his taste for them after back surgery, for a herniated disc, during the summer between his third and fourth year of medical school. But even now Julie isn't convinced that was true. As kind and lovable as Michael was, he lied a lot. In her experience, all addicts do. She was no exception.

Still, it took months of coaxing for Michael to convince her to experiment with him. She eventually gave in, hoping it was something they could get out of his system together. Or maybe she has just hung on to the convenient myth for so long that she now believes it to be true. Regardless, from the moment she first let him inject morphine into the vein at her elbow, she was hooked. She once heard an addict describe the high from opioids as "the warmest hug you will ever feel." It's as good as any description she has heard. But even beyond the otherworldly sense of bliss and contentment she found at the point of the needle, she couldn't have predicted the intensity of the craving. As soon as the euphoria began to wear off, long before any withdrawal symptoms set in, all she could think about was the next high.

As a resident doctor training in anesthesia, Michael had devised an ingenious system of stealing discarded vials of drugs in the operating room. Soon he switched from morphine to fentanyl, which was, and still is, a safe short-acting painkiller when used in the controlled setting of a hospital. In retrospect, Julie has no idea how she functioned as an ER resident during those three months of intense drug abuse. All the lies, excuses, and unexplained absences. She manipulated friends, family, and colleagues, including Goran, playing on their sympathy and their refusal to imagine drugs could be involved. Who knows how long she could have continued—or even survived—had Michael woken up that fateful morning after his overdose?

The nurse pulls Julie out of the memory with a thumbs-up gesture. "We're all good, Julie. See you next month."

"Thanks," Julie mumbles without making eye contact.

She checks her watch and sees that it's still a few minutes before nine a.m., so she decides to walk the one and a half miles from the clinic to the Poison Control Center. The sky is one continuous canvas of blue, and the temperature is ideal. The city's always-generous foliage is particularly lush with the trees and shrubs in full late-spring bloom. Their sweet scents waft around her. And the mountains guarding the city's northern flank are especially inspiring in the dazzling sunshine. By the time Julie reaches the Provincial Toxicology Centre, the new three-story glass-and-steel building located kitty-corner from St. Michael's Hospital, her mood has lightened.

Julie steps inside the main-floor office of Poison Control, where only one of the four cubicles is currently manned. Glen Swinney, who sports a handlebar mustache and diamond ear studs, leans back in his chair with a headset on and his arm resting on his own paunch. At the sight of Julie, the sixtyish Brit gets up and approaches her while still speaking into his headset. "No, Mrs. Glover, your little lad will be fine." He rolls his eyes. "Show poodle or not, two chocolate-covered peanuts are not going to do the pooch in."

As soon as he disconnects, Julie grabs her cheeks in mock horror. "But I hear that chocolate is absolutely deadly for dogs."

"Pretty sure Mr. Peanuts will pull through. If only we could change our greeting to, 'Poison Control, for humans only,' it would cut my workload in half." He leans forward and gives her a quick peck on the cheek. "Good to see your beautiful face, luv."

"Yours, too, Glen." She waves her hand up and down. "You lose some weight?"

"With Darryl's cooking? Never! But Lord love you for lying." He pats his belly. "You're early. None of the other toxicologists are here yet for the meeting."

"Need to drop in on the lab beforehand. Hey, Glen, any more calls about those ultrapotent opioids?"

"Not per se, no. But I did a little snooping. I called a friend who works in ambulance dispatch."

"And?"

"He says they haven't been much busier—above the usual high volume of OD calls—but they've noticed a way higher fatality rate. Practically none of the ODs have made it to hospital."

"The last part makes sense."

"*Sense* is a strong word when it comes to any of this."

"True enough." Julie turns back to the door. "Better go talk to the experts upstairs. I'll see you in half an hour or so."

"I'll be right here, saving lives. Poodle lives, kitty lives, hamster lives . . ."

Julie leaves the office and jogs up the two flights of stairs that lead her into the Provincial Toxicology Centre's open laboratory, which is bathed in sunlight streaming in through a large central skylight. Technicians sit at workstations in front of desktop computers, various electronic analyzers, and rows of test tubes and other lab equipment. The sight always evokes happy memories for Julie of long hours spent in her favorite undergrad biochemistry lab. It reminds her, too, of what a science geek she is at heart.

Julie spots the technician she seeks seated at the third workstation down on the near wall and heads toward her. Young and plump, with blond hair and almost translucently pale skin, Eve McCullough wears a lab coat and goggles. She's hunched over her desk as she carefully pipettes samples into clear vials in front of her.

"Hi, Eve," Julie says as she approaches.

Eve glances over her shoulder and then returns her focus to her task. "Hey, Julie."

"Sorry to interrupt you, but I understand you analyzed the samples from the teenage overdoses."

"Which ones?" Eve asks, while filling another vial.

"Alexa O'Neill and Dylan Berg. Two patients at St. Mike's."

"Guilty as charged."

"You ran ion mobility spectrometry on them, too, right?"

"IMS, yup." Eve thumbs to the center of the lab where a sleek white machine stands with a pop-up screen on top, resembling a futuristic computer terminal from a sci-fi flick. "Old Hal 9000 over there did the heavy lifting."

"And?"

"Confirms the preliminary results. We found low levels of ibuprofen and acetaminophen in the blood. There was a trace of fentanyl. But basically, it was otherwise pure carfentanil."

"How pure?"

"At least ninety-eight percent."

Ninety-eight percent! Even though there's no big surprise in the results, a chill runs through Julie at the idea of such lethal purity. "In other words, poison?"

"Essentially." Eve seals the last of the vials and places it in the small black box beside her. "At the levels of carfentanil we found in their bloodstream, it's a miracle two of them did survive."

Only one of them will, Julie thinks miserably. "Eve, you haven't received any unidentified pills from the VPD for analysis?"

Eve scrunches her nose. "Pills? From the police?"

"From another overdose. By the name of Aiden Wilder. He didn't make it. They found some pills in his desk."

"Nope. Haven't seen anything on a Wilder."

"If I can get you a sample of the pills, could you match them to what you found in the kids' blood?"

"Yes and no. We can't exactly pair metabolites in blood to the parent compounds in a pill."

"No, but if the ratios of carfentanil to fentanyl are the same . . ."

"Would be suggestive, not confirmatory."

"But if you also find ibuprofen and acetaminophen in the

tablets, like you did in the blood sample, then that would be pretty compelling."

"True." Eve considers it for a moment and then nods. "Yeah, if you can get me the pills, I should be able to tell if they're the same as what those kids took."

"Great. Thanks, Eve. You've been a big help."

Julie heads back downstairs to the Poison Control office and joins the toxicologists' meeting that is already in progress. After sitting impatiently through the uninformative and long-winded gathering, Julie grabs a taxi and heads over to the café on Homer Street where she arranged to meet Anson and Theo.

As she climbs out of the cab, Julie spots the detectives seated at an outside table.

"G'morning," Theo says.

"Need a coffee?" Anson asks as she sits down beside them.

"No, thanks, I'm good. Any word on Markku?"

Anson eyes her over the rim of his cup. "So much for small talk this morning."

She meets his gaze with a fleeting grin. "No time for frivolity today."

"Still haven't located Markku," Theo says. "He's definitely known on the street, but we don't have an address for him. And there's no criminal record for anyone by that name in our system."

"Has to be an alias," Anson says.

"It's Finnish, isn't it?" Julie asks.

"Sounds right. Whatever it is, it's rare. We're checking out the few local phone numbers registered with that first name, but so far no matches."

"I just came from Poison Control," Julie says, and updates them on what Glen told her about the high fatality rate among recent overdoses.

Theo nods. "According to the coroner's office, there have been sixteen other overdose deaths, on top of the five teenagers', reported

in the past three days. Twice as many as expected. For six of them—
and counting—the early results point to near-pure carfentanil."

"Only sixteen?" Julie asks.

Anson's brow furrows. "That's not enough for you?"

"If someone were selling pure carfentanil, then we should have
seen a huge spike in deaths over the past three days. Like in the
magnitude of ten times or more."

Theo chews his lip. "What if it's only a single dealer selling one
bad batch of pills?"

"How does that happen?" she asks. "Street-level dealers don't
cook their own supply, do they?"

"Not usually, no."

"Besides," Julie says, "we've had overdoses across the spectrum of
demographics. From IVDUs like Zack to that high-flying developer."

"It's a good point," Anson agrees. "And don't forget the pilot
who overdosed on poisoned coke."

"So maybe we're only seeing the tip of this iceberg so far?" Theo
wonders aloud.

"Maybe only the tip of the tip," Anson mutters into his cup. "Especially if this bad dope is coming from one of the big wholesalers
and we've only seen the first sprinkling to hit the street . . ."

Theo nods. "And we still haven't ruled out the possibility that
some person or group is deliberately poisoning the supply."

Both scenarios terrify Julie, but she keeps her anxiety to herself.
She looks from Theo to Anson. "No other developments?"

"A few," Anson says. "Forensics confirmed that the kids' punch
found at the crime scene contained high concentrates of carfentanil."

"Plus, we got our warrants for the kids' phones," Theo says.
"Babar's already working on them. And I've been checking into that
pilot, Justin Bowles. He's from Toronto. Always flew the same transpacific flight. The airline always put their crews up at the Harbor
Inn after their transpacific flight."

"What does that tell you?" Julie asks.

"There's no way he's going to go through customs carrying coke on him. So he must have bought it when he got to the hotel."

"Couldn't he just buy it on the street?"

"Maybe, but people like him usually get it through a middle-man."

Anson taps his chin. "A bellman or someone else in the hotel. It's worth following up on, for sure."

"I've also been doing some digging into Aiden Wilder," Theo says. "His wife told me he'd been superirritable in the weeks leading up to his overdose, ever since his family doctor cut off his painkiller prescriptions. I think he was new to street drugs. So far, no one has any idea where he got his fake oxys from. But they've also tested positive for nearly pure carfentanil."

"As expected," Julie says.

"Yeah, but look . . ." He pulls his phone out of his pocket, taps the screen a few times, and turns it over to face them. Three bluish tablets—with the typical "80" imprints on the two of them, and the "CDN" marking on the facedown one—are lined up below a yellow ruler. "These were the ones found in his desk."

Julie studies it for a moment. "The color . . ."

"Exactly." Theo swipes the screen and another image appears of a different pile of fake oxys. The shape and markings are the same, but the color is much grayer. He flicks through three or four photos of other piles, none of which are as blue as the ones found in Wilder's desk. "Same shape as the others, but the blue color is pretty distinctive."

"Do you think Forensics could spare one of those pills?" Julie asks.

"What for?" Theo asks.

"For our lab at the Provincial Toxicology Centre. I want them to compare its contents to what they found in Dylan's and Alexa's systems. To see if it's an exact match."

"I'll see what I can do."

Julie motions to the pills on the screen. "This will help. We can add it to our health alert. Warn people to avoid pills of this particular blue and report them if they find any."

"You know my opinion on the usefulness of public alerts," Anson says. "Still, this *is* very good. Looks like we've found the murder weapon. And sooner or later, it's going to lead us back to the source."

As they're discussing the logistics of how best to circulate the images, Hoops appears. With all the ink on his arms, he reminds Julie of one of those movie villains who has stolen the uniform off a dead cop. "Hey, ma'am," he says to Anson as he drops down into the chair beside Julie. "I'll take a half-caf macchiato, extra hot, with sprinkles and sugar-free whip, please."

Anson sighs. "Undercover or not, how have you not been capped in all these years?"

Hoops laughs. "People love me. Especially the gangsters."

"Any lead on this Markku character?" Theo asks.

"Nah. My boys don't know him. Which means he's small potatoes. Near the bottom of the distribution chain."

"So he's not cooking his own fenny?"

"No way. Can't see it."

Theo shows Hoops the photo on his phone. "You ever see fake oxys that look like this?"

Hoops studies the screen. "Not that specific color. No. Text them to me. I'll check around."

"Can't we just raid the local labs?" Julie suggests. "The big ones, at least."

"Great idea, Doc," Hoops says. "Trouble is, we don't know where most of them are. We've got a few under surveillance, but they move all the time. Like coyotes in the night."

"What can you tell us, Hoops?" Theo asks.

"In the last weeks, some of the gangs have been far more active in terms of distribution. And others quiet. At least downtown. For example, the Choudaries and the Sharmas are having a bit of a turf war in Abbotsford. A couple of recent hits. Word is they haven't been venturing downtown at all."

"So who has been?" Anson asks.

"Well, Farhad and the Persians are still the Starbucks of fentanyl distribution on the Downtown Eastside. My boys tell me that, lately, the World Soldiers have switched from meth to fenny. Dumping a whole bunch of it on the street. Not sure where they're getting it from. But never count out Jamie Maddox. He's a wily bastard who's outlasted most of his gang and plenty of the others."

Theo glances over to Anson, before turning to the others. "We busted Maddox once on attempted murder. But our eyewitness—the vic—got cold feet."

"I'm surprised he still had feet at all." Hoops laughs. "And, of course, there's the Triad. These days, that basically means the Jian brothers."

"Who?" Julie asks.

"Wayne and Hugh Jian," Anson says. "Each one of them a world of trouble in a two-thousand-dollar suit."

"A hundred percent," Hoops agrees. "Those two like to play the part of real estate entrepreneurs, but they're as dirty as they come."

Anson turns to Theo. "We need to talk to all of them. And soon."

"Agreed." Theo runs a finger over the image of the blue pills on his screen. "Figure out which one of them decided it was a good idea to peddle ninety-eight percent pure death."

CHAPTER 29

Markku still can't believe how much fluid Elsa has lost. He thought he had seen clients as dope-sick as they came, but they had nothing on Elsa. Her fentanyl withdrawal pounced quickly and violently. Between that and the morning sickness, from a pregnancy confirmed on two separate home tests, she has been vomiting nonstop, but for the last several hours she has only been dry-heaving. Even now, fifteen minutes after he changed the sheets again, she's sweated right through them. He's relieved that she has at least kept down the last glass of water he fed her.

Neither of them slept during the night. Markku didn't dare leave her. In the past twelve hours, he has seen sides of Elsa he never imagined. Her mood swings are dizzying. She has veered from one to another—stoic to whining, determined to despondent, bitter to accepting, and hateful to loving—in an instant. She has begged him for a hit in the same sentence that she has pleaded with him to help her ride it out. She has scared him. She has frustrated him. She has even disgusted him. But he might love her even more now. After all, she's doing it for their baby.

All the while, his phone has been buzzing with messages. He

doesn't care about the ones from impatient customers demanding product. It's the text from his friend Aaron that troubles him. Aaron loves to dick people around for a good laugh, but Markku knows he would never joke about cops looking for him. And his supplier, Reza, keeps pestering him to meet, insisting it's urgent.

Elsa curls up into a fetal position and begins to tremble again. "Talk to me, Markie," she pants. "Distract me. Tell me anything. Tell me about your grandpa again. Yeah, him. The one who used to take you hunting."

Markku smiles. "He was always my favorite. He toughened me up. Taught me about wilderness and survival. Stuff my dad knew nothing about."

"That's why you took his name?"

"Yeah. Dad was such a fucking conformist. Wanted to pretend like he was some kind of WASP or something. That's how I ended up with my stupid first name."

"Blaine! You're definitely no Blaine."

"Always hated it. So after Gramps died, I took his first name. Finnish and proud!"

Elsa suddenly clutches her belly. "I can't, Markie!" Her shaking turns violent again.

"Let me take you to the ER."

"What good'll that do? They won't give methadone for dope-sickness if you never had a prescription before!"

His clients have told him the same. "But maybe if you're pregnant?"

"No hospital, Markie!" Her voice trembles with her whole body. "Shoot me up or just shoot me in the head. I can't do this!"

He runs a damp cloth over her forehead and then hugs her. "You can, El. You will. You're so close. For the baby."

"Fuck the baby!"

"You don't mean that, El."

"No." She sobs. "I'm so dope-sick, Markie. Don't even know what I'm saying."

He clings to her, cradling her in his arms, as she rocks on her side. After several minutes her trembling subsides, and her whimpers die away. He's relieved to finally hear her snoring softly.

He waits a little longer and then inches his arm out from under her body. He rises as quietly as he can. He takes a quick shower and changes, before tiptoeing back to the bed. Satisfied that she's still asleep, he leaves a water bottle on the nightstand and texts her a quick note saying that he'll be back in an hour.

He heads over to the closet in the spare room and opens the safe. He considers revising the combination again, since it's been almost a month since he changed it, but Elsa's in no shape to try to break into anything, so he leaves it as is. He pulls out a few bags of fenny and stuffs them in his pocket. He stares at the gun inside, thinking of Aaron's texts. *Something isn't right.* He grabs the Glock and shoves it into the back of his waistband, before locking the safe.

Markku texts Reza to confirm that he's on his way. He checks once more on Elsa, who's still asleep, before he grabs his helmet, heads down to the garage, hops onto his Ducati motorcycle, and races over to Reza's condo on Alberni Street.

Reza Jazzani, his regular supplier, buzzes him into the building and meets him at the door to his twenty-third-floor unit. "Thanks for coming, dude," the trafficker, who's bald and clean-shaven but hairy from the neck down, says in his thick Iranian accent.

"What's the emergency?" Markku demands.

"Not here," Reza says, glancing around vigilantly. "Come inside."

Markku follows Reza into the living room, with its floor-to-ceiling windows that look out onto the eastern tip of Stanley Park and the harbor beyond. But Markku's eyes are pulled from the dramatic view by the unexpected sight of Farhad Hashemi, who's sitting on the couch in front of the windows and facing him with an arm draped over one of the cushions.

"It's been far too long, Markku," Farhad says in a welcoming tone.

Even though Markku has been buying his supplies off the Persians for almost two years, he has only met Farhad once before, and that was a chance encounter. He glances over at Reza, who shrugs.

"We do need to talk," Farhad says.

Markku's shoulders tense. "About?"

"The Last High. Or TLH, as they're calling it."

Markku frowns. "The what?"

"You know. The bad product that's floating around. The dead teenagers. The stuff the city's warning everyone about."

"What's that got to do with me?"

Farhad smiles, exposing bleached white teeth. "You remember Zack? With the forest growing out of his shirt?"

"What about him?"

"He's a customer of yours, no?"

"I guess."

"He OD'd on The Last High."

Markku's stomach plummets. "How do you know it was the bad down?"

Farhad's smile disappears. "The cops told me. They had no doubt."

This is wrong. "Zack is dead?"

"He is now."

"What does that mean?"

"Turns out your hit was only his second Last High. We had to give him a little push on the next one."

Markku begins to back away from the couch. "I have no idea what the fuck you're talking about."

Farhad stands up. "It's quite simple, Markku. You sold Zack bad dope. And so we had to cover your dirty tracks."

"No . . ." Markku hears footsteps and looks over his shoulder to see Javad, Farhad's hulking bodyguard, standing behind him.

"It's worse than that. The cops have already connected Zack to you. Next, they will tie you to those kids. Can you imagine what would happen if they connect you to us?"

Markku swivels his head to see Javad lunging toward him. He jumps out of the way, thrusts a hand behind his back, and yanks out his gun. He levels it at Javad's chest. Out of the corner of his eye, he can see Farhad glaring at him

"Don't ever forget who you are dealing with, Markku," Farhad warns silkily.

CHAPTER 30

"**W**hat's on the phones, Babar?" Theo asks, before they even reach the cybercop's cubicle at the far end of the Tech Crime office.

"Detective, please. I only received the warrants two hours ago," Babar says without turning away from his screen.

"You texted me," Theo points out.

"Did I say it was regarding the victims' phones?"

Anson taps his fingers impatiently on the partition wall. "What is this? The riddle of the Sphinx?"

Julie rests a hand gently on Babar's bony shoulder. He shifts away from her touch. "Please, Babar, this is so vital."

"All right, let's begin with the phones."

"You're killing me, brother," Anson groans.

"I have only unlocked three of the six."

"Six?" Theo asks. "Not seven?"

"There was no phone found on Joshua Weir." Babar taps his mouse and a series of text balloons pop up on the nearest screen. "Obviously, I haven't had a chance to review all the texts. I did have a cursory scan of the two days leading up to the night of the party. So far the texts are relatively innocuous. No group chats involving the victims. A few mentions of logistics—meeting times and buses and so on—but nothing about drugs or even alcohol."

"Any photos?" Julie asks.

"Only on Rachel Xie's phone, so far." Babar taps a key, and several photos fill the multiple screens in front of him.

They're all set in the same dark den, furnished with old sofas, a Ping-Pong table, and a large-screen TV in the background. Julie recognizes the kids lounging on the furniture—Taylor, Alexa, Joshua, Grayson, and Dylan—from previous photos. It feels surreal to see the teens posing and laughing at the crime scene in images that were clearly captured only minutes before most of them died.

Julie's discomfort intensifies when Babar clicks a button and Alexa springs to life on the largest screen. In the video clip, she raises the plastic cup in her hand and toasts the camera. "Mmm, Nick, your mix is delish!" It's the first time Julie has heard Alexa's voice, and it is hauntingly childlike.

Joshua laughs and wags a finger at her. "Go easy there, light-weight."

"I'm tougher than I look, Joshy!"

The video ends, and the screen freezes on Alexa's beaming smile. Julie's throat thickens.

Anson turns to Theo. "So Nick Gallagher brought the punch to the party?"

"Doesn't mean he was the one who spiked it," Theo says.

"Still . . ."

Theo nods. "I'll talk to his parents again. Lovely people, but they weren't much help the first go-around."

Babar plays two more short video clips that chillingly convey the victims' lethal cluelessness about the impending tragedy but reveal nothing else about where the drugs came from or how they ended up in their drinks. He taps the mouse and another image of a laughing Alexa freezes on the screen. Julie has to swallow away the growing ball in her throat.

"That's all I've recovered so far from the phones," Babar says.

"How about social media?" Anson asks.

"Come on, Detective." Babar shakes his head. "You know that is forbidden fruit until we get separate warrants."

"So why did you drag us down here?"

"Because I found your suspect."

"Markku? How?"

"He has no online presence himself. However, I ran a meta-scan searching for references to him across all social media platforms. I found an Instagram account belonging to an Elsa Durbin." Babar taps his mouse and a photo of a young couple fills the screen. A strikingly pretty girl piggybacks a clean-cut boy as she flashes the camera an almost contagious smile. "The caption below reads: 'Riding my Markku beats walking any day #lookmomnofeet #UberMarkku.'"

Theo points to the image. "You sure it's him?"

Babar clicks the mouse and the man's face fills the main screen. "I took this image and ran it through facial recognition software." Another tap and the photo on the screen morphs to one of a younger man wearing a graduation gown and cap. His hair is longer, and his expression is blank, but it's clearly the same person. "Meet Blaine Saarinen. Aka Markku Saarinen."

"Good work, Babar!" Anson taps the headrest excitedly. "You aren't as useless as I assumed."

"Wish I could conclude the same of you."

"I'm developing a real man-crush on you." Anson laughs as he turns away. "Text us the best images you have of Blaine-slash-Markku Saarinen."

Julie and Anson head out to his car, while Theo stays behind at VPD headquarters to help oversee the manhunt for Blaine "Markku" Saarinen and to book another interview with Nick's parents.

As Julie clicks in her seat belt, she asks, "Where to now?"

"I got to go to Richmond."

"Richmond? Why?"

"Home of the offices of Southeast China Realty."

"The Jian brothers?"

"Yup. Want me to drop you off at the hospital on the way?"

"You're joking, Anson."

His expression turns serious. "This is way beyond the scope of your professional involvement . . ."

"C'mon, Anson, we both know I'm in too deep now not to come with you."

He pinches his lip. "These two . . . they're trouble."

"I'll manage," she says matter-of-factly.

"That, I believe." He sighs as he finally starts the ignition.

Anson drives south along Cambie Street, the busy commercial thoroughfare that effectively bisects the east and west sides of the city. The route leads them away from the mountains and the ocean, past inconsequential new condo buildings and the few nondescript houses still standing, reminding Julie again how blasé Vancouver's cityscape can be without the dramatic natural backdrop.

"Kona," Anson says, apropos of nothing.

"What?"

"The big island of Hawaii." Anson keeps his eyes fixed straight ahead. "It's where Nicole died."

"Oh. I'm sorry . . ."

"First time to Hawaii for either of us. We were island-hopping. We'd rented mopeds that morning." He pauses. "I didn't even see how it happened."

"Anson, you don't have to . . ."

"I stopped to snap a few photos at this lookout. Nicole rode ahead. By the time I got to the scene . . ." He glances at her with a pained smile. "Truck versus moped isn't exactly a fair match."

He clutches the wheel tighter, and she resists the urge to lay a hand on his. "Were you married?"

He nods. "Two good Asian kids. All that crushing parental and cultural pressure. We met during my last year of criminology at Simon Fraser University. We were together four years. She was only twenty-five . . ."

"I'm sorry, Anson."

He shrugs. "It was a lifetime ago."

"Time doesn't always help, does it? At least, it didn't for me, after Michael. More up and down, you know? The littlest things can set me off."

"Yeah."

They lapse into a brief silence as Anson follows Marine Drive west along the Fraser River, which forms the city's natural southern border, before turning onto the Oak Street Bridge. After they cross the bridge into Richmond, Julie says, "This might be the least appropriate segue ever, but do you happen to be free tonight?"

"Possibly. Why?"

"Good friends are having me over for dinner. They're pretty much forcing me at gunpoint to bring a date."

Anson throws her a sidelong glance. "Who could refuse an invitation so flattering?"

"Come on. It'll finally give you a chance to dress up."

A grin creeps across his lips. "If you put it like that . . . OK."

He heads down Number Three Road, the suburb's main commercial strip, and pulls off into one of the side streets that Julie doesn't recognize. They park outside an unimpressive pink building and ride the elevator to a third-floor office. The Chinese lettering of the door sign is larger and sits on top of the English words that read SOUTHEAST CHINA REALTY.

Inside, a petite middle-aged woman with thick glasses and a severe haircut sits behind the desk and types at a computer. She looks up and greets them with a wary smile. Anson addresses her in Mandarin. As they speak, her expression quickly darkens. She picks up her phone and speaks urgently into it.

After she hangs up, she rises and leads Anson and Julie down a short hallway into a plain office with no wall coverings. A fortyish Asian man in a dark suit rises from his desk, as does the shorter man who sits in a chair beside him. Julie hears the door click shut behind her.

Anson nods sternly. "Mr. Jian, Mr. Jian. I am Detective Chen. And this is Dr. Rees."

Li Wei touches his chest. "Please, Detective, I am Wayne." He motions to the other man, who views them blank-faced. "My brother, Hugh."

"Thank you for seeing us," Anson says. "We have a few questions regarding the recent tainted fentanyl on the street."

"Fentanyl?" Li Wei scoffs. "We run a real estate company."

"Of course." Anson holds his palms up apologetically. "And a very successful one, too. I understand you've managed to accumulate properties all over the city."

Li Wei bows his head. "Thank you."

"Much of it from houses you've repossessed from clients—gambling addicts, as I hear it—who default on your loan shark rates."

Li Wei's smile doesn't falter. "Our lending policies are perfectly legal, Detective. Many of our competitors have similar interest rates on such risky loans."

"Yes, but how many of your competitors lend five hundred thousand dollars in laundered bills coated in fentanyl dust?"

Hui glares at Anson, but Li Wei only shrugs. "That was one case. A misunderstanding. There were no charges filed."

"The money was still confiscated as proceeds of crime."

Hui utters a few terse words in Mandarin.

"What I want, Hughie, is to dispense with the bullshit," Anson says.

"What does that mean?" Li Wei asks, his expression now unreadable.

"We know you two are members of the Triad. And that you're

involved in the drug trade. That's not my concern. I'm Homicide. What I'm trying to figure out is who poisoned seven kids."

Li Wei grimaces. "You believe we poison children, Detective?"

"I believe you would in a heartbeat if there were a couple extra bucks in it for you. But what I want to know is how the bad dope reached the streets in the first place and how to stop the flow of it. And you two are among the most likely suppliers."

Hui turns to his brother and mutters something in Mandarin.

Li Wei nods. "My brother is right. If you are going to be so accusatory, perhaps we should involve our lawyer?"

"Good idea. Can't imagine how overworked the poor bastard must already be. But right now we don't have time for that." Anson reaches in his pocket and pulls out his cell phone. He taps it to open the photo of Markku that Babar forwarded to him. "Recognize this guy?"

Li Wei and Hugh examine the photo and shake their heads almost simultaneously.

"You've never seen him before?"

"No," Li Wei says.

Anson taps the screen and conjures the photo of the bluish fake oxys recovered from the developer's desk. "How about these?"

Both Jians view the screen again for a moment. "I am not so good with pills," Li Wei says. "I am more comfortable with traditional Chinese medicine."

Anson runs a hand through his hair. "Either you help us now, or you explain all this at your trial for the multiple murder of those children. And whoever else dies between now and then."

Hui cocks his head. "How would drug smuggler know every pill he sell?"

Li Wei grabs Hui's elbow. "What my brother is trying to say is that even if someone were involved in the drug trade—which we are not—how would they recognize every pill that passed through their business?"

"The color and the imprint are distinct," Julie says. "Are you certain you don't recognize them?"

"Last chance to do this voluntarily," Anson adds.

Li Wei studies the photo again and then rolls his shoulders in defeat. "I wish I could be of help."

Anson turns away in disgust and heads toward the door. As Julie is about to follow, she asks, "Do you know Gary Xie?"

The brothers share a glance of recognition. "The real estate agent?" Li Wei asks.

"That's the one."

"He has represented us on some property sales. Why do you ask?"

"His daughter, Rachel, was one of the victims of those pills. She was sixteen years old. A piano master."

Li Wei frowns. "We must send flowers," he says, and Hui mutters something in Mandarin.

Anson swivels back around and hisses something at them, also in Mandarin.

CHAPTER 31

Hanif Kanji wonders again why he even bothered to show up for the party. He and Jarrod Nader share so little in common now. History alone sustains the friendship. Growing up, Hanif and Jarrod were best friends at their pretentious West Vancouver private school. They bonded as the two non-WASPs in the class—the Ismaili and the Jew—the only kids who didn't celebrate Christmas. But any other similarities they might have shared ended long ago. Each of their strong cultural traditions had funneled them toward professional school, but while Jarrod had chosen law, Hanif had gone into medicine, working now as a family doctor in a growing private practice.

Hanif is proud of his friend for setting a record as the youngest person to be named partner at his law firm, at the age of thirty-four, but the party is exactly what he dreaded it would be. The club music is cranked so loud that walls vibrate in the sub-penthouse, with its twelve-foot ceilings, glistening white kitchen, and gauche prints. The condo is full of loud, snooty lawyers dressed in expensive duds while guzzling overly expensive wine. Based on his recent conversation with one of guests in a skimpy cocktail dress, Hanif suspects that half the women at the party might be escorts. And even if Hanif had any interest in drugs, he would find the little glass bowl full of cocaine that Jarrod had just laid out on the bathroom counter to be over the top. But guests have been scurrying to the bathroom like hungry dogs to a feeding, and a line has formed outside.

Hanif is just plotting a discreet escape when he hears the first scream. More follow. Someone turns off the music, and Hanif sees people gathering around the bedroom door.

He races over and elbows his way into the bedroom. Jarrod and a young woman are collapsed faceup on the bed. Neither is breathing. Their faces are mottled, and their lips are navy. Jarrod's eyes are closed, while the girl's are wide open. *Opioids!* Hanif realizes as soon as he sees her pinpoint pupils.

"Call 911!" he cries out to no one in particular, as he thrusts a hand up to Jarrod's neck. There's no pulse. He darts his hand over to the fallen woman and, after a moment of searching, detects a thready pulse.

"Anyone carrying naloxone?" Hanif screams at the shell-shocked guests. When no one answers, he demands, "Who knows CPR?"

"I do," the young escort to whom he was just chatting volunteers.

"Me, too," one of the other lawyers says.

Hanif motions to Jarrod and says, "Start chest compressions on him."

He positions himself over the female victim, pinches her nose, and blows long and steadily into her mouth, tasting her mint breath spray. He counts to three and repeats. After his fourth exhalation, one of the women watching from the doorway collapses as if she has just been shot. Hanif doesn't even need to look over to make the diagnosis. He gives his victim another deep breath and then motions wildly to the guests nearest the fallen woman. "Do the same as me. Mouth-to-mouth! One long breath every three seconds!"

Hanif has blown two or three more breaths into his victim when he hears a crash of glassware coming from the living room—the sound of another guest succumbing to an opioid overdose.

What the hell was in that glass bowl, Jarrod?

CHAPTER 32

"**L**ook at you!" Anson whistles, as Julie steps out the door of her building.

She hasn't been on a date in months. She's still not certain that tonight constitutes one. As usual in her relationship with Anson, there's ambiguity. But seeing him in a tie and blazer makes her feel better about her own choice of the sleeveless spring dress and pumps, worn with her hair up and mascara applied.

There's an awkward moment of uncertainty at the door, before Julie leans in and hugs Anson, brushing her lips over his cheek. She lingers in the embrace for a moment, enjoying the whiff of his woody cologne. As they pull apart, he hangs on to her elbow for a few extra seconds as they walk to the car. "You clean up good, Doc."

"You don't look so appalling yourself, Detective."

As he reaches forward to open the passenger door for her, she moves her lips to his. He meets her mouth with a surprisingly force-ful kiss and grips the small of her back, pulling her in to him. With the pressure of his chest against her breasts and their touching thighs, she grows more excited with each hungry kiss. She's tempted to drag him back into the building and yank off his tie along with the rest of his clothes on the way up to her unit. But they're already late for dinner, so she wriggles free of his grip.

"Maria and Goran are expecting us," she says, as she skitters her lips over his, before fully separating from him.

He dabs her lipstick from his mouth with the side of his finger and flashes her a playful grin. "Anyone ever mention that you're a lot friendlier in the evening?"

"You just caught me at a weak moment," she says as she lowers herself into the passenger seat.

Anson reaches across Julie to buckle her in and steals another kiss, before getting in on the driver's side. His phone rings just after he pulls away from the curb. He taps a button on the steering wheel and the hands-free speaker engages. "Hey, Theo," he says. "Julie's in the car, so keep it clean."

"Like I'm the one you have to worry about for that?" Theo says.

"What have you got?"

"Markku, or Blaine, is still missing. The address on his driver's license and insurance isn't current. The uniforms are scouring the Downtown Eastside. But so far nothing."

"Probably knows we're looking for him," Julie speculates.

"Who could've tipped him off?" Then Anson answers his own question with a grimace. "We did show the Jian brothers his photo this afternoon."

"And we described him to Farhad as Zack's dealer," Julie says. "At least, I did."

"He'll turn up," Theo says confidently.

"Alive?" Julie asks.

"We'll see. Meantime, couple other things. I called the Gallaghers about their son Nick. Mentioned the mixed drink he brought to the party. They're adamant he wouldn't have spiked it. They're convinced Joshua must've brought the drugs to that party."

"Joshua was definitely the black sheep in a very white sheep crowd," Anson says.

"I went to see Joshua's buddy Sam Dosanjh," Theo says. "Lucky for Sam, he didn't go to the party, but he shot baskets with Joshua only a few hours before. Sam swears there was no mention of drugs, except weed. He admitted that he and Josh smoked a lot of it. Even told me that Josh would sometimes sell some at school for extra cash. But no other drugs. He was insistent on that."

Anson sighs. "Where does that leave us?"

"Well, I'm taking Eleni for a much-needed staycation tonight."

Anson rests a hand on Julie's knee. She covers it with hers and gives it a firm squeeze. "That doesn't sound like you, partner," he says.

"Five boys. Three of them teenagers. You have no idea how bad the house begins to smell after a while." Theo snorts. "We need a break."

"Where are you staying?"

"The Harbor Inn."

"The hotel where the pilot used to stay? What are you up to, Theo?"

"I tracked down Justin Bowles's copilot. My spidey sense tells me they might have been more than colleagues. Regardless, she was forthcoming about the rest. Admitted that Justin would sometimes buy coke through one of the bellmen, but she didn't know which one."

"Theo, you're not planning to . . ."

"If we go to that hotel with badges flashing, the staff is only going to clam up and close ranks. We have no proof. But if, say, a curious traveler with an itchy nose were to check in and start making some discreet requests . . ."

"You're taking over the undercover beat from Hoops now?"

"You got a better idea?"

"As long as the bellman's not an undercover cop himself, you should be OK. Enjoy the staycation. And give Eleni a kiss for me."

As soon as Anson hangs up, he slides his hand higher up Julie's leg.

"Hey, you're distracting your navigator," she says, biting her lip.

"No problem. I got Google Maps."

Laughing, Julie guides him through the quiet West Side neighborhood of Kerrisdale, where many of the streets are named for the local trees. She loves the foliage, especially where Goran lives on Elm Street, which is almost canopied by the leafy branches overhead.

They pull up in front of the beige, stucco-sided house. To Julie, it feels like coming home. After all, she lived with Goran, Lada, and the boys for months in those dark days after her stint in rehab, following Michael's death. And she spent another month back here after Lada died, trying, futilely, to console her good friend.

Goran and Maria are waiting at the front door, his thick arm draped over her slim shoulder. The oversized Croat hovers more than a foot above his petite wife. Julie makes the introductions. Maria—a perpetual hugger—embraces Julie and then hugs Anson, whom she's never met.

Goran pats Anson's back. "So you're the detective who is helping Julija with *her* investigation?"

Anson grins. "It kind of feels that way most of the time."

"Come. Drinks."

Goran leads them into the family room. He tries to foist a big glass of rakija, the fruity Croatian brandy, on each of them, but Julie waves him off, explaining that she is on overnight call for Poison Control. Anson accepts the rakija and takes a tentative sip. "Not bad. Kind of tastes like sake."

"*Sake?*" Goran exhales heavily and looks over to Julie with mock disappointment. "Honestly, Julija, I had been prepared to give this one a chance. But now? *Sake?*"

"Goran!" Maria laughs. "Leave him be."

"I don't mind." Anson turns to Julie with a small grin. "It's not like this one goes any easier on me."

Julie can't help but return the smile. "Someone's got to keep your ego in check."

"Homicide, is this correct, Anson? I cannot wait to hear some of your stories." Goran looks over at Maria. "In the end, it is always the wife, though, is it not?"

Maria laughs. "In our case, it would be justifiable homicide, dearest."

The conversation flows as freely as Goran's drinks. He tries to ply his guests with more alcohol, too, but since Anson is driving and Julie is on call, they both decline his offers. Eventually they move to the dining room and sit down at the ornate place settings Maria has laid out using Goran and Lada's old wedding china. The aromas of herbs and cooked meat waft through the room. Dinner is served over several courses while they discuss everything from politics to films, and even take time to compare their upbringings. Maria grew up comfortably in Manila, the daughter of two doctors, while Goran's parents struggled as farmers in Communist-era Yugoslavia.

After Julie mentions that her dad's parents emigrated from Wales, Anson folds his hands together and proudly announces, "I guess that makes me the most Canadian at this table."

"How do you reach that conclusion?" Goran asks.

"Well, my dad's parents came here from Hong Kong when he was a kid, but my mom's parents were born here. By my calculation, that makes me third-generation Canadian."

Goran laughs. "You win, then."

Anson's expression turns serious. "Never really felt it, though. I always had a bit of an outsider's complex. Like I always had something to prove." He clears his throat. "Just another insecure teen, I guess."

Maria offers him a sympathetic nod. "No shortage of those."

"Speaking of teenagers . . ." Goran says. "How is the investigation progressing?"

"Slowly but surely," Julie says vaguely.

Anson nods. "It's not cut-and-dried. That's for sure."

Goran puts down his fork. "Even before this tragedy, I've never seen anything to compare with fentanyl in my long career."

"How so?" Anson asks.

"I started in emergency during the peak of the AIDS epidemic. Before we had decent treatment. All those poor young men dying while we ran around as useless as medieval barber-surgeons trying to bleed victims of the plague. I thought it was as bad as anything could get."

Anson cocks his head. "This is worse?"

"Statistically, much worse," Julie says. "Last year, over fifteen hundred people died in the province alone from fentanyl overdoses."

"Almost all of them under forty," Maria points out.

"Very true, my heart," Goran says. "HIV, of course, was fraught with politics and stigma, too. Especially in the eighties. But these fentanyl victims are the most marginalized and forgotten ones of all."

Maria nods vigorously. "As a pharmacist, I can appreciate how easy it is to fall prey to drug dependence. How it could happen to anyone."

"Yes," Goran says. "And these addicts have families who love them, too. Who grieve for them."

"Sometimes children, too," Maria adds.

Anson shakes his head. "Don't think I've ever met a user who would choose to end up where they have."

Goran drains the last of the wine in his glass. "And if it weren't for fentanyl, many of them might have recovered. Beat the addiction. Found a meaningful life again."

Julie knows he's not specifically referring to her, but her cheeks burn anyway. Sometimes she forgets how lucky she has been to have overcome fentanyl. Most of the others like her seem to follow the path Michael did—buried by their own parents after a tragically young and senseless death.

"What a disaster! Who talks like this at a dinner party?" Goran howls, even though he raised the topic. "Can we please talk about Trump instead?"

After dinner, the men clear the plates and then head into the den. Julie joins Maria in the kitchen to help her load the dishwasher.

"I like him, Julie," Maria says as soon as they're alone. "A lot. He's smart, and he knows how to stand his ground. Very cute, too. And Gor is really fond of him."

Julie waves the compliment away. "Gor likes everyone."

"I can tell when it's real." Maria gestures toward the den. "They're bonding in there."

Julie warms with unexpected satisfaction. Goran's approval is important to her. It's as close as she will ever come to a father's blessing.

Reading Julie's thoughts, Maria spontaneously hugs her again.

This is my family now, Julie thinks as she squeezes back.

Between the laughter and the affection, Julie hasn't felt so relaxed in a long time. She has totally forgotten that she is on call for Poison Control until Maria says, "Isn't that your phone?"

As soon as Julie picks up on the muffled chime of her ringtone, she rushes over to the foyer and grabs her phone from her purse. The screen shows four missed calls, all from the Poison Control Center. She calls back, and the on-site nurse, Helen, answers in her usual soft tone.

"Helen, hi. Put my phone down," Julie says apologetically. "Were you looking for me?"

"Sorry to bother, Julie, but I need your expertise," Helen says. "I've been fielding a lot of calls about the overdoses at the party."

"From Friday?"

"No. The one tonight."

Julie goes cold. "What party?"

"A lawyer was throwing a bash down in Coal Harbor. A bunch of guests overdosed. They think the cocaine was tainted."

"How many victims?"

"Three dead, so far. There would've been more if some doctor hadn't got the guests to perform mouth-to-mouth on all the victims."

"And the survivors went to St. Mike's?"

"Yes."

"We're on our way." Julie grabs her bag and calls over her shoulder. "Anson, we've got to go!"

CHAPTER 33

Markku eases off the throttle as he rides past his own building again. He has already circled it three times but still isn't convinced the coast is clear.

Do they know where I live? Markku wonders again. He had been so careful. The condo is registered in his mother's maiden name. But their reach is wide, whoever "they" are. If the cops are waiting for him, it will mean a long stint in jail. If the Persians are, it will mean certain death.

I should've plugged Farhad and his goon. If Markku could have pulled the trigger, he would have. But he's not a killer, at least not in cold blood. Instead of shooting them, he backed out of Reza's condo and fled down the fire escape. His guts haven't stopped churning since he hopped on his bike and tore off.

Markku escaped to the first safe place he could think of, Prospect Point. His parents had thrown his eighth birthday party at the scenic lookout, perched at the highest point in Stanley Park, and it has been his sanctuary ever since.

As soon as he parked his bike at Prospect Point and found a quiet spot away from the tourists, Markku called Elsa. He was relieved to hear how composed she sounded, considering the severity of her dope-sickness. It took every shred of strength to keep his voice calm and not to mention what had happened. He considered giving her the code to the safe and instructing her to empty out the money and meet him. But, aware of how many pills were inside, he decided he couldn't trust her with that kind of temptation, not when she was in the grip of withdrawal. So instead he said, "Pack a bag, El. We're going to Whistler tonight. Our special suite. So we can ride the rest of your dope-sickness out there."

Markku knew he couldn't fake his way through another phone call with Elsa—she was too intuitive—so he had been checking in via text every half hour or so. She kept reassuring him that she was coping, even keeping the fluids down. And then, about two hours ago, she told him she was going to take another nap. He hasn't heard from her since.

Markku had spent most of the day in Stanley Park, walking the trails near Prospect Point and biding his time until nightfall. He ventured out only once, in the late afternoon and behind the anonymity of his helmet and visor, to check out downtown. The Downtown Eastside was crawling with uniforms. All of them looking for him, he assumed. He retreated back to the park in a hurry, the worst of his fears confirmed.

Farhad's accusation gnawed at Markku all day long. He even searched photos on his phone of the teenage victims. He studied each of their faces, convinced that he hadn't sold drugs to any one of them. But that was no excuse. He had lots of clients, some of them far too young. Any one of them could have passed, or resold, the deadly fake oxys—TLH, as Farhad had called them—on to the unsuspecting teenagers. Directly or indirectly, Markku was responsible for what happened to those kids, not to mention Zack and anyone else he might have poisoned.

It's now or never, Markku tells himself as he parks his bike in the loading zone behind his building. He tucks his gun into his waistband, under his shirt. His pulse pounds in his ears as he treads to the back door with his helmet still on and visor down. He doesn't remove his helmet until he's inside the elevator.

As the elevator slows to a stop at his floor, Markku pulls out the gun and grabs his phone with his other hand. Once the doors open, he holds out his phone and uses the camera like a periscope to scan the hallway. Seeing no one, he treads down the corridor and opens his door. Steadying the gun in front of him, he takes a tentative step inside. Then another. He stops to listen, but all he hears is the quiet hum of the bathroom fan.

"El?" he calls out, as he closes the door softly behind him.

The silence is oppressive. "El, where are you?"

Nothing.

Markku sprints down to the bedroom. Inside, the covers are pulled back in a heap and there are sweat stains on the fitted sheet. But Elsa is nowhere to be seen. He darts into the bathroom, but she's not in there, either.

"El!" he cries. The panic wells as he drops his gun on the countertop.

Markku rushes into the living room. As he's pulling open the sliding door to the balcony, it hits him like a mallet. Dread rising with each step, he walks down the hall to the spare room, feeling like a condemned man trudging toward the electric chair.

Markku sees her legs before he reaches the open doorway. Elsa is sprawled on her back in the middle of the room. The empty syringe hangs from her elbow by its still-embedded needle. Her blue lips are curved in contentment, and her glassy eyes are peaceful.

Markku lunges over to her. He drops to his knees and holds his ear to her lips. There's no sound. He runs his fingers up and down her cool neck but feels no pulse. He considers grabbing the antidote kit in the bathroom, but he instinctively understands that no amount of naloxone will bring Elsa back. She's already gone.

Markku sits back, wraps his arms around his knees, and rocks silently on the spot. He looks over and notices that the clothes hanging in the closet are bunched back and the safe door is wide open. *Oh, El, you always were too smart for your own good.*

Dazed, Markku stands up and wanders into the living room. Desperate for fresh air, he steps out onto the balcony. He stands at the railing and stares down at the lights of the city below. The dark gray waters of English Bay are barely recognizable in the last glimmers of dusk. Grouse Mountain is only visible by the lights from the gondola track, which make it appear as if it's floating in the sky.

Markku thinks back to the first time he ever saw Elsa, from across the room at the Pacific Rim lounge. Guys were circling her like flies, and she didn't seem to notice him for ages, but when their eyes finally did meet, he knew his life was about to change. Though at the time he had no idea how much. Not only did Elsa become his best friend, she was his only real friend. He didn't need anyone else—except the baby they were about to have. *The love we would've shown that kid . . .*

Markku has never experienced such helplessness. "I can't. Not without you, El," he says aloud. *I did this. It's my fault. All of it. You, Zack, those teens, and God knows who else.*

Markku grips the top of the railing. There's comfort in the cool contact. He feels almost relieved as he swings himself forward and over the top of it.

CHAPTER 34

Julie rushes into the resuscitation room to find a young woman lying on the stretcher in the second bay with her black cocktail dress sliced open along the side. Her eye shadow and mascara have smeared, blending into raccoon-like patterns around her eyes. Intravenous tubing runs from each of her arms, and she's connected to a ventilator.

Dr. Sean Murphy, a gangly ultramarathoner, stands above the patient, flashing a light in her eyes and watching the pupils respond. People are talking in the background, and there's even the smattering of laughter, which Julie finds reassuring. The relaxed atmosphere is so different from the grim pall that hung over the room when Alexa occupied the same stretcher, only four nights earlier.

Julie joins her colleague and friend at the bedside. "What's her status, Sean?"

"She'll be OK. Eventually. Taken a ton of naloxone to revive her just to this point, though." Sean looks up and does a double-take. "Whoa, Julie. Aren't you dolled up! You weren't at the same party as the patient, were you?"

"No. I'm on call for Poison Control."

"They must have a pretty strict dress code for call." He chortles. "We got like seven ODs in tonight. All from the same party. This one's the worst—of the survivors, anyway. Apparently they all stopped breathing at the scene."

A slight, darker man in a blue blazer steps forward from the charting desk. "I'm Hanif Kanji. A family doctor. I was at the party, too."

Sean nods toward him. "Hanif here probably saved all seven of them. Taught the other guests how to do mouth-to-mouth. Like he was running a lifeguarding course during a capsizing or something."

"Several of the guests already knew how to perform it," Hanif says modestly.

Julie shows him an appreciative smile. *If only you had been there at the party with Alexa, too.*

"Can we have a word outside, Dr. Kanji?" Anson asks from the doorway.

Hanif joins Julie and Anson in the hallway. After introductions, Anson says "What can you tell us about this party, Dr. Kanji?"

Hanif's eyes cloud with discouragement. "Jarrod was my best friend from high school. He just made partner at his law firm. He threw a party for himself to celebrate."

"Jarrod?"

"Jarrod Nader," Hanif says. "The party was at his condo a few blocks from here. It was already getting out of hand, and then Jarrod brought out this bowl of coke. Put it out on the bathroom counter like it was potpourri or something. People started to line up. It must have been laced with fentanyl, because it couldn't have been more than fifteen minutes later when we found Jarrod in cardiac arrest." He inhales sharply. "And then other guests began to die."

"You said you were best friends with Jarrod?"

"We used to be, back in school. Life took us in very different directions. I haven't seen much of Jarrod in the past five or ten years."

"Do you know where he bought his coke?" Anson asks.

"No."

"This isn't about finger-pointing." Anson holds up a hand. "It's vital we find out."

"I swear to you, I don't know. I didn't ever do drugs with Jarrod. It's not my thing."

There's nothing defensive in Hanif's tone or posture, and Julie is convinced that he's telling the truth. "How about other friends at the party?" she asks. "Might they know?"

"I really can't say. I didn't know anyone else at the party. In truth, I'm not sure why I even went."

"It's a good thing you did, Dr. Kanji," Julie says. "You saved a lot of lives tonight."

"I suppose," Hanif says, but his tone sounds defeated. "Not Jarrod's. And not the other two, either."

They thank Hanif for his time, and then head down the hallway to escape the hubbub surrounding the resuscitation room.

"Obviously, the crime techs will test the blow, but we know how that's going to turn out," Anson says.

"More carfentanil," Julie says.

"The Last High." He shrugs. "As street nicknames go, at least this one's accurate."

"I hope Markku was his dealer."

"Why?"

"So we only have the one source. Not multiple. Will be easier to prevent more disasters like tonight."

"We're going to have to interview every guest at the party. Hopefully Jarrod told someone who he bought the coke from." Anson shows her a disappointed grin. "So much for our nightcap, huh?"

She punches his shoulder teasingly. "You didn't think I was going to invite you up on the first date, did you?"

"I thought there was an outside chance. I am fairly—" His ringing phone cuts him off. Anson presses a button and brings it to his ear. "Hey, partner. We're just at the hospital now—" He goes quiet and listens, the creases deepening at the corners of his eyes and lips. "Good. Did he say when?"

Julie listens as Anson gives Theo a quick rundown on the overdoses at the lawyers' party, and as soon as he pulls the phone from his ear, she asks, "What is it?"

"Theo just arranged to buy coke from some bellman at the Harbor Inn," Anson says. "Vince somebody."

"The pilot's source?"

He nods. "When Theo told him he was a pilot, too, Vince said something about how he always takes good care of the flight crews."

Julie's chest pounds. "When's it going down?"

"*Going down?* Someone's been watching too many cop shows on Netflix." He flashes a little grin. "Not sure. Vince told Theo it would take an hour or two. He'll call as soon as he hears."

Carol, the veteran ER clerk who acts like she runs the place, marches up and interrupts them. "Oh, Dr. Rees. There you are," she says, as if Julie had been deliberately avoiding her. "Some family member came down here looking for you earlier tonight."

"Who?" Julie asks.

"Ted? Tim?" Carol grimaces. "Sad-looking fellow. He said you took care of his daughter."

"Thanks, Carol." Julie turns to Anson. "I have to go up to the ICU for a short while. I'll text you once I'm done."

As she spins away, he says, "Julie, you look gorgeous tonight . . . even from behind."

"Pig!" she replies playfully, without looking back.

Julie rides the elevator up to the ICU. Elaine and Tom are inside Alexa's glass-walled room, standing on either side of her bed. As soon as Elaine spots Julie, she hurries out of the room with her husband in tow.

Julie leads them into the conference room, which the ICU maintains for holding private, and usually difficult, conversations with families. It's furnished like a den with a comfortable sofa and two padded chairs. Elaine and Tom sit down on the sofa, while Julie takes the chair across from them.

Julie doesn't bother asking how they're doing. She gets the answer from their sunken eyes and sallow faces. "You wanted to see me?" she asks.

"Dr. Dutton told us she's certain Alexa is already gone," Elaine says hoarsely.

"Brain-dead," Tom says in a monotone.

"I am so, so sorry."

"They're going to . . ." Tom clears his throat. "Pull the plug tomorrow."

"Don't use that awful term, Tom!" Elaine turns to Julie. "They're going to take her off the ventilator. Extubate her, right?"

"Yes."

"And then it could be . . . hours?" Tom asks.

Julie nods.

A terrible silence fills the room, but Julie knows better than to try to force it away.

"Dr. Singh spoke to us about Alexa maybe becoming an organ donor," Elaine finally says, and Tom only shakes his head.

Elaine reaches over and clutches her husband's hand. "Tom has serious reservations."

"Oh," Julie says.

"We trust you, Dr. Rees," Elaine says. "You've done so much for Alexa. For us, too."

Julie breaks off the eye contact. All she can see is the extra pain and angst she has caused them by extending their false hope. Julie feels small and ashamed for having defied the hospital's well-reasoned protocol for the use of ECMO.

"We want to hear your opinion," Elaine continues.

Julie swallows the guilt away to focus on her answer. She measures her words carefully before speaking. "As a doctor, I see transplantation as one of the true miracles of medicine. But I understand what an incredibly personal and difficult decision it must be." She turns to Tom. "Can you share a bit more about your reservations?"

Tom stares at her for a long moment, then his stoic composure finally cracks. His face crumples, and tears well in his eyes. "I just want my baby buried whole, you know?"

Elaine throws an arm around his neck and buries her face in his shoulder.

Julie leans toward them, resisting the urge to take their hands in hers. "Of course, Tom. What a natural thing for any parent to want. But it doesn't have to be one or the other."

"How do you mean?" he croaks.

"You can still bury Alexa whole. Donors can even have an open casket at their funeral." Julie pauses. "She will still be your daughter. But part of Alexa can also live on and help keep others alive. That's the beauty of it."

Tom brings his hand to his mouth, as the tears flow freely down his cheeks. "She always had such a big heart. Always cared about others."

"Even when she was just little." Elaine sobs into his shoulder.

Tom turns his face to his wife and they cling to one another in grief. It's all Julie can do to keep her own tears in check as she rises to her feet and leaves them to their intensely private moment.

Just as she reaches the elevator, her phone buzzes with a new text from Anson, which reads: "We found him!"

CHAPTER 35

———————⋀———————•

Li Wei drives the Audi, because it's the oldest car in his collection and the one he is most willing to sacrifice to possible vandalism in the sketchy part of town where he now finds himself.

Hui wanted to accompany him, but Li Wei conjured an excuse, saying that he needed to drop in on their great-aunt in Chinatown. Fortunately, the idea of having to spend even two minutes with the old hag was enough to dissuade his brother. Hui had been growing more bitter and unpredictable by the hour since the detective, who spoke Mandarin with a Shanghai accent, and the pretty doctor accompanying him had surprised them in their own office. Hui had even suggested, with a straight face, that they return the favor and drop in on each of them, though, undoubtedly, his brother meant in the middle of the night and with weapons.

Always so rash, Hui.

But Li Wei appreciates that they can't ignore the tainted fentanyl that is circulating on the streets. The teenagers and the other victims don't bother him. The dead never do. It's the attention this new product is raising that alarms him. Not only is it bad for business, it's dangerous. The police are nosing around far more than before.

And at tense times like these, truces easily crack, and gangs quickly turn on one another. War becomes inevitable.

Li Wei wishes the detective had left him a photo of those pills. They looked familiar, but the color wasn't quite right. Still, he cannot be certain that they weren't produced in his own East Vancouver "factory." The cop's visit also reminded him of how strangely talkative Bunsen had been the last time he saw him. *And why had the fool suggested he needed more carfentanil?*

Li Wei has no option but to test his own supply. And he has never trusted the sophisticated gadgetry. No. He prefers the time-honored method that Triads have been using in Guangdong for generations.

Li Wei slows the car the moment he spots the repellent woman in the fishnet stockings who is stumbling along the curb beside him. As soon as he has come to a full stop, near the corner of Powell and Hawkes, she leans her haggard face and drooping breasts through his open passenger window.

"Oh, mister," she coos. "Baby doll can take such good care of you."

"How much?"

"What's your fancy, sir?"

"Oral."

"Because you're so cute, I'll do it for a hunny."

"Fifty."

"Fifty?" she cries. "I can't be giving it away."

Li Wei begins to roll up the window.

"OK, OK! Fifty!" She wedges her arm through the window.

"Get in."

Li Wei drives in total silence. He keeps the windows down, which only partially ventilates the stench of her body odor and sickly-sweet perfume. Seven or eight blocks later, he pulls into a parking lot off East Cordova in the heart of the industrial area. He parks at the very back, away from the lights.

As soon as Li Wei turns off the ignition, the woman leans toward his crotch, reaching for his zipper. *I will definitely have to burn this suit.* He catches her wrist in his hand and gently pulls it away.

She jerks free of his grip, sits bolt upright, and thrusts a hand into her purse with surprising deftness. "Don't you fucking dare mess with me!" She waves her purse without revealing what, if any, weapon she keeps inside.

Li Wei holds up his hands. "I have no intention. I thought you might want something to relax you first." He slowly reaches into his pocket and extracts the baggie full of powder, crushed from a few of the pills that Bunsen supplied them the day before.

She eyes him suspiciously but with obvious interest. "What is it?"

"Fentanyl."

"I don't have my rig on me."

"This is ideal for snorting."

She studies him for another wary moment, but the temptation proves too much for her. "Will you do some, too?"

"Of course." He holds the baggie to her. "Ladies first."

She doesn't hesitate as she snatches the baggie and skillfully taps a generous portion of powder onto the back of her hand, between thumb and forefinger, without spilling a flake. She leans forward and inhales it all in one nauseatingly wet snort.

She flops back in her seat and dangles the baggie out to him. "Oh, baby, me like."

Li Wei takes it from her and pretends to fuss with it, but she pays little notice. In less than a minute, her eyes glaze over and she begins to mumble a song. Soon even that noise dies away as her eyes close and her arms drop limply to her sides.

Li Wei slips the baggie into his pocket and watches. After a minute or two, when he is convinced she has stopped breathing, he reaches over to touch her neck. She startles as if he has just shocked her. She darts a hand for her purse without making contact. "Fuck you," she slurs. "What you trying to do?"

Li Wei slides a hand into his back pocket and pulls out his wallet.

He digs out a fifty-dollar bill and tosses it into her lap. He reaches across her and opens the passenger door. "Get out."

"What? Here? Where am I?"

"Out." He nudges her by the shoulder.

She fumbles for her purse and the loose bill before she rises awkwardly from the seat. She misses her first step and falls sideways onto the gravel with a scream.

Li Wei slams the door behind her. Satisfied that his product is not the contaminated fentanyl, the so-called TLH, he throws the car into reverse and backs away as the hooker flails on the ground.

CHAPTER 36

A ghostly sprinkling of lit boats and freighters drift in the dark harbor below her, while Grouse Mountain floats above. Julie feels a bit sheepish for noticing the tranquil beauty of the nighttime view from the balcony when, thirty-six floors below her, Markku's body lies splattered across the sidewalk.

She turns back toward the condo's interior, where Anson is inspecting the sliding door. "Wonder what his last thoughts were before he jumped," she says.

"You're assuming he did jump."

"You think he was pushed?"

"Wouldn't be the first time with gangsters." Anson gestures to the glass, behind which a white-suited crime scene technician is examining the kitchen cabinets. "For all we know, someone injected the girlfriend with drugs and then tossed Markku over the railing."

"To cover up any links to them?"

"Wouldn't that be convenient? If Markku were to literally take the fall for all the bad down killing people out there?"

She sees his point. "Markku couldn't have done it alone."

"Nope. He's just a street-level dealer—I mean, clearly a very successful one—or used to be, anyway—but he didn't cook the bad pills. He only distributed them."

"And probably only some of them. We might never find out if he's the one who sold the drugs that killed the kids."

"It would help if we find some TLH pills here." He turns away from the balcony. "Let's go check out his stash."

Julie pads through the living room after Anson, both wearing the shoe covers mandated by the crime scene technicians. They enter the spare bedroom and stop at Elsa's feet. The young woman lies faceup on the hardwood. Her neck is craned, and one leg is bent under the other knee. The deadly needle still sticks out of her arm.

Julie appreciates that Anson has to consider every possibility, but she has seen too many overdoses to doubt the authenticity of Elsa's. Julie experiences a pang of sympathy for the dead woman and even her drug-dealing boyfriend, because she understands how it feels to discover your partner dead from an overdose you facilitated. The guilt might even outweigh the grief, and they compound each other in a vicious cycle. *Lucky I wasn't on the thirty-sixth floor when I found Michael.*

"So many past tenses in this case," Anson says as he reaches inside the open wall safe and pulls out a bag of pills.

"Is it OK to touch that stuff?"

"Yeah, I cleared it with the guys in white. They've already catalogued everything in here." He opens the bag and extracts a large baggie full of gray fake oxy pills. He digs his hand back in, but it comes out empty. "There's no coke in this safe."

"None?"

"Not a sniff."

"Maybe he sold it all? To the lawyer for his party?"

"A guy who had high-powered clients such as lawyers and pilots . . ." He wags a finger at her. "No doubt doctors, too . . ."

"No doubt." She looks down, trying to hide her sudden embarrassment from him.

"You'd think he would need a constant supply of coke on hand for such an elite clientele. All Markku has in here is fentanyl. And lots of it, too."

"Good point."

He waves her closer. "I want to show you something."

She crosses the room. He holds up the baggie to the overhead light, and their heads touch as she studies the pills inside. "Notice anything?" he asks.

"The color. Only gray. No blue like the tainted pills they found in the developer's desk."

He lowers the baggie but keeps his forehead pressed to hers. "Exactly."

"So Markku might not have been the one selling the lethal coke *or* even the pills of TLH?"

"Maybe not."

Julie straightens, hit by a sudden thought. "But if someone did kill Markku, they could've easily swapped out the drugs, if they were in the safe. Even better way to make it seem like there's no connection between TLH and whichever gang is manufacturing it. By making it look as if their dealer wasn't peddling any."

"That's a possibility, too. Another, more likely scenario is that there are multiple dealers of TLH, and Markku just sold out of his stock. Either way, we need to find out who supplied him. And I know who can help there."

"Hoops?"

"Yup."

Anson's phone chimes and he glances down at the text. "We got to run, Julie."

Theo is alone when he opens the door to his hotel room for Anson and Julie.

"Your mark hasn't shown up yet?" Anson asks, as they step inside.

"No," Theo says, closing the door quickly behind them. "Should be soon, though."

"Where's Eleni?"

"Went back home to the boys." Theo cracks a small smile. "Apparently she doesn't find undercover sting operations to be all that romantic."

"I think they're kind of sexy." Julie glances at Anson. "A bit risqué and risky."

Anson grins. "Get your head out of the gutter, Doctor."

Theo's thoughtful gaze moves from one to other. "Speaking of undercover, what were you two up to tonight dressed so fancily?"

"Just this dinner thing we had to go to."

"Ah. One of those things."

"Yup," Anson says, and quickly changes subjects. "Listen, I'm not convinced Markku was the primary dealer of TLH."

"Why not?"

Anson summarizes what they learned in their search of Markku's pad.

"So what killed his girlfriend, then?"

"Users are still dying from plain old fentanyl overdoses," Julie says. "Three of them every day in this city."

"True," Theo says. "But this week, most of them are dying from TLH."

"I didn't say Markku wasn't dealing it at all," Anson says. "I'm just not convinced he's the main guy."

There's a quick rap at the door. Theo shoots his finger to his lips and nods toward the bathroom. Anson and Julie tiptoe inside. Anson pulls the door behind them but leaves it open just a crack.

"Sorry, was just in the can," Julie hears Theo explain to the person at the door.

"No worries, mate," the muffled voice replies in an Australian accent.

"You were able to get it?" Theo asks.

"I did, indeed."

"Come in, then, Vince. My wallet's over here."

Julie hears footsteps and the sound of the door closing.

"Oh, by the way," Theo says. "I probably should've mentioned it earlier. I'm not really a pilot. I'm actually a detective with the Vancouver Police."

"What the . . . ?"

"Me, too," Anson says, as he shoves the door wide open and bursts out of the bathroom, with Julie following.

The good-looking Australian backpedals so quickly that he stumbles and almost trips. "You can't do this! It's entrapment or something, isn't it?"

Theo steps over and grabs him by the wrist and spins him against the wall. "Actually, we can, Vince. Unless you don't have five grams of coke on you. Then I'll have pie on my face."

"You can't," Vince pleads. "With a criminal charge, they'll deport me, won't they?"

Anson shakes his head. "Not while you're doing jail time here."

"The good news is, Vince, we're not really looking for you," Theo says as he lets go of his arm.

Vince turns to face them, his face creased in confusion. "You . . . you still want the blow?"

Theo shakes his head. "We want your supplier, Vince."

"Oh. Christ."

"A name and a number . . . an address, if you have that, too."

Vince's eyes go wide, and he shakes his head fearfully. "I . . . I can't do that."

"That's too bad," Theo says.

"Hey, Vince, you remember that pilot, Justin?" Anson asks. "The one you used to bring a little pick-me-up for after his transpacific flights?"

Vince doesn't respond but his eyes go even wider and his lower lip begins to quiver.

"Don't know if you heard, but your coke killed him," Anson says matter-of-factly. "These days we call that murder. Not manslaughter anymore. So you won't have to worry about being deported for ten years, minimum, mate."

The tremble in his lip worsens, but Vince says nothing.

Julie can't hold her tongue any longer. "People are dying, Vince. The coke you've been supplying is poisoned. You understand what that means?"

Vince waves his hands in front of his face. "All right, all right! His name is Wade."

"Wade who?" Theo asks.

"Don't know. I swear!"

"How do you get ahold of Wade?"

"It's one of those dial-a-dope deals." Vince's voice cracks with panic. "I just text him. We arrange a meet-up."

Theo and Anson share a glance, before the older detective turns slowly to Vince. "OK, then. Time to arrange another meet-up."

CHAPTER 37

Wade can't sit down, at least not without swearing aloud. *That fucking ape Jamie Maddox must've broken my tailbone!* Wade heard the crack the moment he landed on his ass. He can't remember feeling anything as painful, not even the time his appendix burst. How he would love to lodge a bullet in the back of Jamie's thick skull. But he calms himself with the thought that the World Soldiers are a dying species and, undoubtedly, someone else will do him the favor, likely sooner than later.

Wade feels cooped up in his apartment, but he's in no hurry to leave, either. Even beyond Jamie's unprovoked assault, his intuition is telling him to be careful. And there is nothing and, certainly, no one, he trusts more. It has kept him alive and out of jail ever since he boarded that bus, at the age of fifteen, and escaped his dying hometown and unfortunately still-living dad—that volatile, violent son of a bitch. Wade stole from the backpacks of three other riders on that drive to Vancouver, and he has stayed on the wrong side of the law ever since, without facing anything more than a single misdemeanor possession charge in the past fourteen years.

But there's no loyalty in this line of work. Customers will move on after one missed call or a single late drop. Wade has already ignored seven or eight dial-a-dope requests. And with all that paranoia swirling around TLH, some of his most frequent customers have gone missing in action. For the first time in ages, Wade is feeling uneasy about his cash flow.

He has also ignored his most dependable fenny supplier, who keeps texting and saying that he needs to talk. But Wade is flush with fentanyl, so he doesn't need the hassle.

And then there's Vince—that Australian bellhop with the perma-smile he'd love to wipe off his face—who has already texted three times tonight. Normally Wade would have told Vince to fuck off, but the bellhop is looking for a way bigger quantity of coke than usual, and at a premium price, too, for some rich English tourists planning a huge party in their suite.

For a quick three grand, Wade is sorely tempted to ignore his wary gut and show these foreigners as good a time as he did that asshole lawyer Jarrod.

CHAPTER 38

Anson hasn't said more than a few words since picking Julie up this morning. She wonders if he's disappointed by how suddenly their night ended. By the time they left the hotel with Theo, shortly after two a.m., the accumulated exhaustion and stress of the past few days crashed down on her all at once. With only a quick goodbye to the detectives, she hopped into the first cab in line outside the lobby and headed straight home. She fell asleep with her makeup still on.

Julie suspects, though, that Anson's shyness relates more to how their relationship has changed after the date. She's a little confused herself. But as she views his angular features in profile, she realizes that she's eager to get closer to him—it's an urge she barely remembers. She reaches over and caresses the back of his hand. His lips break into a slight smile, but he keeps his eyes on the road and both hands on the wheel.

"When do you think we'll hear from Wade?" Julie asks.

"If Wade and Markku are one and the same, then never."

"You think they are?"

"Probably not."

Theo hung on to the burner phone that Vince used for buying his drugs, but so far Wade hasn't responded to any of the texts they sent under the Australian's name.

"These drug dealers don't exactly run nine-to-five businesses," Anson continues. "Nine a.m. is like the middle of the night for them. And they disappear for a million reasons. Sometimes they never come back."

"That sucks," she mutters.

"Let's assume Wade is the guy who provided the bad coke the pilot took. We know he didn't cook it himself. He's only a retail-level distributor."

"But he can lead us to the supplier. And the cook."

"Maybe. Maybe not. Those drugs pass through a murky convoluted chain. Gangs sell to one another. And every gang has its own hierarchy. It could be that Markku, Wade, and ten other plugs are all peddling TLH right now."

"I don't think so, Anson."

He frowns at her. "Why is that?"

"Simple epidemiology. Do you have any idea how many daily opioid users there are in this city?"

"Thousands."

"Exactly. So if the main supply had already been tainted with pure carfentanil, after five days we should've seen hundreds and hundreds of overdose deaths. It'd be as if Vancouver's water reservoir were poisoned with sarin or cyanide. They should be dropping like flies."

"So why haven't they?"

"Not sure. But it's probably just a matter of time. Maybe Wade is the first dealer whose tainted supply has hit the street. And he sells to Markku. Or vice versa."

Anson rubs his face in frustration. "So like Theo said, the tip of the iceberg."

"More like what you said: the tip of the tip. Anson, deliberately or not, if those TLH pills go mainstream . . ."

"There won't be enough space in the morgue." He sighs.

"Any morgue."

His phone rings, and he answers it on the car's speakerphone.

"Hey, pal, heard you were looking for me," Hoops says cheerfully.

"Yeah, did you hear we found our guy Markku?" Anson asks.

"I guess if you call scraping someone off the sidewalk 'finding' . . ."

"The point is we need to work backwards now, Hoops. We couldn't get anything off his phone—it was in no better shape than him. We're hoping you might know who supplied him."

"Funny, that. I was just talking to one of my undercover boys. He had heard a solid rumor on Markku's connect."

"Who?"

"Guess."

"Really? We're going to do this?"

"You know how boring it is at my desk today? Humor me . . ."

"The Jians?" Julie ventures.

"Doc!" Hoops cries. "Are you still saddled with Chen?"

"What can I say? I drew the short straw."

"I feel for you, Doc. Good thought on the Jian brothers, but no. Word is Markku always bought wholesale from the Persians."

"Farhad Hashemi?" she asks.

"One and the same. Lovable sociopath that he is."

Anson thanks Hoops, and as soon as he disconnects, he turns to Julie. "We need to talk to Farhad again. On our turf, this time."

Before she can comment, her phone rings and she brings it to her ear.

"Hey, Julie, it's Kam."

"Hi, Kam. What's going on?"

Kam clears her throat. "Just thought you would want to know that Alexa O'Neill is coming off the ventilator this morning."

"Yeah, thanks. I spoke to her parents last night. I really hoped they were going to opt for organ donation."

"But they did. We'll be procuring the organs soon."

"Oh, wow, that's . . . good."

"Not only that, but one of the recipients is right here on the unit."

"Who?" Julie asks, not willing to get her hopes up.

"A young mother with postpartum heart failure."

"Chloe!"

"You know her?"

"I admitted her from the ER. When will they be going to the operating room?"

"An hour or so."

"Thanks for letting me know, Kam. Really," she says as she hangs up.

Before Julie can even ask, Anson says, "I'll drop you off at St. Mike's."

As Julie steps through the door of the ICU, she runs into Harold Mott, who's dressed in surgical scrubs, on his way out. She breaks the cold silence by saying, "I heard Chloe is getting her transplant this morning."

"You heard correctly."

"I'm happy for her."

His eyes are expressionless. "This doesn't make it right, Julie."

"I didn't say it did."

"But you probably are thinking now that the ends justify the means."

"I don't care about that. And I certainly don't give a fuck how this will reflect on the critical review of my case." She doesn't even realize she's jabbing her finger at him until it's shaking in front of her. "All I'm thinking is how pleased I am for Chloe and how sad I am for Alexa's family. Nothing more, nothing less."

He scoffs. "They didn't get a second chance, did they?"

"No, and I know your family didn't, either, with Michael." Once the words start flowing, she can't stop them. "I know he was your favorite nephew. And I know you blame me for everything that happened. But guess what, Harold? You can't blame me a tenth as much as I blame myself."

He squares his shoulders. "Well, I don't know about that."

"I didn't set Michael down his path any more than he sent me down mine. We were two people who found each other. What happened to him could've just as easily happened to me. Why can't you blame the disease or the drugs, just a little?" She pivots and walks off without waiting for his response.

The sight of the O'Neills on the other side of the glass hovering over their daughter, for what will be the last time, wipes away her indignation. Julie wonders if it was a mistake to have come. Just as she turns to go, Elaine rushes out of the room and over to her. She wraps Julie in a tight hug. "We decided, Dr. Rees," she sobs.

"It's the right decision, Elaine."

Elaine nods against her shoulder.

"Alexa is going to save other lives," Julie says.

"I hope so."

"As a matter of fact . . ."

"Yes?"

Julie realizes she's not supposed to discuss specific organ recipients with the donor's family, but she feels compelled to tell her. "The woman who's going to get the heart transplant is right here in the ICU. A young mother. A lovely person."

Elaine pulls away. "Could we . . . meet her?"

Julie has never faced the situation of a donor and a recipient being on the same unit. She assumes it must be against protocol to introduce them, but that doesn't stop her. *What the hell does it matter now if I break one more rule?* "Let me go ask her."

She hurries over to Chloe's room. Chloe is breastfeeding her baby while her husband sits beside the bed. She greets Julie with a heartwarming smile. "You heard about the donor?"

Julie reciprocates the grin. "I did. And I wanted to ask you a big favor."

"A favor? From me?"

"The donor's parents, they're right here. Their daughter . . . she's only sixteen. They are good people, Chloe." Julie lays a hand on her shoulder. "They want to meet you. But, of course, it's totally up to you."

Chloe doesn't hesitate. "I'd be honored."

Julie collects Tom and Elaine and leads them back to Chloe's room. The introductions are stiff and awkward. Tom stares down at the floor. Elaine breaks the silence by asking, "What's the baby's name?"

"Maya."

"Maya, pretty," Elaine says. "I loved to breastfeed Alexa. I hated to stop. Remember, Tom?"

He nods.

Chloe pulls Maya from her breast. "Would you like to hold her, Elaine?"

Elaine hesitates, but Chloe smiles encouragingly and holds the baby out to her. Elaine tentatively takes Maya and cradles her in her arms. After a moment, she looks up at her husband with misty eyes. "Oh, my God, Tom. She's so beautiful. Do you remember?"

He closes his eyes and nods again.

Chloe looks from Elaine to Tom and back, and the tears begin to roll down her cheeks. "What you're going through . . . I don't have the words . . ."

"Lex loved babies," is all Elaine says.

"Lex was a giver," Tom mutters. "She would've wanted this."

Chloe glances at her husband. "We will never be able to thank you or Alexa for this incredible blessing. Never ever."

Elaine cuddles the baby tighter. "This is thanks enough." She passes the baby to her father and leaves the room with a small wave. Tom follows.

Julie goes over and gives Chloe a loose hug, careful not to press on any tubes or lines. "Look forward to seeing you when you're off the pump."

"Me, too. Thank you, Dr. Rees. For everything."

As soon as Julie leaves the ICU, she takes out her phone to call Anson, but it vibrates in her hand and his name pops up on the screen. His text reads: "It's arranged!"

CHAPTER 39

Li Wei sits, with his cup to his lips, at the window of the overpriced French coffee shop, but he doesn't even take a sip. The French have no idea how to brew tea. The cup is only for show. Hui sits on the other side of the table with his hands clasped on the table, brooding silently.

Li Wei doesn't like it. Any of it. His esophagus is on fire. But he could find no reason to counter Hui's logic, and so here they are.

Li Wei plays the scene from his office earlier this morning over in his head, looking for a fault that he still can't find.

"It's the filthy Persians!" Hui barked, hovering over his desk.

"What about them, brother?"

"The dealer—Markku." Hui butchered the pronunciation. "The one who was selling TLH. He jumped off his balcony last night. Or the Persians threw him. Either way, he is dead."

"Are you saying Markku worked for the Persians?"

"I confirmed it, yes."

"But we supply the Persians."

"We were supposed to, weren't we? That was the deal."

"So that is why the pills the detective showed us looked different in color? They weren't ours?"

"No, they weren't."

The implication hit Li Wei hard. "So not only have the Persians been making deals behind our back, they're also poisoning the supply on the street?"

Hui only grunted his affirmation.

"They have been setting us up!"

"I have been telling you for months that we need to take care of the Persians." Hui glared at him. "Sometimes, brother, it would do you well to talk less and listen more."

The memory of the conversation shames Li Wei. He is supposed to be the strategic one. The one who foresees the real threats and differentiates them from the rest of the noise.

In an act of concession to his younger brother, Li Wei has taken care of all the arrangements. But he hates leaving any detail to chance. He needs to be present when it happens. "Always too controlling," his young wife sometimes tells him in that shrill giggle that he used to love. In this rare instance, she isn't wrong.

Li Wei looks out the window and to his right. At end of the block, at the intersection of Alberni and Thurlow, he views the parked blue Porsche Cayenne with the tinted windows. He knows the engine is running. He shifts his gaze to the front of the restaurant, directly across the street. The orange-jacketed valet stands on duty. A few customers drift in for lunch. But there is still no sign of them.

Another twenty minutes pass, and the server pesters them into ordering expensive, overly sweet confections. Hui is as still as ever, but Li Wei sees the growing impatience in his brother's usually impassive eyes.

Finally, the front door to Cena opens and the goliath, whom Li Wei recognizes as the bodyguard Javad, steps out. Li Wei reaches for his phone and taps send on the prewritten text, which reads: "Go!"

The brothers' heads swivel simultaneously. They watch as the Porsche SUV slowly pulls away from the curb. Li Wei looks back to the restaurant's door, but there is still no sign of Farhad. The bitterness in the back of his mouth intensifies, as the Porsche crawls closer to where the bodyguard stands, alone.

Just as the car almost reaches Cena's entrance, the door flies open and a laughing Farhad steps out of the restaurant motioning to the valet for his keys.

In seconds, the Porsche comes to a stop directly in front of the Jians' window, obscuring Li Wei's view of the entrance. He hears the crisp rat-a-tat-tat and the shriek of windows shattering. There's a moment of absolute silence, broken by scattered screams outside and the squeal of the SUV's tires as it rockets off.

When Cena's entrance comes back into view, Li Wei sees the bodyguard, the valet, and Farhad all lying crumpled in different poses across the sidewalk. None of them move.

The coffee shop erupts with cries and yells—pandemonium—as chairs fly, tables wobble, and customers rush for the back exit.

Li Wei takes one more bite of the pricey macaron before he pushes his chair back, rises, and casually follows Hui out the front door. His stomach feels better than it has in days.

CHAPTER 40

Anson's car screeches to a halt in front of the police barricade at Burrard and Alberni, startling the uniformed cop who was trying to wave him past.

"Keep moving, no stopping!" the young cop shouts at him.

Anson hops out of the car, waving his ID. "Detective Chen, Homicide."

"Oh." The young cop visibly calms. "The vics are down there out front of Cena. A couple other detectives are already on scene."

Julie and Theo climb out, too. Anson leaves his car where it is, and the three of them hurry down Alberni toward the emergency response vehicles that are clustered in front of the restaurant.

Julie spots the three bodies ahead on the sidewalk, each draped with a black tarp. Uniformed officers mill around Cena's entrance. Hoops is with them, gesticulating urgently as he talks to two of the cops. But he breaks away as soon as he sees them.

Hoops's expression is uncharacteristically grim as he approaches. "Some morons just poked a very large bear. Actually, more like a starving grizzly."

Anson points in the direction of the corpses. "This is an occupational hazard for them."

"Most. Not Farhad. He was untouchable in this town. Until today."

"We were on our way over to talk to Farhad about his connection to Markku," Theo says.

"Yeah? Well, he's going to have even less to tell you than usual," Hoops says, though his tone isn't jovial. "I was no fan of Farhad. Trust me. But he was good at keeping the peace in that world. Now?"

"Gang war?" Julie says.

Hoops pulls his hands apart and simulates the sound of an explosion.

"Who were the other two victims?" Theo asks.

"Javad Madani, his bodyguard and shadow. And some parking attendant named Patrick Gowan. Irish kid here on a one-year work visa. 'Come see Vancouver, and get your head blown off.' Poor bastard." He shakes his head in disgust. "It's not a drive-by unless at least one innocent bystander gets pegged."

"So it was a drive-by?"

"Middle of downtown, in the middle of the day. It was fucking brazen." Hoops sounds almost impressed.

"Suspects?"

"A witness caught some cell phone footage of the getaway. Blue Porsche with tinted windows. But unless it really was an eighty-one-year-old pensioner behind the wheel, the license plates were stolen."

Anson eyes Hoops intently. "Who's behind it?"

"Right now your guess is as good as mine. The Persians control a huge part of the fenny trade. Any one of the other gangs would have reason, out of jealousy alone." Hoops roughly scratches his cheek. "Always the possibility of an inside job, too. A lot of secession planning happens that way in this world."

"Any historical grudges?"

"A couple years back the Persians went to war with the World Soldiers. And they won."

Theo looks at Anson. "Jamie Maddox?"

Hoops nods. "There isn't a crime in this city where that snake shouldn't at least be on the suspect list. But if Maddox is behind this, then he has bitten off *way* more than he can chew."

"The Jians?"

"Always. And never count out the East Indians, though that'd be a two-front war for them, as they're going at it with each other in the valley right now."

"Best guess?" Theo asks.

"Ask me tomorrow," Hoops says. "Word will eventually filter onto the street. It always does. Meantime, we're just scratching the surface."

"Thanks," Theo says. "Will you keep us posted?"

Hoops nods curtly. "This is not good, guys. Not good at all. Brace yourselves."

As they head back toward the car, Theo says, "It's got to be related to TLH."

Anson nods. "I'm thinking that whoever knocked off Farhad either blamed him for distributing the stuff or was trying to cover up their own involvement."

"Or both," Theo says. "Time to see Jamie Maddox and the Jian brothers."

"What about Rachel Xie's dad?" Julie suggests. "The Jians admitted to being in business with him. And his daughter was one of the victims. That's quite a coincidence."

Anson turns to her, arms folded in feigned indignation. "Who are the detectives here? You want me to come over to St. Mike's and start operating on your patients?"

"It's a good idea, partner," Theo says. "Let's start with Gary Xie. See what he knows."

They climb back into the car. As Anson pulls onto the street, he asks, "Have we confirmed the logistics for Wade's takedown tonight?"

"Think so. Let me double-check." Theo taps a number on his screen and then brings the phone to his ear. "Hey, it's Theo. Is the garage all set up for this evening? Second level, right?" He listens for a moment. "Good. OK, we'll meet you there around six." He looks as if he's about to hang up but he stops to listen further. "Interesting. Thanks."

"What?" Anson demands before the phone is even off his partner's ear.

"Forensics got the drug tests back on Markku's girlfriend and on the pills from inside his safe."

"No carfentanil in either, right?" Julie speculates.

"Not a trace."

"Which means Markku probably wasn't the guy distributing TLH. Right?"

"Maybe not," Anson agrees.

Her heart sinks. "So TLH is still out there."

Theo shrugs. Anson says nothing. They drive in silence until, five minutes later, Anson pulls up to a shiny new office tower on the corner of Georgia and Richards. They ride the elevator up to the Gary Xie's twenty-ninth-floor office.

Anson speaks Mandarin to the strikingly pretty receptionist, whose eyes are such an intense tint of walnut that Julie is tempted to ask her if they're real or colored contacts. A few moments later, Gary appears at the desk. He guides them all back to his spacious office, offering tea or coffee, as if they have come to close on a home purchase. But once they're all seated, his affable façade gives way to a look of concern. "Have you learned more about Rachel? How it happened?"

"Nothing concrete yet, Mr. Xie," Theo says.

"I see." Gary sits back in disappointment. "How can I help you today?"

"We wanted to ask you about the Jian brothers," Anson says.

"Yes?" Gary sits up straighter again. "What of them?"

"They told us you buy and sell houses for them."

"Three. No, four. And I only represent them for the sales, not their purchases."

"Why is that?" Anson asks.

Julie realizes he already knows the answer. She remembers him outlining to the brothers themselves the Jians' system for repossessing the houses of overextended gamblers who default on their brutal loans.

Gary holds out his palms. "They have only ever asked me to represent them on sales. The Jians are very . . . private. They're not the type of people who like to be asked questions."

"I couldn't agree more with that assessment. Why do you suppose that is?"

Gary only looks down. "It's not my business."

"It kind of is. Especially if the money is dirty and you're helping to launder it."

Gary's head snaps up and he inhales sharply. "I'm just a real estate agent."

"A real estate license isn't exactly diplomatic immunity in the eyes of the court."

Gary speaks rapidly in Mandarin to Anson, pleading.

Theo cuts him off. "We're not here to investigate money laundering, Mr. Xie. We're trying to find out what happened to your daughter and the other four kids who died."

"Five," Julie can't help but say, realizing that by now Alexa must have already died on the operating room table, during the organ donation.

Gary looks at them desperately. "But the Jians?"

"Are some of the biggest fentanyl suppliers in the city," Theo says.

"It's entirely possible their drugs were what ended up in your daughter's drink," Julie says.

Gary stares at them for a long moment and then hangs his head in shame. Julie can see that he is making the mental bridge back to his daughter's possible killers, and she feels for him.

"We need your help, Gary," Anson says.

Gary nods. "They are bad people."

"We know."

"The Triad."

"That, too."

"I didn't know about the fentanyl." His voice is heavy with defeat. "Extortion. Loan sharking. Human trafficking. Smuggling. I suspected drugs, too, but I didn't know about fentanyl."

Julie glances over, expecting a sarcastic comment from Anson, but he only nods sympathetically.

"I never asked about their business. It would have been reckless to do so. Frankly, I did not want to know. I never asked to represent them. They came to me. They were told I was the best at getting top dollar. They did not give me a choice."

"We believe you," Theo says. "All of it. But you've been in business with them for, what . . . three, four years?"

"Three."

"Think, Mr. Xie. Something might've slipped in that time. Something that can help us?"

"Rachel . . ." Gary mumbles. He appears lost in thought for a long while, but then he looks up slowly, and his face creases with recognition. "That old house."

"What house, Gary?" Julie asks.

"All the properties I've sold for the brothers have been on the West Side. All sold for at least four million. But last year, maybe eighteen months ago, I was going to list a house for them in the southeast corner of the city. In Champlain Heights. It was very run-down. Only worth land value. We were going to list it at just over a million."

"Going to?" Julie asks, confused. "You didn't?"

"At the last minute, Li Wei told me he changed his mind. Said they had another use for it. I assumed they meant it as a rental prop-erty. But . . ." They wait for him to finish. "None of their properties on the West Side ever had tenants. They were all vacant."

Anson leans forward. "You have the address, Gary?"

Gary nods while he types at his keyboard.

Theo turns to Anson. "Better get a search warrant."

"Or if we want to get inside anytime soon . . ." Anson says, his expression dead serious, "I've got a better idea."

CHAPTER 41

As Wade straps on his red helmet—*Safety first, Mom*, he thinks, chuckling to himself, appreciating that protection has nothing to do with it—he again considers not going. That Australian dipshit Vince sounded so desperate in his texts. *Too desperate.* But in the end, Wade finds it irresistible. If a group of filthy rich Brits want to spend a hundred dollars a gram—plus Vince's markup—on thirty grams of blow, then Wade sees it as his duty to separate them from their cash.

Still, his gut is sounding the alarm. That's why he's chosen to dress in full bike gear with helmet, sunglasses, and a riding jacket, instead of just the usual jeans and T-shirt that he would have normally worn for such a short downtown ride on his cruiser bike.

Wade cycles past the hotel's entrance without spotting anyone familiar, not even Vince, who is supposed to be on duty. He doesn't read too much into the bellman's absence, assuming he is probably already on break, since their rendezvous is supposed to be in five minutes. Wade rides by the entrance of the underground parking lot a second time before he's convinced there is no unusual activity out front.

He dismounts his bike on the side of the road, about three car lengths from the garage's entrance, and pretends to pump his tire as he surveils it. Six-thirty passes, and Wade hears his phone vibrate inside his seat pack—undoubtedly a text from Vince wondering where the hell he is.

Wade watches for another five minutes. Nothing changes.

Three grand for two minutes' work! What kind of loser would leave that on the table? he thinks as he swings his leg, gingerly, over the bike's crossbar.

CHAPTER 42

Julie had to plead with Anson and Theo to let her accompany them. Theo was the first to relent, but Anson was harder to wear down. It was only after she played the guilt card, pointing out how many volunteer hours she had devoted to helping them with the medical aspects of the case, that he grudgingly agreed to let her observe from the back seat of the car.

The adrenaline courses through her veins as Julie leans between the two front seats. The anticipation is comparable to that delicious feeling she still remembers all too vividly of drawing up the next hit in a syringe. Every passing second heightens the excitement. Not only is she on the front line of a police takedown, but they might be closing in on the source of this ultralethal poison.

Julie has a good view of Vince from the rear driver's-side window. It probably doesn't help the covert operation that the twitchy bellman can't keep still, but she supposes it won't matter even if he does give himself away. There are six other cops waiting to pounce the moment Wade shows his face. *If* he shows his face.

"He's nine minutes late and counting," Anson mutters as he checks his watch again.

"Patience, partner," Theo says soothingly.

No one says a word for a minute or so, until Theo's phone buzzes with a text. "Wade?" Anson demands.

"No. Hoops is just confirming that they've got a surveillance team in place outside the dump in East Van the Jian brothers own."

"But no search warrant?" Julie asks.

"We still need probable cause," Theo says.

"They're *gangsters*," she says, frustrated.

"Not convicted. And even if they had been, we'd still need more."

"Like what?"

"Often we end up stealing their garbage. If we find suspicious chemicals in there, we get our warrant."

Anson scoffs. "I like my idea better. Talk a neighbor into reporting a funny smell or something that we would have to go check out."

"Not kosher, partner."

"Whatever. It would probably stand up in—" Anson stops mid-sentence and sits up straighter when a cyclist wheels past them in a red helmet and shoes with tips that reflect the overhead fluorescent lights.

The radio crackles with the voice of the tactical operations officer in charge. "Stand down. It's not him. There's a bike locker on level P4."

They lapse into vigilant silence. A minute or two later, the same cyclist rides by them coming up the ramp. "What?" Anson drums the steering wheel with his fingers. "No bike locker?"

They watch as the rider throws a friendly wave to Vince and continues up the ramp.

Anson suddenly hits the ignition. The voice crackles on the radio again. "Engines off! Vince didn't give the signal."

Theo's head snaps toward him. "Anson?"

"Check out Vince!" Anson says as the car lurches forward.

Julie saw it, too. Vince stilled the moment the cyclist rode past him, and his head followed him all the way out of the garage. Even as they gun past Vince, his gaze is still turned in that direction.

Anson slams on the brakes at the exit, and two pedestrians freeze a foot or two from his bumper, bracing for impact. One of them flips them the finger.

"Police! Move!" Anson cries out his open window, and the two scurry out of the way.

Theo grabs the radio. "Mark heading east on Cordova on bike! Red helmet. Black bike."

Theo points up to the next intersection on West Cordova, and Julie sees the red helmet round the corner onto Richards Street.

Anson tears after him. As they turn onto the same street, the cyclist glances over his shoulder and then darts down the first lane he reaches. Anson pounds the steering wheel as he waits for more pedestrians, including an older man with a cane, to clear the lane's entrance.

"Move it, granddad," Julie grumbles, sharing in his impatience.

By the time they go again and gain on him, the cyclist has already reached the far end of the lane and is turning onto Cambie Street. Anson hits the gas. They fly around the corner after him. Julie spots the cyclist half a block ahead, heading toward the iconic steam clock in the heart of Gastown. He swerves right and peddles directly into oncoming traffic on the one-way Water Street, igniting a chorus of honking horns.

Don't lose him! Julie wants to scream.

Anson is all focus as he flies down Carrall Street and turns onto Abbott Street.

"Blood Alley!" Theo calls into the radio, and Julie sees the back wheel disappear down the old lane that was once home to rows of slaughterhouses but is now a trendy pedestrian-only thoroughfare. "Box him in from the other side!" Theo says as he hops out of the car.

Anson circles the block and abandons the car, doors open, in front of the Cambie Street entrance to Blood Alley. With her heart pounding in her throat, Julie follows him down the lane, which is teeming with restaurant-goers, tourists, and other pedestrians.

She glimpses Theo approaching from the other side, but there's no sign of the cyclist or his bike. They weave around a pack of slow-moving tourists with a guide in front who is shouting in what sounds like German. Julie doesn't even see the face of the last member of the group, who wears shorts and a T-shirt and dawdles close behind the others. But as she looks down, she notices reflectors on the tips of his shoes.

Her head snaps up. "Hey! You!"

The man surges ahead. He shoves the woman closest to him, who falls forward, knocking her friend down, too. The cyclist bolts ahead down the lane.

Julie runs after him, but Anson overtakes her in a few strides. Before the man even reaches the end of the lane, Anson lunges and tackles him by the legs, toppling him to the pavement.

CHAPTER 43

Wade paces behind the table in the small interview room, his ass aching and his frustration growing by the minute. Whatever damage Maddox had caused his tailbone, that Asian cop doubled it when he tackled him onto the pavement. *How long are these assholes going to make me wait?* He again considers asking for a lawyer but decides against it. He wants to get a sense for himself just how much they have on him, and it won't help to lawyer up.

Wade knows he only has himself to blame. The moment he saw Vince inside the garage, he suspected the fucker had set him up. The Australian, who had always been as laid-back as they come, was bobbing from foot to foot as if standing on hot coals. So Wade kept his head forward and cycled on. Before he even rounded the ramp down to the third level, he spotted two men sitting inside a parked sedan, confirming his suspicions. He counted two other similarly occupied unmarked cop cars on his deliberately slow ride back up the ramp. On his way out, he cycled closer to the still-fidgeting Vince and waved as if politely acknowledging a stranger. But as he wheeled past, Wade hissed, "One word, and I'll put a bullet through your eye!" He reached the street without hearing any sirens and, for a few blissful moments, thought he had escaped their trap. Until he heard the tires squealing behind him.

The door to the interrogation room flies open and chases away the miserable memory. The cops Wade recognizes from the alley enter. The hot chick who screamed bloody murder at the sight of him is nowhere to be seen, but the Chinese guy who looks like he walked straight out of an Asian *GQ* precedes the older, frumpy one, who could be manning the counter of an Italian deli.

They grab seats on the other side of the table, and the older cop speaks first. "Wade, I'm Detective Theo Kostas, and this is Detective Anson Chen. Won't you please sit?"

"I'd like to, but I'm too sore from the act of police brutality," he says, firing Anson a glare.

"You understand that you're under arrest for a PPT—possession for the purpose of trafficking?" Theo asks.

"Yeah, you better call CBC and CNN. You just cleaned up the whole drug mess in this city by busting a guy with a couple ounces of coke on him."

Theo smiles, while Anson remains stone-faced. "We have to start somewhere, don't we? We do have a big drug problem in this city, especially this past week."

Wade recognizes the slow warm-up act, but he only shrugs.

"Since TLH hit the streets," Theo continues.

"What's that?"

"The Last High, Wade. Ultrapotent narcotic. Killing people left, right, and center." Theo pauses. "Wonder if we'll find any of it in the coke we confiscated from you."

"Hope not," Wade says, knowing that, thankfully, he hadn't ground any fentanyl into that particular batch. "If so, I'd like to have a word with that Australian asshole who sold it to me. So would my best friend's fiancée, I bet. Could've killed the groom and his entire wedding party. Me included."

"So Vince is your dealer, then?" Anson speaks up. "Not vice versa?"

"Yeah, why?" Wade grimaces. "What did he tell you?"

Anson doesn't reply, but the two detectives share a quick glance. Theo reaches for his phone. "Wade, weren't you curious as to why we kept you waiting so long?"

"Curious? No. Pissed? Yes. It's been over four fucking hours."

"Let me explain anyway. Search warrants take time to acquire. They take even longer to execute. In fact, crime techs are still in your place as we speak."

Wade's gut clenches, but he reminds himself to keep moving and show no sign of concern.

"The boys tell us you did a good job concealing your stash in the false panel under the dryer," Theo continues.

Wade stops in his tracks.

Theo taps the screen on his phone, and then he turns it toward Wade. "Look what they found."

Wade glances at the photo of the same bag of fake oxys he was sorting through earlier in the afternoon. "Not mine," he says, forcing the defiance back into his shocked system.

"Must be the last tenant's?" Theo suggests.

"Nah, I was just holding it for a buddy."

"You don't know much about the law, do you, Wade?" Anson says.

Theo advances the photos to a close-up of the pills. "I once took my kids to the M&M's flagship store in New York. Couldn't believe all the different colors and shades of candies they had. Kind of reminds me of the different shades of gray-blue we found in your fentanyl pills." His finger hovers over the bluest of the tablets. "These ones are interesting. Know why?"

The hair on Wade's neck bristles, but he just shrugs again.

"We found the exact same ones on this high-powered businessman who overdosed in his office. Aiden Wilder. Ring any bells?"

Wade shakes his head.

"Anyway, turns out these are TLH pills. Pure carfentanil. So, ipso facto, Wade, you were the one peddling The Last High."

"Death, Wade," Anson adds. "You're selling death."

"Hang on a second!" Wade holds up his palm. "Even supposing those were mine—and I'm not saying they are—I'm no cook. If I did happen to have them on me, then I had no fucking idea. And if I did have a bag like that, I'd dip into it myself from time to time. So I'd be at as much risk as anyone else. Hypothetically speaking."

Theo nods sympathetically, as if he accepts Wade's explanation at face value. "Let's get back to the blow for a second. Do you know a lawyer by the name of Jarrod Nader? Pardon me, wrong tense. *Did* you know him?"

Wade pretends to consider that for a moment, all the while wondering how Jarrod died and feeling oddly pleased that he had. "Nah, can't place him."

"Jarrod was marking a milestone last night. He'd made partner and bought a ton of blow to celebrate with friends. But it turns out that the coke was laced with TLH. Jarrod died instantly. So did two others. A bunch more would have, too, if it weren't for a very astute doctor at the party."

Wade wills his voice to be calm, mentally calculating whether they could link Jarrod's death back to him. "Don't know the dude."

"All right." Theo sighs. "How about Justin Bowles?"

"Who?" Wade says genuinely.

"The pilot."

"Nope. Not a clue."

"That makes sense," Theo says. "Seeing as how you didn't sell to him directly. But we know that you did sell the coke to Vince, who passed it on to the pilot. And you'll never guess what happened next."

"He OD'd," Wade says through gritted teeth.

"We have you for that one, Wade. Dead to rights, as they say."

Anson shakes his head. "The courts these days—with all the public outcry around the fentanyl epidemic—they don't just charge drug trafficking anymore. Not even manslaughter. Nope. They call it murder now. Ambitious prosecutors even go for premeditated."

Wade's guts are afire, but he manages to keep his tone in check. "All you got is that Australian prick's word against mine."

"You figure, Wade?" Anson says with eerie confidence. "You heard about those teenagers, right? Six of them died of the same TLH overdose. Innocent kids. Devastated parents."

"I heard something, yeah."

Theo holds up his phone again. "I want you to look carefully at these photos. These victims." He taps the screen and the face of a young girl appears. She doesn't even look old enough to be in high school. Theo slowly scrolls through six more photos, while Wade cements his expression in a squint of full concentration, trying to give away nothing. "Did you sell to any of these kids?"

"Show me again," Wade says, pretending to care.

Theo swipes through them all a second time.

Wade lets his shoulders rise and fall and then shakes his head. "Sorry."

"Jesus," Anson snorts. "You're in more trouble than you can begin to dream of. You really want to take the fall for all of this, Wade? We have you on felony possession, holding the most lethal drug the street has ever seen. We already connected you to the pilot's death. With minimal detective work, we'll link you to others."

"*But.*" Theo takes over. "We know you didn't cook those TLH pills. We're running out of time to find out who did before a bunch more innocent people die. So, if you give up your supplier, it'll go a long way to helping your cause."

Wade looks from Theo to Anson and back. "How long?"

"We'll talk to the prosecutor. If you name your supplier, *now*, we can drop the murder rap. Leave it as a simple PPT."

Wade's intuition tells him that he has to offer them something if he hopes to find a way out of this nightmare. *Why not take a bit of sweet fucking revenge along the way?* "OK, but you can't let him know it was me, or I'm dead."

Theo nods. "It stays in this room. You have our word."

CHAPTER 44

Λs Anson pulls to a stop in front of her building, Julie checks her watch and sees that it's a few minutes before one a.m. She pushes open the passenger door, but he stays in his seat and leaves the engine running.

"Come on, Detective," she says. "You need a glass of wine every bit as much as I do."

"I guess." He turns off the ignition. "As long as it's the stuff only you doctors can afford."

Shaking her head, she climbs out of the car. "You need to find yourself an ophthalmologist or dermatologist, not a poor old emergency doctor."

"Until I land a case involving a visually impaired killer with bad eczema . . . guess you'll just have to do."

She buzzes them through the main door. Inside the elevator, they stand close enough that their shoulders rub. She distracts herself by focusing on the recap he shared of Wade Patterson's interrogation. "How much do you believe of what Wade told you?"

"With that guy? The bare minimum."

"How about what he said about Jamie Maddox?"

"I don't doubt that Maddox is Wade's supplier. Or at least one of them. Wade's admission should be enough to get us a search warrant on Maddox's place."

The idea of searching yet another suspect's home dampens her mood. "We're still not there, are we?"

He gently lifts her chin toward him. "We're closer than we were yesterday. We'll get there, Julie. Trust me."

"God, I hope so."

His stare intensifies. "I know you saw those kids when they first came in. And I realize you have to deal with the carnage from fentanyl at work every day. But . . ."

"Yes?"

"It's like you've taken this whole case so . . . personally. Right from the get-go."

She clears her throat. "If you'd seen Alexa that night . . ."

She is saved from further explanation when the elevator opens to her floor. They tread in silence to her unit, but before she opens the door, she turns to him and says, "You need to know something about me, Anson."

He kisses her softly on the lips. "I want to know everything about you, Dr. Rees."

"Inside," she says as she pushes the door open, turns on the light, and pulls him over to the kitchen counter. "Sit. Wine first."

She pulls two glasses down and then selects a bottle of twelve-year-old Bordeaux that she has been saving for a special occasion, although she never expected it to be a confession. She uncorks the bottle, pours two generous glasses, and sits down beside him.

Julie stares straight ahead, and Anson seems to know better than to rush her. Finally, she says, "I'm an addict, Anson."

He slowly lowers his glass. "An addict?"

"I've been sober nine years now, but once an addict . . ."

"Julie, I don't . . ." He glances at the wine bottle. "What were you addicted to?"

"Opioids. Morphine at first. Then fentanyl." She pauses. "Michael, too. He was an anesthesia resident. He used to steal it from the operating room."

"Wow. That's risky, isn't it?"

"If he'd been caught, it would've cost him his career." She pauses to have a slow sip of wine. "In the end, though, it cost him way more than that."

Anson lays a hand on hers. "I'm sorry, Julie."

She feels a deep flush warm her face, but she doesn't try to hide it this time. "It was my fault," she says in a small voice.

He squeezes her hand. "How so?"

"It was the three-year anniversary of our first date. Michael wanted to take me out to celebrate. But all I could even think about was that next high. Craving it like a drowning woman craves air. I convinced Michael to stay in. We . . ." Her voice cracks, refusing to cooperate. She hasn't shared these details with anyone except Goran, and that was nine years ago. "We went and shot up in bed. We used to be so careful with the dose, but by then we were beyond reckless. I . . . I passed out. Michael . . . he must've taken another hit, because when I woke up, the needle was still in his arm. Was the very first thing I noticed. Not that he was cold or blue or not even breathing. No, I focused on the only thing that mattered to me by that point. The needle."

Anson pulls her in closer. Her head falls into the crook of his neck. "None of that makes it your fault, Julie."

"If I didn't—"

"You were doing what addicts do. Enabling each other. It could've just as easily been you."

She lifts her head up. "Do you know how many times I wish it had been?"

He views her impassively for a few moments. "I'm no stranger to survivor's guilt, Julie."

"Not like this, though. Not when you're the one responsible."

"Don't be so sure."

"What's that mean?"

"Nicole." It's his turn to go silent for a spell. "When I told you how she died, I neglected to mention that the whole thing was my idea."

"The mopeds?"

He nods. "Nicole said she didn't feel safe renting those bikes. She had never done it before. She worried about the winding roads. I convinced her it was fine. That it would be an adventure." He swallows hard. "One of the last memories I have of Nicole is her wagging a playful finger at me and saying, 'You better not get me killed, Constable Chen.'"

Julie puts down her glass and throws both arms around him. "Oh, Anson, I am so sorry."

CHAPTER 45

The leather chair is Li Wei's favorite. Or, at least, it's positioned in his favorite spot. From where he sits, he can see out the living room window to the Fraser River as it meanders behind the palatial property on Southwest Marine Drive. He has a clear view of the air traffic control tower of Vancouver International Airport on the far side of the river. He loves to watch the steady stream of planes taking off and landing. To Li Wei's eyes, airports represent escape and, therefore, freedom.

The Jians only foreclosed on this house three months earlier. But even in the weeks leading up to the repossession—as it became clearer that the owner, a rich widow with terrible luck at the blackjack tables, was not going to be able to meet the weekly forty-thousand-dollar payments—Li Wei knew it was destined to become his home. There was no dispute over it, either, since Hui had no interest in the house, claiming the location was too remote and the grounds too sprawling.

Both of those attributes now work in their favor. After the hit on Farhad, the Jians had to be prepared for retribution. And the house—with its gated, single-point access—doubled well as a fortress, especially with four guards posted out front, including the same shooter who took down Farhad.

Hui stomps into the room and disrupts Li Wei's peace. "How long are we planning to hide here like cowards?" he demands. "It's as good as losing face."

Li Wei swallows his sigh. "Another day, no more. Just until we are certain the Persians aren't looking for us."

"Would be the last mistake they ever made. Besides, I hear the Persians already think the Indians are behind the shooting." Hui shows a rare smile. "Let them sort it out between themselves."

"The choice of car was inspired, brother," Li Wei says, crediting Hui for choosing the same model and blue color of Porsche—right down to the custom wheel package—driven by one of the most hot-headed of the Sharma brothers, Ravi, who was known to have hated Farhad.

Hui drops into the chair across from him, reaches for his phone, and begins to text. *Even his typing is aggressive*, Li Wei thinks, as he watches his brother bash the screen with his thumbs.

As another plane swoops down smoothly across the river, Li Wei reviews the situation in his head for the umpteenth time. "I want to talk to him again," he says.

"Who? The cook?"

"Yes, the one with the foolish nickname," Li Wei says.

"Why? I thought you tested the sample on the whore and found it to be clean."

"*Those* particular pills were not contaminated. There are others. It's not just that he forgot we had already given him the carfentanil. No. It was the look on his face when I reminded him."

Hui raises an eyebrow but says nothing.

"Like someone who had just been caught in a lie."

Hui considers this for several silent seconds. "All right, when you free us from this self-imprisonment, we will go see him." And then he smiles.

CHAPTER 46

"**W**hat time is it?" Julie mutters as she wraps the sheet tighter around her naked body, but not before stealing an appreciative glance of Anson's toned body.

"Seven-fifteen," Anson replies as he sits up straighter in bed to read the text that just sounded the notification that woke her.

"What's going on?" She touches her earlobe and realizes that her earrings are still in.

"Theo says the search warrant got approved."

"On the house in East Van?"

"No. For Jamie Maddox's condo."

"That's good."

"It could be." He puts down the phone and begins to caress her neck.

She withdraws from his touch, hit suddenly with a morning-after-the-first-night self-consciousness that she hasn't experienced in ages. "That tickles," she says.

"Just exactly how drunk were you last night?" he asks.

"I wasn't drunk at all. You didn't even let me finish one glass of wine."

"Then why are you acting like you just woke up beside some terrible drunken mistake you made at a bar?"

His laughter eases her discomfort, and she rolls over into his open arms.

Their sex is less hurried and more tender than it was the night before. After they'd bared their hearts and shared their deep secrets, animalistic passion overtook them. They fumbled for clothes and tore them off before even reaching the bed. Need and release supplanted everything else. But this morning the sex is more intimate and even more intense, with the added familiarity of one another's bodies. Julie would be happy to linger in bed with Anson all day long, chatting, laughing, and making more love, but Theo is expecting them.

Julie has a quick shower and Anson rinses off even faster, but they still are the last ones to reach the exclusive condo complex in the heart of Yaletown, outside of which Theo and the rest of the search team have already assembled. Uncertain of the resistance they might face, Theo has arranged for four uniformed VPD officers to accompany the three crime scene technicians through the front door of the building. When one of the technicians questions Julie's presence, Theo explains that she is their toxicological consultant who needs to accompany them to help identify any substances found.

As they ride the elevator to the penthouse, Theo looks from Anson to Julie and back. "Rare to see you wearing the same shirt two days in a row, partner," he says wryly.

Julie has to suppress her laugh as Anson's face reddens. They step off the elevator and head down to the only door on the northwest side of the building.

Anson knocks firmly. When no one answers, he pounds on it with the side of his fist. "Jamie Maddox!" he yells through the door.

Nothing.

Anson pounds again, raising his voice even louder. "This is the Vancouver Police Department. Open up now!"

"What the fuck do you want?" a muffled growl comes from behind the door.

"We have a warrant to search the premises."

The voice doesn't respond.

"If you do not admit us in the next ten seconds, we will be forced to break down the door."

A few tense seconds pass before the dead bolt clicks and the door swings open. Jamie hovers on the other side, standing at least six-four and weighing probably two hundred forty pounds. He wears sweats with a sleeveless T-shirt that shows off his bulging tattooed shoulders, one of which supports a red-crested macaw. The parrot whistles at the guests and then says, "Hello, hello," in a creepy, high-pitched tone.

Jamie's eyes narrow as he recognizes Anson and Theo. He folds his arms. "You two pricks just won't let it go, will you?"

"Funny, that." Anson grins. "We're both kind of anal about attempted murder."

"Attempted murder, my ass," Jamie scoffs as he rubs the thick stubble on his cheek. "I was the one protecting myself."

Theo raises the signed writ in his hand and pushes the door open farther. "We're not here to relitigate old cases, Jamie. We have a warrant to search the contents of these premises."

"What for?"

"Possession for the purpose of trafficking."

"This is such bullshit!" Jamie flings his arm up and the bird squawks, flies up momentarily, and then drops back down to land on his bare shoulder.

Behind Jamie, a skinny blond-haired woman, who looks twenty-ish and wears only black panties, covers her breasts with her arm as she scurries across the hallway and into a room. Seconds later, another naked giggling young woman, who's curvier and has darker hair, follows the path of the first one.

"No more stalling," Anson says as he pushes the door fully open and walks right past Jamie. The parrot hoots in excitement as the rest of the team files in. Julie follows them into an expansive living room with chocolate-brown hardwood floors and oppressive black leather furnishings. Aside from the striking water view through the floor-to-ceiling windows, the only other color comes from a few gaudy prints hanging on the white walls in a hodgepodge of asymmetry. The room smells of stale sushi and cigarettes. Random pieces of clothing are strewn over the furniture. Empty champagne bottles and half-full cocktail glasses stand among the open food containers that are scattered over the coffee table.

The cops slip on latex gloves, as the team wordlessly divides up the unit to search it. The two girls, now dressed in shorts, tops, and runners, emerge from a bedroom, acting as if the cops don't exist. Each kisses Jamie on the lips. One of them strokes the parrot and says, "Bye-bye, Ronald," in a singsong tone that the bird mimics but says instead, "Fuck you, fuck you."

The other one laughs and says, "See you after our spin class, babe." And the girls leave together.

Julie wanders from room to room and watches, admiringly, as the cops conduct their meticulous search, sorting through drawers, cupboards, and every sort of container they encounter.

"Detectives, in here!" a voice calls from the same bedroom the girls just vacated.

Julie joins Theo and Anson inside the room, beside the large walk-in-closet, where the bald technician leans over a waist-high safe that appears to be bolted to the floor.

"You can't touch that!" Jamie says as he enters the room behind them, the parrot gone from his shoulder.

"Actually, we can." Theo turns to face him. "This warrant covers the entire contents of your condo, including this safe."

"Well, I'm not giving you the combo. So you're fucked on that score."

"Not exactly. We'll just call for the engineers and they'll either drill it open here or rip it out of the floor and do it at our offices."

"What do you figure, Jamie?" Anson asks. "You're the first drug trafficker to have his own safe?"

Jamie shakes his head adamantly. "I want to talk to my lawyer."

"You're just stalling the inevitable by—" Theo stops at the sound of the mechanical whir coming from behind him.

All eyes turn to the technician who is pulling the safe door wide open.

Jamie's face scrunches. *"What the fuck?"*

The technician shrugs and taps the far back corner of the safe. "The six-digit combination is written here, on the side. Guess no one bothered to change the default factory setting."

Theo and Anson share a look before they both break into laughter. "Looks like Ronald might be the brains behind this operation," Anson jokes.

The levity drains quickly from the room, though, when the technician extracts a large baggie full of pills from inside the safe. He pulls out several other bags loaded with pills and powders, before removing wad after wad of tightly wrapped bills, mainly hundreds.

Anson looks over to Jamie, who's now flanked by two uniform cops, one of them as big as he is. "This probably isn't going to help your case."

Jamie glares at him but holds his tongue.

Anson steps over to the safe. Ignoring the cash and the other substances, he collects the four bags of gray pills that Julie recognizes as fake oxys. He carries them into the bathroom down the corridor and lays them side by side on the counter, under the bright glare of the hanging pendant lights. Julie watches as he and Theo examine each bag together, moving the contents around but being careful not to open the bag. Even before Anson catches her eye, Julie recognizes that none of the bags contain any of the bluish TLH pills that they found at Wade's place.

Anson returns the bags to the technician, leaving him to his careful cataloguing of the safe's contents. They head into the living room to find Jamie sitting on the sofa and speaking on the phone while the same two cops stand on either side of him. "Let me call you back," he says at the sight of the detectives.

"Where are the other pills?" Anson demands.

Jamie crosses his thick arms again. "I want to speak to my lawyer."

"The blue pills. You know? The ones they're calling TLH."

Jamie leaps up from the sofa as if someone shot at him. "No fucking way you're pinning that on me! I got nothing to do with that shit."

"We have good reason to believe that you might be the source," Theo says.

"Which asshole told you that?"

"That we can't say. But we do have a witness."

Jamie jabs a finger at the detectives. "Fuck you and fuck your witness! I have nothing to do with TLH. And that's all I'm going to say until you let me talk to my fucking lawyer!"

"Time will tell," Theo says. He nods to the closest of the two police officers, who pulls a pair of handcuffs off his belt.

Jamie doesn't resist as the officer spins him around and cuffs his hands behind his back, while the other officer pulls out a laminated card and reads from it. "Jamie Maddox, we are arresting you for possession for the purpose of trafficking. You have the right to retain and instruct counsel without delay. You also have the right to free and immediate legal advice from duty counsel. Do you understand?"

"Fuck you."

"We'll take that as macaw for yes," Anson says.

Fifteen minutes later, they've also found two handguns, a shotgun, a semiautomatic rifle, and on the bedroom nightstand a pile of loose cocaine dust, with a razor beside it. After Animal Control has extracted the parrot and the technicians have confiscated the drugs, weapons, and all the electronics, including cell phones, the uniformed officers lead Jamie away in handcuffs.

Theo, Anson, and Julie gather outside on the sidewalk under the warm June sunshine. "I sort of believe him," Julie says. "That he's not distributing TLH."

"Or maybe he's distributing it without even knowing it," Theo says.

Anson nods. "And maybe he's distributed it all already. To dealers lower down the pecking order like that scumbag Wade. That's why there might not be any in his safe."

"So where does he get his drugs from?" Julie asks.

"He's not going to tell us jack." Anson sighs. "But maybe Hoops knows?"

"Jesus!" Julie mutters, disheartened. "These drug traffickers are like Russian nesting dolls. You open one up and there's another inside it. Their chain of supply never ends."

Anson's smile is undeterred. "More like a Rubik's Cube. We just need to get all the colors aligned. We're getting close. I feel it."

Theo looks as if he's about to add something, but he's stopped by the sound of his phone ringing. "Kostas," he says as he brings the phone to his ear and listens a moment. "Maybe ten minutes?" Another pause. "OK, see you then."

Julie and Anson view him expectantly. "Babar wants to see us," he says with a shrug.

They drive together to VPD headquarters and head straight down to the Technical Crime Unit. Babar is seated, as usual, at his corner cubicle with all his computer screens lit up in front of him.

"I might have something for you," Babar says in lieu of a greeting.

"We missed you, too," Anson says.

Babar only sighs. "The warrants came through yesterday for the social media accounts on the phones. As we suspected, many of the conversations between the teenagers occurred through Snapchat. That data is, of course, inaccessible. And aside from the expected overly suggestive teenage photos and other mundane posts, Instagram and Facebook haven't revealed much of use."

"Can we dispense with the pertinent negatives?"

Babar shoots Anson a disparaging glance. "But they also communicated through WhatsApp. Some individual conversations and a few smaller group chats."

Anson snaps his fingers. "And?"

"I found this snippet of conversation on Grayson Driscoll's phone from late in the afternoon on the day of the overdose." He types a few keys and a short series of text bubbles appears on the screen in front of him. "This group only consisted of Grayson, Joshua Weir, and Dylan Berg."

Theo points to the screen. "Who says what?"

"This top one is from Joshua." Babar motions to the first text, which reads: "Big doubts about the plan tonight, D."

"D?" Julie asks. "As in Dylan?"

"I would assume so, since Dylan replied to it." Babar points to the next text, which reads: "It's totally cool, Josh. Trust me on this one."

There's only one other text bubble below it that Julie recognizes, by the color, as having come from Joshua. "Fuckin useless old phone acting up. Cell receiver not working again. Getting Wi-Fi only. Gonna leave it behind. Meet you at yours."

"Explains why Josh's phone wasn't found at the crime scene," Theo thinks aloud.

"Nothing else?" Anson asks. "What about Dylan's phone?"

Babar shakes his head.

"Meaning he deleted his copy of the whole conversation?"

"Yes." Babar runs a finger up and down the screen. "Look, I can't be certain, but experience and logic tell me that this conversation was longer. And this is the only snippet that Grayson didn't delete."

Theo studies the texts. "The 'plan' Joshua mentions could be anything. Doesn't necessarily involve drugs."

Anson stares hard at his partner. "What else could it involve?"

Theo slowly nods. "We better go ask Dylan."

A thought hits Julie so suddenly that she grabs Anson's arm. "There's someone we should go see first!"

CHAPTER 47

Bunsen has barely slept since the Jian brothers' visit. For once, it's not the demands of work that are keeping him awake.

He has taken his lab apart. Inspected every nook and cranny. He has run a sample of the powder from every single container through his portable analyzer. And he still hasn't found the missing carfentanil.

Li Wei was right. Based on the minuscule proportion Bunsen adds to his recipe, he should have had enough carfentanil to last for months. He could kick himself for letting it slip to the brothers that he didn't. Those sharks don't miss a thing.

If the carfentanil were just lost, Bunsen could easily improvise without it. He adds such a tiny amount to the finished pills that it contributes little more than the garnish to a steak. What terrifies him is where the unaccounted-for carfentanil might have ended up.

When the story first broke about the teens who died from a mass overdose, Bunsen wrote it off as the unfortunate collateral damage of an ugly world, in which he only plays a very peripheral role. But as more reports surfaced about TLH, he began to wonder if there could be a more direct link to him. And as soon as he realized that his supply of carfentanil was missing, the terror took hold.

Bunsen scours his brain again, trying to remember which batch he prepared when. It had to have been last week sometime. He drags the fridge out of the wall and removes the exposed floorboard. Not only does he hide his money here, but he also keeps small samples—two or three pills, at most—of every batch of fake oxys he produces. As a student of colors, he likes to compare and contrast the results.

Bunsen removes the little baggies that contain a few pills each with the production dates written in felt pen on the outside. He lays them side by side on the counter beside his laptop, where, on a hidden file, he stores a list of the tints and concentrates of coloring he added to each batch. The results vary from almost pure gray to bluer hybrids of gunmetal, slate, and even cobalt.

Bunsen focuses on the four lots he made last week—five, if he includes the much smaller supply he made for his other, secret customer. His eyes are drawn to the sample pills from that fifth batch, as they had emerged almost Copenhagen-blue. Bunsen is always more deliberate in adding blue coloring to his "off-sales," as he likes to think of the clandestine product for his only other client. Not only for artistic reasons. It's smart business and a necessary survival skill to ensure the Triad doesn't recognize their pills among someone else's stock.

As he studies the pills, Bunsen hugs himself, fighting off an imaginary chill. Everything comes flooding back to him. It had been a particularly hectic deadline for that specific pill-run, even worse than usual. He was so exhausted when he finally had the chance to make those Copenhagen-blue pills. And, he concedes, he might have sampled too much of his own product by the time he ran that batch, just before dawn. It would have been so easy for him to have mixed in the wrong ingredient.

His fingers tremble as he pulls one of the blue pills from inside the little baggie, crushes it, and loads a sample into the analyzer. He tastes the vomit in the back of his throat even before the analysis is complete and the screen lights up as "strongly positive" for carfentanil.

His breath catches in his throat. *What if the brothers know, too?*

CHAPTER 48

Sheila Weir meets them at her front door in the same clothes she was wearing on their last visit. Her hair is a greasy bird's nest, and the bags under her eyes are now black sacks. She reeks of tobacco and a stale unwashed scent. Julie wonders if Sheila might have slipped from grief into a full depression.

"Who's this?" Sheila motions to Theo with fingers that hold a lit cigarette.

Theo offers her a sad smile. "I'm Theo Kostas. Another detective on this case."

"Great. More tax dollars and still no arrests. You said there were developments?" she asks without inviting them in.

"Yes," Anson says. "We have a drug dealer in custody who may have sold TLH—that lethal carfentanil—to the kids that night."

"What's his name?"

"Wade Patterson." Anson pauses, but when there's no recognition on her part, he adds, "It's still unconfirmed."

"Sold them to who? 'Cause, like I told you last time, it sure as hell wasn't my Josh! No way, no how. I know my own boy."

Theo nods sympathetically. "We get it, Mrs. Weir."

"Sheila!"

"Sorry, Sheila. That's why we've come. We've been going through the phones of the other kids." Theo summarizes what they've learned from Babar's analysis. "But Joshua's phone wasn't found at the scene. And we have reason to believe he might've left it at home that night."

"Last few weeks, Josh had been complaining about his phone. It would only work on Wi-Fi." Sheila swallows. "He had a good job down at the water taxi on Granville Island—he never asked for much—but he did ask me for a loan for a new phone." Her voice softens as she speaks of her son. "I told him we weren't like his rich friends and that he was just going to have to wait for his next paycheck. What he didn't know was that I'd already bought him a new Android phone with all the bells and whistles. I was just waiting . . ." She has to pause again. "To surprise him. His birthday would've been next week."

Julie lays a hand softly on Sheila's bony shoulder, half expecting her to recoil from the touch, but she holds still. "Josh's old phone might help us put the last pieces together, Sheila."

"How?" Sheila mumbles, unconvinced.

"If Josh hadn't deleted the text conversation with Grayson and Dylan, then maybe we'll be able to figure out what happened that night." Julie rubs Sheila's upper arm. "Do you know where his phone is?"

Sheila stares past them for a while and then, without a word, turns and trudges back into the house, leaving the door open behind her.

They follow her up a narrow flight of stairs and down a carpeted corridor. She stops at the second door and opens it. Inside, Julie is surprised to discover that Joshua's room is tidy and even smells fresh. The bed is made, and the desktop is meticulously organized, with a row of books sorted against the wall, a collection of car magazines fanned out, and a single framed black-and-white photo of a prepubescent, grinning Joshua with his arm around his mom; both of them wearing windbreakers and standing in front of a waist-high tent. Julie is moved that, despite Sheila's self-neglect, she has kept her son's room so pristine.

Sheila opens the top right drawer of the desk and pulls out a cell phone with a web-shaped crack across the screen along with a charging cable. She plugs it into the wall and then holds down a button on the edge of the phone. The screen lights up with the manufacturer's logo and, after a moment, the passcode screen appears.

"Don't suppose you happen to know the—" Anson starts to say but stops when Sheila types in the passcode with a yellowed finger and the home screen appears.

"I told you we shared everything. No secrets," she says to no one in particular. "Where's this supposed conversation?"

"In WhatsApp," Theo says.

Sheila swipes her finger through a few screens until she finds the WhatsApp icon. As soon as she taps it, a list of chats appears, but Julie is too far from the screen to read any of the names.

"What am I looking for again?" Sheila asks.

"A group chat with Dylan, Grayson, and Joshua," Theo says.

Sheila studies the screen for a moment, scrolling up and down through conversations. The longer she scans, the more deflated Julie feels, assuming Sheila isn't going to find the one in question. Just as her hope is slipping away, Sheila holds the phone out to Theo and says, "Here."

Theo accepts it with a nod of thanks. The others all crowd around him, reading the screen over his shoulders. Julie's heart pounds in anticipation when she recognizes the last few texts that Babar already showed them. She leans in closer as Theo scrolls a finger up the screen, and the earlier section of the conversation comes into focus. "Joshua didn't delete it!" Julie blurts.

"No," Theo says. "Look . . ."

"It's the best stuff," reads a text from Dylan that is time-stamped as Thursday at 8:35 p.m. "Better than booze. You don't get sloppy or nothing on it. Just SUPER friendly."

"What if the girls don't want to take it?" Grayson asked in response.

"We can dissolve it in a drink. No taste to it."

"Not cool!" Joshua responded, adding an angry emoji for effect.

"We do it all the time back in TO," Dylan wrote. "Works every time. Makes the girls SO friendly. You won't believe it!"

"I'm out," Joshua replied.

"How about you, G?" Dylan texted.

"You sure it's safe?" Grayson wrote.

Dylan responded with a one-hundred-percent emoji.

The next text in the sequence is time-stamped from Friday morning at 10:42. "Your weed guy came through, G," Dylan wrote. "Gave me a number. Pick-up is after lunch."

Grayson responded with a thumbs-up emoji.

"Got it!" Dylan texted at 3:15, but no one replied.

The next text is from Joshua at 5:42. "Big doubts about the plan tonight, D."

And the only two texts that follow are the ones Babar already showed them.

"You see that!" Sheila cries. "Josh wanted no part of it! He was way too classy for any of that devious roofie shit!"

Julie wraps Sheila in a gentle commiserative hug. "He was," she murmurs.

"Not sure we can say the same of Dylan, though," Theo mutters.

They thank Sheila for her help, promising to be in touch as soon as they know more. Sheila stands on the doorstep, her face blank and a freshly lit cigarette dangling between her lips. Her sad eyes seem to follow them all the way back to their car.

As soon as they drive away, Julie calls the hospital, only to be told that Dylan has already been discharged. She is grateful when the unit clerk goes to the effort of looking up the name of the hotel, the Nelson, that was listed in his electronic medical record as the local address where his parents were staying.

Anson dials the Nelson on speakerphone. As soon as he explains his official capacity, the unquestioning front-desk clerk tells him that the family checked out less than half an hour before and were on their way back to Toronto.

They race straight to the airport. Anson weaves through traffic, driving as though his car has lights and sirens. Theo works the phone, trying to track down Dylan's flight number and gate.

Anson slams on the brakes in the no-parking zone at the departures drop-off area. As they hop out of the car, Theo flashes his badge at the indignant parking patrolman who storms toward them.

They rush inside the terminal not knowing what time or from which gate the Berg family is departing. At the security checkpoint, Julie stands back while Anson and Theo negotiate with an RCMP officer. A few minutes later, they're cleared to bypass security.

Inside the departure terminal, Theo checks the electronic board and notes the gates of the next three Toronto-bound flights. They hurry down the hallway, stopping at the first of those departure lounges. The flight isn't scheduled to leave for another ninety minutes and the lounge is almost empty, but Julie spots Dylan, sitting alone at the end of a bank of chairs. His head is down, with earbuds in, as he watches a video on his tablet. He doesn't even notice them until they're standing over his chair.

"Hello, Dylan," Julie says.

He looks up, and as he yanks the earbuds out, his eyes go wide at the sight of them. "Oh, h-hi."

"Where are your parents, Dylan?"

"They went for lunch. I wasn't hungry."

Anson and Theo sit down in the seats on either side of him, while Julie stands in front of him.

"Do you know why we're here, Dylan?" Anson asks.

The boy shuffles in his seat. "No."

"We found the WhatsApp chat group. The one between you and Grayson and Joshua." Anson pauses for effect. "Joshua hadn't deleted it."

Dylan freezes, looking as if he's afraid to breathe.

Julie kneels in front of him. "You told us you didn't remember anything from that day," she says in a gentle tone. "That's not really true, is it?"

Dylan's jaw trembles as he slowly shakes his head.

"We need to know what really happened at that party."

Dylan hesitates. "I just wanted them to think I was cool like them."

"Joshua and Grayson?" Julie asks.

Dylan nods, eyes glued to the floor.

"So you decided to spike the drinks?"

"At parties in Toronto we sometimes dissolve E into drinks. The girls usually know it's there, but they still drink it."

"E? Ecstasy?" Anson asks. "Not fentanyl or heroin?"

Dylan grabs his head in his hand. "No way! I'd never do those kinds of drugs! The guy I bought it from swore it was pure E."

"Which guy?"

The psoriatic blotches on Dylan's face go redder and his eyes moisten. "The guy. I don't know his name. Joshua's weed dealer gave me the number. Dial-a-dope, he called it. I texted, and the guy met me downtown."

"And this dealer told you he was selling you Ecstasy?" Theo asks.

Dylan nods frantically. "He insisted I buy four tablets even though I only wanted one. He said there was a hundred-fifty-dollar minimum."

"What did you do with the other tablets?"

"I flushed them down the toilet. Before the party. I was staying with Gray's family, and I was worried his mom might find them."

Theo pulls out his phone and summons a photo of the bluer fake oxys found in the developer's desk to show Dylan. "Is this what they looked like?"

"Yes! The one I kept, anyway. Couple of the others were darker . . . grayer." Dylan sobs. "The guy, he promised me they were all pure E! I asked him a bunch of times because of the difference in color."

Julie shakes her head, feeling simultaneously sorry for and furious with the distraught kid. "It was wrong either way, Dylan," she says quietly.

"I know. It was so wrong. I am so sorry. If I could go back . . ." Dylan's face crumples and the tears stream down his red cheeks. "Should have been me, not them."

Theo flips through the photos on his phone until he finds the one he seeks. He shows Dylan a photo of Wade Patterson. "Was this the guy who sold you those pills?"

Dylan opens his mouth, but he's crying too hard to speak now. He just closes his eyes and nods.

CHAPTER 49

Wade shifts gingerly on the chair. But the moment the two detectives sit down at the interview table across from him, he forgets about his sore ass. Their expressions are unreadable, and the older one is as polite as ever. But Wade sees it in their eyes. They know something. And whatever it is, it's not good.

"You need a water or a coffee, Wade?" Theo asks.

"Yeah," Wade says, eager to stall. "Coffee. Cream and two sugars."

Theo gets up, opens the door, and speaks through the crack. "Just be a couple minutes," he says as he sits back down. He digs a hand in his pocket and pulls out his phone. "Meantime, I want you to look at this."

Wade rolls his eyes. "Another slideshow?"

Theo smiles. "Just the one photo. You saw it last time, too." He shows Wade a photo of the kid with the weird blotchy rash on his face.

Of course Wade remembers the nervous little wuss. He recognized him the last time the cops showed him the photo, too. The kid probably had never ridden a bus or worked a day in his life and yet the little mamma's boy shows up on the Downtown Eastside with a wallet full of cash demanding E. *What a goddam waste of my time!*

He should've just bashed the kid in the head and taken his wallet, but no, he tried to do right for the spoiled little shit. The kid was looking for drugs, so Wade sold them to him at a decent price. *Was it my fault that I'd already run out of E?*

But Wade only shrugs.

"You sure you don't remember him, Wade?" Anson says. "Because he sure as hell remembers you."

"So he says."

Anson leans toward him. "No, Wade, he doesn't just say. He has a whole text exchange with you on his phone. Right down to your dial-a-dope number."

Theo nods. "It's irrefutable, Wade."

Wade looks from one detective to the other. His mind races, desperate to find an out. But he can't see one. "I'm a low-level street plug. Someone approaches me, I sell them shit. You know all of this."

"But Wade, you sold TLH to a bunch of kids," Theo says.

"You might as well have planted a bomb under a minivan," Anson adds.

"I didn't know what the fuck it was!" Wade says, unable to keep the panic from his voice anymore. "I thought it was just fenny."

Anson lunges forward and grabs his shirt collar, twisting it tightly around his throat. "You told Dylan it was pure E! *You fucking monster!*"

Theo reaches over and tugs on his partner's outstretched arm. Anson releases his collar, and Wade drops back into his seat.

"He's right, Wade," Theo says calmly. "You could've just as easily killed them with fentanyl. This isn't trafficking. You're facing multiple counts of murder here."

Wade feels the walls closing in on him. He didn't escape that prison of a small town just to end up in a real jail for the rest of his life. "There was no intent. Any other dealer would've done the same. The kid wanted drugs. I sold them. End of story."

"It's only the beginning of *your* story," Theo says. "How it ends totally depends on how much you cooperate."

"With what?"

"We need to know where TLH came from," Theo says.

"I already told—"

"Don't give us more bullshit!" Anson barks. "Jamie Maddox didn't sell you those TLH pills. He didn't have any to sell!"

"Who did, Wade?" Theo asks. "Help us stop this from happening again."

Staring into Theo's understanding eyes, Wade realizes it's over. He has lost. Everything.

"We need a name," Anson prods.

"A name, huh?"

"It'll help your cause," Theo says. "And it will save lives."

Wade sees that he's out of options. The sudden sense of futility and defeat is paradoxically calming. He looks from Theo to Anson. "Here's a name for you," he grunts. "Gordon Kattenhorn."

"Kattenhorn?" Anson squints. "The defense lawyer?"

"Yup." Wade sees the fury reignite in the Asian cop's eyes, and it gives him a glimmer of satisfaction. *Why the fuck would I help my own executioners?* He sits back. "Get me my lawyer."

CHAPTER 50

"Look at you, Julija," Goran says as soon as Julie steps into the ER doctors' office.

"What are you on about, Gor?" she says as she walks over to her mailbox.

"I haven't seen you this smitten since . . ." He stops without finishing the thought. "Even Maria says it's so."

"That poor woman. Having to put up with you all the time." She chuckles. "But please thank her again for the wonderful dinner on Tuesday. We had a great time."

"Us, too. We really like your detective, Julija." He wags his finger. "Perhaps Maria even likes him a little too much? Handsome devil that he is."

She grins with pride. "I like him, too. Maybe a little too much."

"So you might actually keep this one around, Julija?"

"I just might."

Goran clutches his chest. "Hallelujah!"

"Don't jinx it, Gor!"

"I won't. I won't. It's good to see you here, though. I still remember when you used to be a doctor."

"It's only been four days since my last shift," she says, although in truth it does feel more like four months. "And I'm working all weekend."

He pushes the stack of reports in front of him away. "How is the investigation going?"

"Not bad. They've arrested the dealer who sold the carfentanil to the kids. A particularly nasty piece of work."

"In a particularly nasty line of work."

"True. Also, we figured out that Dylan Berg spiked the others kids' drinks."

Goran frowns. "The boy who survived?"

"Yeah."

"Such cruel irony." He sighs. "The only survivor . . . Like when a drunk driver kills a bunch of innocent people and just walks away from the accident."

"Yes and no. Dylan thought he was buying Ecstasy, but the dealer sold him opioids instead. Even if there was no carfentanil in the pills, those kids could've just as easily overdosed on the fentanyl he deliberately substituted for E."

"But this is good, no? You have cracked the case wide open, as they say?"

"The problem is that we still don't know who supplied the dealer with TLH."

"So we could still see more overdoses?"

"There's no 'could' about it, Gor. If we don't choke off the source, and soon, then there will be a lot more cases. And other Alexas, no doubt." She experiences another twinge of grief for a girl she never even knew.

He nods understandingly. "How did the transplant go?"

"That's one of the reasons—paperwork aside—I've come in. To see how Chloe is doing."

"It's strange isn't it?"

"What is?"

Goran leans back in his chair. "This fentanyl crisis has changed the medical landscape in so many unexpected ways. Even beyond all the senseless death."

"How so?"

"Organ donation, for one. For years, the wait list for new kidneys, hearts, and livers had been growing longer and longer. Fewer people willing to donate their organs. But just yesterday I heard on the radio that the transplant wait list has never been so short."

"I heard that, too."

"These young people found brain-dead from fentanyl overdoses . . . they're like some kind of macabre bumper crop of new organs." Goran raises his shoulders. "Helpful if you're waiting for a new liver, I suppose."

"But not much help to the victims or their families." Julie thinks of Alexa's parents again. She hopes they took a sliver of solace from meeting the recipient of their daughter's heart, but she doubts it could even begin to compensate in any meaningful way for their loss.

"And what of the psychiatric emergencies?" Goran persists.

"How do you mean?"

"Surely you've noticed we're seeing fewer psychiatric patients these days."

"Of course. Everyone here has."

"I'm told the psychiatric-related visits have plummeted by almost thirty percent, Julija. And trust me, it's not because of some epidemic of mental wellness. Go stand in rush-hour traffic at the Oak Street Bridge for a few minutes and you'll appreciate the sad state of mental health in this angry city." He snorts. "So where have the psychiatric patients gone?"

"Fentanyl overdoses."

"Exactly. The most fragile psychiatric patients have always been the most vulnerable to drug addiction, have they not?"

"It makes sense when you think how many of our addicts are

SAMI," Julie says, referring to the term for the dual category of "substance abuse and mental illness" that describes so many of St. Michael's inner-city patients.

"I was speaking with a psychiatrist who runs the outreach program on Gore Street for homeless schizophrenics. He says they've lost one-third of their patients to fentanyl in the past two years. One out of three, Julija! Can you imagine? Where will it end?"

"I have no idea, Gor."

Goran slumps in his seat. "No one does. Not even me. And I think I know everything, at least according to Maria."

She musters a smile. "I do know the first step is getting this TLH poison off the streets."

"Let's hope." He gets up, walks over to her, and drapes an arm over her shoulder. "How are you holding up, Julija?"

The whiff of his menthol aftershave is comforting. Still, she just says, "I'm fine."

"This investigation . . . Right from the moment when the ambulances rolled in with that little redheaded child and the others . . . It cannot be easy for you."

She hesitates a moment, but she knows he won't let it go. "It's not," she says, without looking at him.

He grips her upper arm a bit tighter but says nothing.

"I hate to admit it, Gor, but Harold was right. As I ran the resuscitation on Alexa, I kept thinking about Michael. Had the same feeling as when I was pumping away on his chest in CPR, even though it was obvious he was dead. I knew Alexa wasn't going to make it, either, but I just couldn't stop myself."

"I was in the room, too, Julija. I didn't stop you, either."

"This case has brought everything back. Truth is, those memories are never far away. And to be honest, I think I want to keep them close. Why else would I choose to work in an inner-city ER and moonlight as a toxicologist?"

"Guilt is a powerful motivator, Julija."

"It's not only guilt."

"What else could it be?"

"Deterrence."

"Deterrence?"

"From the temptation." She looks away in embarrassment and hurries to add, "I haven't touched so much as an aspirin in the past nine years. But I can still remember my last high like it was yesterday. I've never known such bliss. And the hunger for it never really goes away." She wriggles free of his arm and turns to him. "I'm an addict, Gor. Temptation will always be there. So maybe I need to be reminded on an almost daily basis of the devastating cost of using."

Goran studies her for a long moment and then slaps the desk. "So what if you do? I keep my size-thirty-four pants hanging in my closet. Haven't fit into them for twenty years. But I keep them around to remind me the cost of eating too many *kremšnita*, those custard pastries sent down from heaven." He grins. "Now, there is a bliss like *I* have never known."

The laughter feels like a weight lifting from her. "You always know the perfect thing to say, Gor!" She leans forward and hugs him tightly. "I really love you."

"*Draga.*"

Julie hears her phone ringing in her bag and breaks off the embrace. She pulls it out and, seeing Anson's number, answers it. "Hi, you."

"Hey. We're going to have postpone dinner tonight."

"Why's that?" she says, hoping she kept the disappointment from her voice.

"We just got word from Hoops. It might be going down."

CHAPTER 51

Bunsen hurriedly zips up the backpack and lays it on the bed. He'll have to leave all his winter clothes behind, along with most of the summer gear, too. He even has to abandon his top-of-the-line Marantz turntable. But he did find space for the most precious vinyls in his collection, including an original pressing of Miles Davis's *Kind of Blue*, which is worth almost as much as the cash stuffed below it. The bills fill almost half the bag. *Lazy asshole!* he chastises himself again for not having already exchanged his savings into cryptocurrency. Even Holly—who he once joked "couldn't tell a Bitcoin from a chocolate coin"—had encouraged him to deposit his money somewhere more secure. Now he'll have to lug it around like a homeless person, providing he even manages to escape the house. And he won't be taking Holly with him, either. It wouldn't be fair to expose her to the risk and, besides, their relationship has been in its death throes for months.

Bunsen hasn't slept since he spotted the brown van pull up across the street yesterday evening and park in a grassy spot where vehicles hardly ever stay. He can't tell who's watching him, but since he's never seen the van before and it's remained there ever since, he's convinced someone must be. At this point, if he were certain the cops were the ones watching, he would just march over and turn himself in. But if it happens to be the Triad's men in that van, it would be faster and less painful to just throw himself in front of traffic.

Taking his own car isn't an escape option, since it's parked across the street from the brown van. His only hope, as he sees it, is to wait for the cover of darkness and then sneak out the back lane on his mountain bike. And pray no one is stationed there, too. From there, he has no specific plans. Escaping his own home is his major focus and biggest hurdle.

Bunsen is tempted to take a small bump from the container of fentanyl powder on his table, but he forces himself to resist. *Remember how you ended up in this mess in the first place, idiot!* Even the slightest impairment in his judgment could lead to further disaster, so instead he fills the coffeemaker with fresh water.

Just as he scoops the third spoonful of ground coffee into the filter, his hand freezes as the external motion detector beeps on his cell phone. His eyes dart to the video screen above the fridge, which is hooked up to the outdoor surveillance camera. He recognizes Hui's face on the monitor. The coffee grounds begin to spray before Bunsen even realizes his hand is shaking.

The doorbell chimes. As his pulse throbs in his ears, Bunsen considers forsaking his backpack and bike and just fleeing on foot down the lane. *But how far could I get?*

The bell rings again. He rushes toward the door feeling as if he is running into enemy fire.

Li Wei is smiling as he steps inside the house with a briefcase in hand. Even Hui's scowl is less pronounced than usual, as he follows his brother, carrying a matching case.

"The next batch isn't . . . um . . . ready, Mr. Jian," Bunsen stammers. "I wasn't expecting you."

"Not to worry," Li Wei says. "There has been a change of plans."

Bunsen feels the blood rush from his face, wishing there were something nearby to grab hold of.

"A rush order." Li Wei lifts his briefcase. "Do not worry. There will be a bonus for you, of course."

Bunsen breathes again. "For when . . . will you need it?"

"Tomorrow evening."

Hui points toward the lab in the kitchen. "No mask? No fan?" he demands.

Bunsen shakes his head. "Everything is sealed right now. There's no need."

Li Wei and Hui stride down the corridor toward the kitchen-cum-lab. Bunsen follows. As they pass the open door to his bedroom, his stomach plummets. But neither of the brothers seems to notice the backpack on the bed.

Bunsen stands across the kitchen counter from the brothers. Li Wei lays his briefcase on the countertop and pops it open, while Hui continues to hold his in his hand. "You still need more carfentanil, correct?" Li Wei asks as he reaches inside the case.

Bunsen shakes his head, sensing more danger. "No. You were right about it. I checked after your last visit. I'm flush." He forces a laugh. "After all, when it comes to that stuff, a little goes a very long way."

"True." Li Wei smiles. "But a lot can get you into trouble. Very quickly."

Bunsen's mouth goes dry and, at a loss for words, he can only nod.

Li Wei's hand lingers inside his case. "Since we brought you a fresh supply of carfentanil, can you please show me how much you have left?"

"Yeah . . . of course . . ." Bunsen struggles to swallow away the sudden constriction in his throat. "It's all sealed up, though." He scours his brain for a possible out. "If we're going to open that container, I probably should fire up the fans and get the breathing masks out."

"I see." Li Wei nods as he reaches to close his briefcase. "Perhaps it's not worth the effort, then?"

Bunsen's shoulders sag and it's all he can do to hold back the sigh of relief.

But as Li Wei shuts the lid, his hand emerges with a gun in its grip. He points it casually at Bunsen's head. "I think now is the time for more honesty."

Bunsen throws his hands up in front of his face, palms outward, uncertain himself if it's a gesture of surrender or futile self-protection. "I don't follow you, Mr. Jian," he croaks.

"A few days ago, policemen showed me photographs of pills." Li Wei casually waves the barrel of the gun as he speaks. "They were a color that I have never seen before." The barrel stills. "But the markings looked very familiar."

Bunsen shakes his head helplessly.

"These pills apparently were the same ones people are calling TLH." The smile finally leaves Li Wei's lips. "Do you have any idea why, aside from the color, they look so similar to our product?"

Bunsen feels his legs begin to tremble. He understands that admitting anything about TLH would be tantamount to putting the barrel of that gun into his mouth and squeezing the trigger. "Apart from the quality, there's nothing special about the pill press machine you ordered for me," Bunsen spurts. "The pills are supposed to look alike. On the street, you know? I've never seen them come out blue before." *Asshole!* He goes cold as soon as the words leave his lips.

"Did I say they were blue?"

"I . . . I just assumed."

Li Wei nods. He motions the gun toward the hallway. "And the suitcase on your bed . . ."

"It's a backpack!" Bunsen cries. "My girlfriend—Holly—and me . . . we were going to go camping . . . for her birthday."

Li Wei raises an eyebrow. "Her birthday again?"

"I'm sorry, Mr. Jian. I've never . . . had a gun pointed at me. I'm really flustered. It's hard to . . . um . . . think."

Li Wei turns to his brother and mutters a few words in Mandarin. Hui only grunts in response, as he flips his own briefcase onto the counter and pops open the lid. Li Wei motions with the gun to the nearer of the two wooden chairs at the breakfast table. "Bring that here, please."

Bunsen hurries over and grabs the chair, imagining he can feel the barrel of the gun trained on him as if it were a hot laser beam. By the time he sets the chair down in front of the brothers, Hui is holding a thick roll of duct tape.

"Why . . . what's that?" Bunsen asks as he shuffles back away from it.

Li Wei levels the gun at his head again. "Sit."

Bunsen drops into the chair.

Li Wei motions to the armrests. "Arms there, please."

"I don't understand," Bunsen says as he rests his wrists, palms down, on the armrests.

Hui roughly grabs Bunsen's right arm and begins to tape it down to the chair with tight loops. "You don't have to do this . . ." Bunsen pleads.

"Do you know much about the Triad?" Li Wei asks as Hui continues to tape.

"No."

"Our origins go back to the early days of the Qing dynasty. Older than the Mafia. We have outlasted dynasties and regimes. Our society was, and is, based on strict Confucian principles, including a dedication to the absolute truth. You understand?"

Bunsen nods, his exposed fingers cooling from constriction as Hui reinforces and tightens the tape binding him from his elbow to his knuckles.

"Symbolism is also vital to us." Li Wei pulls up the sleeve on his left arm to reveal a tattoo of a black-lined triangle with a single bar running through it near the center and parallel to the base. "Most of us have these 'heaven and earth' markings. You see?"

Bunsen nods as Hui tears off the tape and then shuffles around to the other side of the chair and begins to secure his left arm.

Li Wei puts the gun down on the countertop and steps over to

Hui's briefcase. "Another symbol—of sorts—that we are famous for is the form of our punishment." He calmly reaches inside the brief-case and extracts a black-handled meat cleaver. "Some call it 'the chop-chop.'"

Bunsen's breath catches, and he struggles involuntarily against the binding.

"Stop!" Hui barks.

The fist smashes so unexpectedly into his nose that Bunsen hears the crack before the pain shoots through his face. Despite the agony, he stills out of reflex.

The room goes horribly quiet, except for the sound of tape unraveling and the tapping of the blunt edge of the meat cleaver against Li Wei's palm. Bunsen tastes the blood dripping from his nose and tries, pointlessly, to raise his wrist up to wipe it away.

Li Wei takes a step closer, and Bunsen pulls away in his chair.

"Stop," Hui growls again, and Bunsen complies.

Hui straightens up and steps behind the chair. Bunsen looks frantically over his shoulder as he feels the first strip of tape wind around his chest. In a minute or two he is secured so firmly to the chair's back that he can only inhale in shallow breaths.

Li Wei stands to the left of the chair. "Shall we try again?" he asks in a pleasant tone, as he raises the meat cleaver in his hand.

Bunsen desperately tries to flex his fingers, but he has nowhere to pull them, with his arms so firmly bound to the chair.

"What happened to our carfentanil?" Li Wei asks. "The truth, please."

But Bunsen realizes that the truth is a death sentence. "I . . . I don't know," he stutters, in full panic now. "I followed the recipe. Always. I used the same—"

Li Wei's arm swings down, leading from the elbow.

For a moment Bunsen feels disembodied—as though he's watch-ing himself in a movie. It's only after he hears the crunch of bone and sees his ring and little fingers drop to the floor that the scream forms in his throat.

CHAPTER 52

———————————/\/\———————•

Julie's hands feel clammy as she huddles beside Hoops in the back seat of Anson's car. Heads almost touching, they lean toward the two front seats, listening to the conversation over Theo's speakerphone.

They pulled up only a minute or two before, about fifty feet behind the unmarked police "dump car"—one of the disguised vehicles the VPD uses for surveillance operations. In this case, the dump car is an old converted brown van with tinted windows to hide its occupants. The van is parked across the street from the run-down bungalow under surveillance. The skies are still too bright in the waning dusk for them to risk getting out of their car and approaching the van without being spotted from inside the house. Instead, they speak over the phone to the two undercover cops, Derrick and Meghan, inside the dump car.

"Run us through exactly what you saw," Theo instructs them.

"The Jian brothers drove up twenty-five minutes ago in that Mercedes across the street," Derrick says, and Julie's eyes are drawn to the car with the matte-black paint job that is parked across at the far end of the block.

"Just the two of them?" Theo asks.

"Yeah."

"Then what?"

"They stayed in the car for a good ten minutes," Derrick says. "We were worried that they might have made us, but I think they must've just been on the phone, because they eventually got out, went around to the trunk, and pulled out two briefcases. They lingered there for at least a minute, and—"

"Did you see any weapons?"

"Negative."

"They had their backs to us," Meghan says. "So we can't know for certain."

"And the brothers have been inside the house ever since?" Theo asks.

"Yes. About fifteen minutes or so."

"Have you heard anything?"

"No. The night team dropped a wireless spy microphone outside the window. We haven't picked anything up on it so far."

"OK." Theo looks to Anson and then glances over his shoulder to Hoops. "For now, we wait."

"You can't just go in?" Julie asks.

Theo shakes his head. "No warrant and no probable cause."

"What about the suspicion of weapons in those briefcases?" Julie asks.

"That would never hold up," Theo argues.

"Then again, you heard the officer," Anson says. "They couldn't see, and maybe—"

"*Did you hear that, Meghan?*" Derrick's agitated voice cuts Anson off.

"Yes!" she cries. "A scream. On the window mike!"

Anson jabs his hand inside his jacket and pulls his gun from its holster. "We just got our probable cause!" he says.

Theo nods as he and Hoops also hurriedly unholster their firearms. "OK, we're going in! Derrick and Meghan, we need you to cover us," Theo says as he reaches for the radio. "This is Sergeant

Kostas. We're making an emergency entry at 3081 East Fifty-Eighth. That's three-zero-eight-one East five-eight! Need all available cover units to attend code three! And a canine unit if available!"

When Julie moves her hand toward the door handle, Hoops snaps, "You stay right here, Doc!"

Anson's head swivels toward her. "Don't even think about it, Julie!"

She opens her mouth. "But . . ."

Theo turns to her with a glare she's never seen before. "Not a *fucking* inch, Julie! We'll call you when it's clear."

Julie falls back into her seat as the three cops launch out of the car.

She can't remember feeling as tense or helpless. She barely breathes as she watches them run carefully, but without hesitation, toward the front door, where they're joined by the two other cops. Weapons drawn, they assemble in two rows, with Theo, Hoops, and Anson standing at the front and Derrick and Meghan behind.

Julie is overcome by sheer dread. The idea of something happening to Anson terrifies her. It takes all her restraint not to reach for the door handle as Hoops raises his foot to kick in the front door.

CHAPTER 53

Li Wei doesn't show it, but there is something about a mutilated hand that always turns his stomach. He almost gagged when Bunsen's middle finger hit the floor and rolled toward him. Li Wei tries not to focus on the bloody stumps where the three fingers used to be as he raises the cleaver again.

Bunsen opens his mouth wider to scream again, but the gag Hui stuffed between his teeth absorbs most of the sound.

Li Wei has witnessed his share of fear over the years. It's as essential an element of his business as the legal contracts and the expensive suits—all of them required to establish the level of respect necessary to survive in their world. But it's been a long time since he has seen the degree of terror that is now dancing in Bunsen's eyes.

"The human hand is an interesting piece of machinery," Li Wei says. "It can function well without the last three fingers. But remove the thumb or the index finger . . ."

Bunsen gags into the restraint.

"Are you ready to tell us about the carfentanil?" Li Wei asks.

Bunsen nods frantically.

Li Wei motions to Hui, who yanks the gag out of his mouth.

"It was just a mistake!" Bunsen blurts.

Li Wei purses his lips. "The TLH pills?"

"Yes! I was so tired. I'd been up all night pressing pills. I couldn't see straight. The last batch . . . I mixed up the recipe. I must've used pure carfentanil in the mix. Didn't even realize it for days!"

"Thank you for your honesty," Li Wei says in the most sympathetic tone he can summon. "What I do not understand, though, is where those pills went."

"I have no idea." Bunsen gulps. "It was only a small run. The end of the batch. They probably—"

Li Wei sighs. He nods to his brother, who stuffs the gag back into Bunsen's mouth. "You see, we have checked with our entire distribution chain." A noise that sounds like a cell phone alarm beeps twice and stops Li Wei momentarily. He waits a few seconds but hears nothing more, so he continues. "Those pills never ended up within our distribution sphere. So we can only conclude that you must have sold them elsewhere."

Bunsen's eyes go wide as coins as Li Wei slowly raises the cleaver again.

Just as he's about to swing again, a loud crash freezes his arm. He swivels his head toward the sudden blur of activity in the hallway.

"Police!" a voice booms. "Drop your weapons! On your knees now!"

Li Wei sees three policemen advancing in crouches, with guns extended in their outstretched arms. Just as he lets go of the cleaver, he catches a blur of movement out of the corner of his eye. Two bangs explode in his ears, and he sees the flash from the barrel of Hui's gun.

One of the cops topples sideways at the same moment as gunfire erupts from the hallway. The noise is deafening. Li Wei hears Hui crash to the floor without even seeing him fall.

Li Wei has no idea if he himself has been hit as he crumples to his knees.

CHAPTER 54

"**O**fficer down!" Theo's voice booms over the radio, startling Julie. "Need paramedics, code three!"

Anson? Julie grabs her head in her hands and rocks in her seat. *No! Not again!*

Long seconds pass as she wrestles with the urge to leave the car. The low hum of static over the radio taunts her. "What's happening, dammit?" she mutters at the unresponsive device.

"Premises secure, all clear!" Theo finally calls through the speaker. "Julie, we need you!"

She flings the car door open and sprints for the house. Her breath catches in her throat as she mounts the front step and flies without hesitation through the open doorway.

Inside, the eerie quiet only compounds her dread. It takes her a moment to digest the mayhem. In the dimness of the kitchen, she cannot make out who is lying where.

"Over here, Julie," Theo calls.

She ignores everything else until her eyes find Anson in a corner of the room. She exhales at the sight of him upright but kneeling alongside Theo. But her relief is short-lived. A very pale Hoops sits slumped between the two detectives against a wall. Anson uses both of his hands to squeeze Hoops's upper biceps, but blood still leaks out between his fingers.

As Julie rushes over to them, she takes note of the others in the makeshift lab. Hui lies motionless on his back, the shirt over his chest covered in blood, while Li Wei is facedown with his hands cuffed behind and Derrick's knee between his shoulder blades. Meghan stands beside her partner with her gun still leveled at Li Wei. Another man is taped to the chair beside them, his clothes stained, his swollen nose pushed sideways, and blood oozing from his mutilated hand.

Julie kneels in front of Hoops and grabs his uninjured left arm at the wrist, feeling for a pulse. It's fast and thready but easy to find. His eyes are glassy and his face ashen, but he is breathing. "Can you hear me, Timothy?"

"It's Hoops," he croaks with a small grin.

"OK, Hoops, you're in shock, but you're holding your own." She steals a quick look at Anson, who shows her a fleeting reassuring grin. The wail of sirens drifts into the room.

Julie turns her attention to Hoops's upper right arm just below the armpit, from where, despite the pressure of Anson's hands, alarmingly bright blood continues to pulse. The bullet must have clipped his brachial artery. "Your belt, Theo!"

He whips off his belt and passes it to her.

"Keep the pressure on, Anson," Julie says, as she threads the belt between Anson's hands and Hoops's armpit. Once it's looped, she pulls it as high up the arm as she can and cinches it as tightly as it will go. "Don't let go, Anson." She looks over to Theo. "Take the end of the belt and pull as hard you can."

"That wimp?" Hoops grunts. "I'll bleed out in seconds."

"Well, maybe if you didn't juice up on 'roids and pump your arms into such huge targets . . ." Anson jokes, and Hoops's pale lips curve into a slight smile.

The blood dripping between Anson's fingers slows dramatically as Theo takes the belt out of her hand. "OK, slowly lessen the pressure between your fingers, Anson." She watches intently as he complies, and the blood flow slows even more. "Good."

After a few more seconds, Anson says, "I'm barely holding him now."

"OK, you can let go," she says as the wail from the sirens reaches a crescendo.

Anson pulls his hands away as slowly as if he were setting down a cracked crystal bowl. No more fresh blood drips from Hoops's arm. Julie grabs her phone and turns on its flashlight. She leans in closer until she spots the entry wound through the blood-caked sleeve on the inside of his upper biceps. She knows better than to explore the site at all, but she quickly pats down the shirt over the right side of his chest, which is also damp with blood.

After carefully palpating the area, she says, "All the blood on your shirt is from your arm, Hoops. The bullet hit an artery. But the tourniquet's working. You're going to be OK."

Hoops nods toward the Jian brothers and Bunsen. "And them?"

"Hui is dead," Anson says. "Li Wei's alive. Sadly. Their cook lost a bunch of fingers. But he'll make it. Everyone else is OK."

The paramedics rush through the door. Theo waves them over. "Here!"

Theo and Anson clear the way for the two paramedics, both of whom Julie recognizes from the ER.

"Dr. Rees?" the larger one, Lauren, says in surprise as she crouches down beside her.

"Long story. Single GSW to the proximal biceps with an arterial bleed. Controlled by proximal tourniquet. No other identified injuries. GCS fifteen. Peripheral pulse weak but present. Grade two hemorrhagic shock," Julie says, summarizing the location and extent of the gunshot wound and the degree of subsequent blood loss.

Another pair of paramedics burst through the door and, as soon as Theo motions, head past them to the man duct-taped to the chair. His moans indicate that he's still alive despite his closed-eyed still- ness.

When Julie looks up again, the other two cops have lifted Li Wei to his feet. As he shuffles past them, he looks over at Anson with a glare of sheer contempt and mutters something in Mandarin.

"You're the disgrace!" Anson fires back in English. "You bring shame to our heritage."

CHAPTER 55

As little Maya fusses in her arms, Julie tries awkwardly to rock the baby back to sleep.

Chloe chuckles. "Just bounce her up and down a little, Dr. Rees. She loves that."

Julie grins self-consciously as she holds Maya under the arms and bounces her. The baby quiets in moments.

Julie is delighted to see Chloe free of the external heart-lung bypass machine and most of the other tubes, except for one intravenous line. "I can't believe how well you've responded only a couple of days after getting a new heart, Chloe."

"Yeah, but this heart works. Unlike the last one."

Julie offers a solemn grin. "It's a good heart."

"The best," Chloe agrees. "I'm . . . I'm going to stay in touch with Tom and Elaine. They want to. And so do I."

"I'm sure it'll help them to know what a great second chance Alexa has given your family."

A pained look crosses Chloe's face as she reaches out to tickle Maya's toes. "I wish that was true. Can't imagine anything would help after losing your child."

"Not now, no. But maybe in time."

Chloe's eyes mist over. "How can I ever thank you, Dr. Rees?"

"For what?"

"Saving my life. Twice. First in the ER that day, and then again with . . . Alexa."

Julie looks down at Maya, not wanting to be reminded of her role in prolonging Alexa's life after she was already brain-dead.

"Dr. Mott said you made a difference," Chloe continues.

"He did?"

"Yeah."

Julie finds more satisfaction than she expected from the comment. She doubts it will affect Harold's pursuit of a formal review of the case, but it's enough to know that he gave her a little credit.

Maya begins to fuss again, despite the bouncing. "I think she must be hungry," Chloe says, extending her hands toward the baby. "I'll try to feed her again."

Julie passes Maya to Chloe. "I'll let you both rest now. I'll drop in on you again soon."

Julie wraps mother and baby in a very gentle hug, cognizant of Chloe's major chest incision, and then heads downstairs to the surgical ward.

Anson and Theo are standing at Hoops's bedside, inside his private room. The undercover cop's arm is wrapped from shoulder to elbow and supported in a blue sling. But his complexion is pink, and the glimmer is back in his eyes. Julie has already heard from the vascular surgeon that Hoops's operation went well, and the artery was repaired without any permanent damage to the arm.

"How's the patient?" Julie asks.

"Good," Anson answers for Hoops. "Now we're just trying to teach him how not to walk directly into the line of gunfire."

"Advice from this one?" Hoops rolls his eyes. "Only man alive who color-coordinates his outfit for a gunfight."

"When are you going home?" Julie asks.

"Want to go now. Hospital food is gross," Hoops says. "But my doc says I need another twenty-four hours."

Anson chuckles. "You're just itching to cash your first disability check, aren't you?"

"I seriously do *not* remember asking you to visit."

"Lucky you, Hoops, because we have to get going anyway," Theo says, pulling his partner by the arm. "Apparently Jason Moskowitz wants to talk."

"Who's he?" Hoops asks.

"The Jians' cook. Aka 'Bunsen.'"

Julie nods. "They were able to reattach Bunsen's three severed fingers. His surgeon thinks there's a good chance he'll keep them."

"Oh, goodie." Anson sighs. "Maybe he'll even be able to return to work soon?"

Hoops reaches for the pole holding the bag of intravenous fluids with his good arm. "I wanna be there when you grill this clown."

Theo shakes his head. "Not yet, Hoops."

"You know the VPD policy? I think it's rule 432-C . . ." Anson motions to Hoops's hospital attire. "No conducting official interrogations with your bare ass hanging out of a hospital gown."

"Knowing them, they probably do have that policy." Hoops snorts. "You better get back to me with the whole rundown of what he cops to."

"Will do."

After saying their goodbyes to Hoops, Julie and the detectives head over to the adjacent surgical unit. "Li Wei has lawyered up," Theo says. "Won't tell us boo. But between that home lab and his financials, we have a mountain of evidence on him."

"And the rest of the TLH pills?" Julie asks.

"There were only a couple left in Bunsen's lab, and we collected all the ones from Wade's stash. Hopefully Bunsen can tell us where the rest of them are."

They reach another private room, this one guarded by a

uniformed policeman. Inside, there's a second cop seated by the bed who gets up and leaves as soon as Theo shows his ID. Julie realizes Bunsen is under arrest, but she suspects the uniforms are also there to protect him from potential retribution by the Triad or any other gangsters.

Bunsen sits up in the bed with his elevated arm in a cast from above the elbow to his outstretched fingers, which are wrapped in bulky bandages. He looks otherwise healthy.

Theo makes the introductions, then says, "We understand you wanted to speak to us."

"I want to make a full confession," Bunsen announces.

"You are aware of your right to counsel?"

"Don't care about any of that. Those fuckers were going to cut me apart, piece by piece."

Anson nods. "All right, then. Tell us about TLH."

"It was a huge fuckup on my part," Bunsen admits, and tells them how he cooked up TLH by mistake while under the influence of drugs himself.

"How many pills in total?" Anson asks.

"A small batch. Two hundred."

"How can you be sure, when you were mass-producing so many pills for the Jian brothers?"

"Because those specific pills were for a side order. And I could only skim so much off the top without getting noticed."

Theo frowns. "Side order?"

"After I made my usual huge runs for the Triad, I would fire off a custom batch for a private client. I always colored them differently from the other fake oxys—a lot bluer—so the Jians wouldn't suspect me. Turns out they did anyway."

"This private client?" Anson demands. "Who is he?"

"A real douchebag."

"Wade Patterson?" Julie guesses.

"Yup. That's the prick."

"How did you connect with him?" Theo asks.

"A couple years back I was in university finishing my chemistry degree. I started to dabble in drugs. A little coke and Adderall here and there, to help me study. Wade was my dealer."

"And he led you to the Jians?"

"Not directly. I got into debt with Wade. It got ugly. He told me my only way out was by cooking up pills for him. We set up a small lab in my apartment. Turns out I had an aptitude for it. Soon I'm cooking for other dealers. Word got out, and then the Jians found me. They set me up in that dumpy house." He shakes his head. "And the rest is history. Pathetic history."

Anson stares hard at him. "We're going to need you to testify against both Wade and Li Wei."

Bunsen's face lights up. "Will be my absolute pleasure, Detectives."

After leaving Bunsen, they head out of the hospital and gather beside Theo's car in the parking lot.

Even though Julie is hugely relieved by the news that the small batch of TLH is accounted for, she feels unexpectedly demoralized over what she just heard. "All this . . . death and misery, for what?" she muses aloud.

"How do you mean?" Theo asks.

"This whole trade boils down to nothing but callous greed and stupidity," she says. "There was no master plan here. Just a collection of epic screwups. A lazy cook who carelessly whips off a batch of pure poison. A spiteful asshole of a dealer who thinks it would be fun to play Russian roulette with kids' lives. And a misguided teen who wants to win over girls by spiking their drinks."

Anson nods. "All of it fueled by the greed of the Jian brothers."

"The whole thing would be laughable if it weren't so horribly tragic."

Theo looks from Anson to Julie. "But if what Bunsen told us is true, then there shouldn't be any more TLH on the street."

"*If* being the pivotal word," Anson says.

"I believe him," Julie says. "But what about the next time one of these cooks screws up and runs off another lethal batch?"

Theo nods, and then smiles. "Let's celebrate the victories when we can. At least one crisis has been stopped and more deaths averted."

"You're a wise man, Theo." Julie pats his shoulder. "So what happens to Dylan now?"

"Probably ends up with a custodial youth sentence."

"A bigger break than he deserves," Anson says.

"How so?" Julie asks.

"The Crown could have bumped him up to adult court and charged him with manslaughter," Theo explains. "Instead, looks like they'll try him as a young offender for criminal negligence causing death. He might get six months of juvenile detention time."

"If that," Anson says. "No matter what, he's going to get off a hell of a lot easier than his six friends."

"Still," Julie points out. "He has to live the rest of his life with what he did."

"No denying that." Theo thumbs to Anson. "What do you say, partner? You and I have one heck of a report to craft."

"Can't wait. I'll meet you back at the office, OK?"

Theo nods his understanding and turns to Julie. "It's going to be weird not working with you day-to-day, Julie. I got to say, you make a solid detective. It's been a pleasure."

"Totally mutual." Julie hugs him. "Thank you, Theo. For everything."

Appearing a little embarrassed, Theo slips out of her arms. He climbs into the driver's seat and leaves with a quick wave.

After Theo's car pulls away, Anson says, "It *is* going to be weird not working with you anymore."

Julie grins. "It's not like I'm going anywhere."

"Oh, I know." He strokes her cheek. "I just hope you're going to make an easier girlfriend than you do a colleague."

"Don't count on that!" she says with a laugh, as she pulls him closer and locks her lips to his.

A sense of contentment warms her. She's acutely aware that the fentanyl crisis won't be controlled anytime soon—if ever—but Theo is right, they've subdued the single deadliest drug threat to ever hit Vancouver's streets. There's immense satisfaction in that. And now that she has connected with someone who understands how guilt can compound grief and turn it into an emotional prison, perhaps it will be a little easier to finally let go. And maybe she won't feel so alone anymore.

ACKNOWLEDGMENTS

I write, first and foremost, to entertain, but I also strive to enlighten readers with what I've learned while researching the subject matter behind my story. In the case of this novel, I've been unknowingly doing research for the past twenty years while working as an emergency-room physician in a hospital that sits at the epicenter of the opioid crisis in one of the hardest hit cities.

This is a work of fiction. But I am convinced an almost identical calamity could unfold today on the streets of Vancouver, or any other city. To call the opioid epidemic a tragedy is a sad understatement. In my province alone, thousands—most of them under forty—have died from overdoses. And it's likely even more still will. The victims range from addicts to first-time dabblers or, sometimes even, as portrayed in this novel, people who are unaware they ever consumed opioids. The stats or demographics don't move me as much as the emotional toll on those affected and their loved ones. I wanted to convey that sense of the suffering, loss, and helplessness. And how this crisis could, and does, touch almost anyone.

While I live the medical side of this disaster almost every shift I work in the ER, I had to rely heavily on a friend in law enforcement to understand the criminal elements that are driving the illegal fentanyl trade. Because of the sensitivity of his ongoing work, I can only identify him as JD. But I'll be forever indebted to JD for sharing his boundless knowledge and reviewing the manuscript so painstakingly to ensure it was authentic as possible. He lent this story heaps of street cred.

I'm fortunate to collaborate with such gifted and supportive editors as Anne Perry, Bethan Jones, and especially Laurie Grassi, who invests so much time and energy into bringing out the absolute best in my writing. I'm delighted to be working with the talented folks at Simon & Schuster, particularly in the Toronto office, including Nita Pronovost, Gregory Tilney, David Millar, Felicia Quon, Jillian Levick, and Kevin Hanson, whose guidance has been unfaltering. This is the eleventh book in a row where I've depended on the feedback and wisdom of my wonderful first-pass, freelance editor, Kit Schindell. And I'm grateful for the counsel of my agents, Henry Morrison and Danny Baror.

There are so many others I could acknowledge. Writing is often considered a solitary pursuit, but in my case, it does take a village, including the many friends and family members who listen to the early pitches, read the rough drafts, and support me through the ups and downs of the unpredictable process. Thank you, all of you.

As always, I want to thank you, the readers, who inspire me to keep going. While, of course, I want you to enjoy the story, I hope it will also make you a little more aware of a terribly indiscriminate and potentially stoppable killer that is ravaging our communities.

ABOUT THE AUTHOR

DANIEL KALLA is the internationally bestselling author of *We All Fall Down, Pandemic, Resistance, Rage Therapy, Blood Lies, Cold Plague,* and *Of Flesh and Blood.* His books have been translated into eleven languages, and three novels have been optioned for film. Kalla practices emergency medicine in Vancouver, British Columbia. Visit Daniel at danielkalla.com or follow him on Twitter **@DanielKalla.**

Also by

DANIEL KALLA

"A tightly plotted thriller, energetic
and completely believable."
Booklist

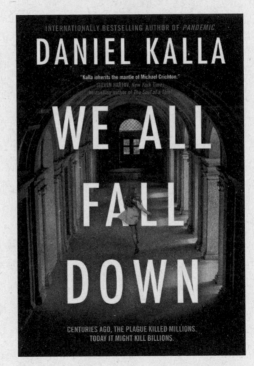

"Michael Crichton ought to be looking
over his shoulder."
The Chronicle Herald

SIMON &
SCHUSTER